the tender grave

sheri reynolds

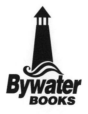
Bywater
BOOKS

Ann Arbor
2021

Bywater Books

Print ISBN: 978-1-61294-193-6

Bywater Books First Edition: March 2021

Printed in the United States of America on acid-free paper.

Cover designer: Ann McMan, TreeHouse Studio

Bywater Books
PO Box 3671
Ann Arbor MI 48106-3671
www.bywaterbooks.com

This novel is a work of fiction.

For BB

I.

Dori was still a little high. Her blood vessels pulsed all through her scalp, like she was a cartoon character and someone was sketching her a wig that very minute, bearing down with a marker and drawing every strand of fake hair on her oversized fake head. She felt cartoonish, and her timid cartoon-blood crept fretful through her blood vessels. Why was her blood so bashful, and why did it move so slowly? She pictured her blood cells like little hunchbacks all in a line, a chain gang of hunchback blood cells in a comic book of their own, staggering along one frame at a time, going nowhere. She scratched at her scalp and was surprised to find that her hair was still wet from the shower. She didn't feel quite real.

As the lights of the bus station came into view, bright in that hour before morning, yet somehow still dingy-looking, her mom veered to the side of the road and pumped at the old Buick's brakes. The brakes didn't half work anymore; the tires were worse, already bald, and it had started to drizzle, so the tires had more than the usual trouble catching.

It made her sick, how they jerked, and then jerked, and then slid to a stop, still a full block from the depot in that rural, run-down North Carolina town.

Her mom clicked on the car's interior light and dug through her pocketbook, finding at last the envelope with *rent* scribbled in tiny tight letters right where the stamp should go. Dori watched her count out what money she had—not enough for rent, anyway—turning all the crumpled bills in the same direction and straightening them out before handing them to Dori. She'd use that envelope again.

"Alright, darling," her mom said. "Time to go."

Dori unclipped her seatbelt and tucked the money into the pocket of her jeans, but as she reached to open the door, her mom said, "Hang on." From the glove compartment, beneath the owner's manual, her mom produced a second envelope, this one her tire fund. She licked her finger and counted through another small stack of tens and fives.

"What will you do?" Dori asked.

Her mom slammed shut the glove box, shook her head and shrugged. She pulled out a cigarette, lit it, and took a deep drag. "I'll make do," she said, holding in the smoke a long time before she exhaled. "I've got no choice."

The thick smoke lingered between them. Dori tried to hold her breath. The chain gang of blood cells stomped their little boots inside her newly drawn head. "I'm sorry, Mom," she replied. "Try not to drive on the highway, okay?" A deacon at their church who was also a mechanic had told them they shouldn't go over thirty on those tires.

"Just get out," said her mom, but Dori couldn't. Not yet.

Her mom sighed, took off her glasses, and wiped her eyes with the heels of her hands. Dori could see fingerprints smudging the lenses of her glasses, and so she lifted them from her mom's thigh and cleaned them on her T-shirt before giving them back.

"Thank you, sugar," said her mom. She took Dori's hand and squeezed it, then kissed her first knuckle and her second, and said a prayer that God would watch over her and keep her safe. "Now, please, just go."

The sun wasn't yet up, but the milkiness of the coming day pushed through the dark. Dori didn't look back. She was still a little drunk and took care not to stumble as she crossed the potholed parking lot, reciting to herself, "Don't step on the crack or you'll break your momma's back." She tried not to cry when she heard those threadbare tires squeal off.

Most of the seats on the bus were already taken. Dori pushed her way along the narrow corridor, her overstuffed backpack grazing the shoulders of passengers along the aisle. She tripped over a sneaker nudged into the walkway but caught herself before she fell. Halfway back, she found a spot next to a skinny brown-skinned granny and dropped into it as the bus began to roll. She had the worst headache of her life, so she closed her eyes and tried to ignore the heavy thumps escaping a stranger's earphones.

She hadn't been to bed, not all night, and though she'd brushed her teeth before she left, her mouth already tasted stale. She suspected it might taste that way forever, whether she brushed or gargled again or not: her new reality, her life the flavor of bile.

She hugged her backpack and tried to rest, but in her dreams she was a never-ending bass note, a note trying to slip around the edges of the bud in somebody's ear and disappear.

She wished that she were dead, and that her boyfriend Cane were dead, and that the world as she knew it had scorched to ashes. She wished she'd never been born.

In her mind, she went round and round, like her mom's old patched tires with no treads left, no way to get a grip on anything. It made her hate her mom—that she drove around on old bald tires. Then it made her cry—that she might never see her mom again. Round and round, a circle of hating and sorrow.

At a later stop, when her seatmate got off, she threw herself against the window, pushed her pack into the neighboring space, and tried to sleep in spite of a crying baby and the dings and sizzles of a video game on somebody's phone, no headphones. But images from the night before kept intruding: the spray of blood across her favorite coral cami, the blood splats on her canvas flats, her mom still in her nightgown shoving Dori fully clothed into the shower and scrubbing her down, saying, "Oh, my Lord. My dear Lord Jesus," then stripping her and rubbing soap into the stains on her clothes, bits of grass and clumps of dissolving dirt swirling around the palest pink water at their feet. The images interwove with the screeches of the bus's brakes, the one-sided phone call of somebody desperate to make it to New York before his brother died, the driver's announcements of this station or that one, the rustle of passengers coming and going.

Dori woke with a glaze of diesel exhaust clinging to her skin, an oily coating across her nose and forehead. Someone had stolen her backpack by then. At least she'd had the good sense to keep her wallet in her pocket—a back pocket that buttoned—and her mom's cash buried deep in front. She still had money, but no spare clothes and no phone. She knew better than to use the phone, of course, but it had all her pictures on it. So she'd turned it off, wrapped it in a T-shirt, and stashed it at the bottom of her pack. Now her pictures were gone, too. She had no food or water and no toothpaste or deodorant, which she needed. A ripe fear pooled in the pits of her arms. She couldn't escape her own stink.

The bus driver was no help. The passengers around her had seen nothing. She wasn't sure where she'd been when she'd closed her eyes or how many bus stops they'd passed. The driver suggested she file a police report in Richmond, but she couldn't do that. She couldn't talk to the police when she was probably *wanted* by the police, or would be soon.

At the terminal in Richmond, she got off anyway with plans to board a different bus—one headed for the Virginia coast and toward the older half sister she'd never met. Maybe her sister would welcome her, if she was lucky. She bought a bagel from a vending machine, but even with the cream cheese, it was too tough to eat. It reminded her of taking communion, and how sometimes the host would just swell inside your mouth, huge and unchewable, and wasn't that fitting—to be so full of the body of Christ that you couldn't even swallow?

When the next bus came, she threw away the bagel and boarded. She told herself not to be afraid. Plenty of times she'd pictured

4

running away, taking her backpack and heading cross-country. This wasn't so different—just another kind of adventure—and for a while, she was glad to be anonymous and traveling light. But fear kept surging up, sour in her mouth and in her guts.

She tried to pray, but why would God listen? She was a trouble-maker. She knew about the wages of sin.

It wasn't long before her imagination highjacked that bus and drove it directly toward Hell, that charred and fiery chasm she'd heard so much about. She tried to focus on the pine trees, green and supple, passing by the dirty bus window, but Hell kept coming back, how her skin would crisp and blacken and flake away. She could hear her dad's voice, preaching and crying and beseeching God to save them all from eternal damnation. But Dori knew her soul was unredeemable. She would writhe in the flames for all eternity. She'd earned it.

All along that eastbound route, she kept peeking up and catching glimpses of the bus driver's eyes in the oversized rear-view mirror. He stared her down, relentless. He could be the grim reaper himself.

It was almost like Hell, the next bus station in Norfolk, where she spent half the night hiding in the grimy women's bathroom and the other half huddled on a painted metal bench. But the next morning, the bus that carried her across the Chesapeake Bay and onto Virginia's eastern shore was spacious and quiet, and the transit van she took for the final leg of her journey was nearly empty. She had two seats to herself to stretch her legs across. The driver, a cheerful snaggletoothed woman who played gospel music and sang along, wished Dori a blessed day as she dropped her off at the edge of a bayside fishing village, the town where her older half sister supposedly lived.

Dori walked the rest of the way, peeking back over her shoulder even as she passed through the tiny business district, beyond the rows of houses, and down to the water. There was a breeze coming off the water, and she decided to rest there a while, calm herself there. She'd made it. She settled on a rock jetty that separated the public beach from what was left of a fallen-in dock.

The dock itself had washed away, and all that remained were the pilings: weather-worn, leaning, jutting up from the sandy bay floor and marking off the tide. Some of the pilings were twenty feet tall; others had worn to nubs. They looked like the ribs of some decomposing sea beast. Terns and pelicans kept vigil from the irregular tops of posts.

The place was eerie and peaceful at once, but it wasn't entirely private. For company, Dori had a chatty little boy playing in the algae along the shoreline.

"It's just like salad," said the boy. "Salad for stingrays and sharks." He picked up a leaf of the slimy-looking sea lettuce, shook away clumps of sand and brine, and stuffed it into his mouth.

"Yuck," said Dori. She'd never been to that beach before, had never seen that kid before, had never tasted seaweed in her life and didn't want to.

But she was hungry. Except for some cheese puffs she hadn't eaten since the too-tough bagel the day before.

The boy spit and giggled. "It's gritty, but it don't taste that bad. Be better with ketchup, though. You want some?"

"No thanks," she said. She wished he'd scat. That's what her mom used to say when she wanted alone time and Dori was being a pest: "Scat!" But this kid was going nowhere.

The air was thick and muggy, and the gray sky faded into water the color of knives. In the distance, church bells rang three times and played a hymn she recognized, though she couldn't remember the words.

The boy said, "You're not supposed to be down here. This is the working beach. The tourist beach is down yonder." He pointed south, where a few beach chairs and umbrellas randomly freckled the sand. "This ain't where you go to get a suntan. I'll tell you *that*."

Dori shrugged. "What are you doing here then?"

"I ain't no tourist," said the kid. "I'm waiting for my daddy!" He motioned to a man in waders walking out among gray pilings, a five-gallon bucket in one hand, a crab line in the other.

Dori *wished* she was on vacation. "I'm not a tourist either," she replied.

That seemed to satisfy the boy. He was maybe seven, wormy-looking and brown from the sun. He wore only a pair of cut-off shorts and scratched at bug bites all over his arms and back and belly, his legs, and even his head. Red welts peeked from beneath his crew cut, some of them scabby.

The boy found a stick and dragged it along the shoreline, holding it up to impress her with the seaweed and lettuce he'd harvested.

"That's nasty," Dori called back.

"Is not," he said. "I'll show you how to make tater chips." He rinsed some of the lettuce in the clearer water just beyond the gunk that had settled over the rocky place where bay met sand. Then he climbed up onto the jetty next to her. "Once you clean it, you just tear it into pieces and stretch it out on the rocks like this." Carefully, he draped each bright green leaf on the sunny granite. "You wait for it to dry out good and crunchy," he explained. "Then you got tater chips."

From out in the water, the boy's father hollered, "Hey, Randy, quit bothering that gal and bring me the net."

"I ain't bothering nobody," the kid yelled back, but he scrabbled down the rocks and waded out. While he was gone, Dori climbed down, too, and paced that empty strip of beach, finding oyster shells and pieces of broken bottles littering the edges, bits of rock and dried-out legs of dead crabs in the sunshine. The pilings were shorter closer to shore. You could peek right down into the hollowed-out centers of some of them and find cracked shells or stuffed-down candy bar wrappers.

Dori rolled up her jeans and splashed her way just far enough to stand among those pilings with their seagulls perched atop. It was such a quiet place: softly lapping water, occasional squawks of laughing gulls, a good place to clear her head and work up her nerve before she went searching for the older half sister she'd never met.

She would need to look cute, even though she couldn't possibly be cute, given all she'd been through the past couple of days. She'd need to be charming. She could still be charming—or at least she could try.

She examined the posts and found tiny black snails and hairy-looking grasses growing against the wet wood. She found barnacles and algae, and in the distance she saw the boy's father thigh-deep and pulling in one crab after the next, surprising them as they feasted on what grew along those posts.

In a while the boy ran back to find her.

"Hey," he called, "What's your name?"

She wondered if she should make up a name, but in the end, she told the truth.

"You wanna be my girlfriend?" he asked.

"I'm too old for you," she said and laughed. She was seventeen, but could pass for twenty. "Besides, I got a boyfriend already." Just thinking of him made her choke.

The boy shrugged and said, "That's okay. I'll show you my hideaway anyhow." He led her up the bank to a hot place where the high tide couldn't reach, talking all the while. Dori was glad to be distracted. They stepped over rocks and broken bricks, then to hot sand pocked with holes from ghost crabs shying from the sun. Creeper vines and grasses masked a place where trees had tipped over, leaving wiggly roots partially exposed and partially embedded in the ground. Trees with scoliosis, their lowest branches grew against the sand.

The boy pushed back some vines to reveal a shady, shallow cave beneath one tree's contorted branches. "Come on in," he said.

He had a little braided rug in there and some plastic army men he kept inside a rusted cookie tin. He crouched on the rug, and Dori sat beside him, and he introduced her to his army. The vines and leaves against her neck kept making her think there were spiders on her. Again and again she slapped at nothing.

"You come here every day?" she asked.

"Just Sundays," said the boy. "My granny's sick, so we bring groceries every Sunday. Then me and Daddy come down here and crab while Momma visits and rolls her hair."

"Oh," she said.

"Momma fixes chicken and puts it in Mason jars so Granny can eat it all week long. She don't eat that much, though."

Dori's belly grumbled.

"Sounds like you could eat a whole jarful of chicken," said the boy. "Does your granny live here, too?"

"No," said the girl.

She didn't mention her older half sister. She hoped her sister hadn't moved away. She had a name and an address, memorized long ago from an envelope with a postmark so faded you could hardly read it. As soon as she worked up her courage, she planned to scope things out.

"I'll show you where my granny lives," the boy offered. "It ain't far."

Dori couldn't care less, but it was such a relief to have somebody to talk to, somebody safe. So she followed Randy out of the cave, and he led her down to the water, then around some rocks on the far side of the pilings, and back to sand again. From there, he pointed out a small bungalow that sat alone about a quarter-mile inland, huddled between squatty, fat trees at the far edge of the town. "That's my granny's house," he said.

"Does she live there by herself?" Dori asked.

"Yep," said the boy.

"Maybe you should move her to the nursing home so she can hang out with other old people."

"She's too old and set in her ways," said the boy. "She don't even go to church no more. Only place she goes is therapy—to get her broke shoulder worked on. Every Tuesday morning at eleven. You ever been to therapy?" he asked.

"No," she said.

"It feels good," he said. "Some Tuesdays I sneak on the table next to my granny and let the therapist stretch all my muscles."

The boy's father called to him again: "Randy! Get over here!"

"You better go," said Dori. "He sounds mad."

But Randy didn't hurry. He just shrugged and made squiggles in the sand with his toes. "If you be my girlfriend," he said, "I'll tell you a secret."

"You're a mess," said Dori. "I already told you, I've got a boyfriend. You wouldn't want me to two-time him, would you?"

"Well, yeah," said Randy. "It's a really good secret."

"Okay," she said. "Just tell me."

Randy grinned. "Back before I was born," he said, "when I was still in my momma's belly, I had a pair of magic flip-flops. But they fell off when I was coming out."

"Oh yeah?" said Dori.

"They're probably still in my momma's belly somewhere."

Dori laughed and said, "You think?"

"If I had them flip-flops, I could jump from here to that pier way down yonder." He pointed to a place so far down the beach that you could barely make out the people fishing. "Just leap right up and land way over there."

"I need me some shoes like that," said Dori.

"I can still remember them," Randy told her, "from when I was a tiny baby, not even yet borned."

Just before sundown Dori went exploring. She found the avenue where her older half sister supposedly lived and followed the sidewalk to the address—a wooden two-story house with over-grown oleanders around the porch. She even knocked. A dog barked from the other side of the window, but nobody answered. So she left and wandered to the main drag, where the hardware store was closed, and the coffee shop was closed, and the clothing store was closed, and the convenience store was closed.

But the art gallery was open, with people crowded inside it. She leaned against the corner of the building and watched as people came and went, some of them still holding cups. She was thirsty, and so she rolled down the cuffs of her jeans and brushed away the sand. She ran her fingers through her newly chopped-off hair to release the tangles, and she held up her chin and stepped inside. An old lady handed her a brochure with the name of each painting and the price, then pointed her toward the snacks.

Dori ate cheese and crackers and looked at landscapes; strawberries and carrots as she studied seascapes; peanut butter cookies while she considered the portraits and the abstract art. She knew about gallery openings. Her mom was an artist, off and on, and she wondered if her older half sister might be an artist, too. She looked around at the people, imagining which of them might be her mother's child from a previous marriage and a lifetime before. She drank two bottles of water as she admired bowls carved from fallen trees. There were even tiny paintings of sailboats on sand dollars, and it occurred to her that if she could dig up sand dollars—something she'd done once with her mom when they'd visited a different beach—she might sell them to one of the artists and make a few quick bucks.

She checked the list of artists, in case her older sister might be a painter, but there was no Teresa King listed there.

Before she left, she used the bathroom and took another bottle of water for the road.

That night she slept in the boy named Randy's cave, curled up on his little rug, hidden behind a curtain of vines, but it wasn't a good sleep, thanks to biting flies and mosquitoes. She had a stick handy to warn away foxes or wild dogs, but none of those showed up. She had a broken beer bottle to slash the throat of anybody who got too close, but she didn't need that either. All through the night, she was startled by random cries, maybe of seagulls. She hoped it was seagulls. She didn't sleep much or well.

Early the next morning, she collected things left behind on the public beach: a sand bucket, a towel, a pair of superman pajama bottoms, and she stashed them in Randy's cave. She even found a raft washed up on some rocks beneath the pier, and since no one was around to see her, and since it was a blue canvas raft, like so many others you could buy, she took it.

11

Before it grew too hot, she walked the streets again. The whole town was only eight square blocks, not counting the harbor, so it didn't take that long. This time when she passed her older half sister's house, she saw a Black man with a baby come out. What if her sister had taken up with a Black man?

Could she live with her sister if she'd taken up with a Black man?

"Excuse me," she called. "Does a woman named Teresa King live here?" and the man shook his head.

"Nope," he said. "Don't know her."

Inside her mind, everything slowed. It was good, in a way— that her sister didn't live there with a Black man. But where would she go? Thoughts snarled and tangled over one another as she toed the broken sidewalk, considering.

"Did you buy this house from a Teresa King?"

"No," said the man. He opened the van door and put the baby in a car seat. "We bought it from some people named Lewis, I believe, but that's been two years. You could ask at the realty company about the lady you're looking for. They might be able to help you."

She took the long way back to the beach, wandering the perimeter of that town and even walking past the driveway to Randy's granny's house, wondering if the old lady had an extra bedroom, if she needed someone to cook and clean. She didn't know what to do, and so she returned to the beach and ate green potato chips and tried not to panic. She didn't have a backup plan. Her jeans were already loose in the waist, and they'd been snug to start with. Her stomach felt empty as a clamshell pecked clean by a seagull. She rode out on her raft and cried awhile, then splashed her salty face with salty water.

When she'd gotten too much sun, she paddled in and dragged the raft to Randy's cave. She used the sand bucket to dig it out deeper and wider, wide enough to wedge the raft inside.

Then she had a bed, and so she napped there, hot and sticky and sad, hidden behind green vines with trumpet flowers the color of sunsets hiding their pistils deep inside their blooms.

Later that night, on the pier, she met an older boy fishing. They talked a while, went for a walk down by the harbor, and she agreed to give him a blow job in exchange for ten dollars and a trip to the McDonald's out on the highway. She asked for twenty, but he negotiated, and anyway, a blow job was no big deal. She figured she'd given at least fifty blow jobs by then. Maybe a hundred. But the entire time she kept thinking about Randy's magic flip-flops. As the boy tugged at her head, insisting on his rhythms, she imagined springy shoes that could bounce her anywhere, if she could just figure out where she'd left them.

At the drive-thru, he ordered her a kid's meal, which pissed her off, but what could she do?

He got her drunk on beer, and being drunk felt fizzy, a fizzy-delicious holiday from all her worries. So she went with him back to the pier where he cast his line a time or two for a last chance at a kingfish or a flounder. In a while, when it was dark, he packed away his fishing gear, and they walked on the beach, and he told her about the little railroad town that had died out with the railroad. "Used to be," he said, "they dumped raw sewage right in the bay. But now this place is coming back. They cleaned up the bay and built a sewage treatment plant."

They walked down toward the fallen-in dock, and he told her about the ferries that once traveled back and forth across the mouth of the Chesapeake Bay. The clusters of posts in the deeper water where Randy's dad crabbed had been guides for the ferries themselves, bound together in order to be strong enough for a boat like that to bump against as it pulled in or loaded or set off for Little Creek.

He led her around the point, past the place where you could see Randy's granny's house, and farther down the beach, where there was no one, not even fishermen checking nets, and hardly any light. He told her that they used to dump the trash right into the water there—since that part of the beach was considered out of town. But now, with new ordinances, with the town council trying to attract tourists, Waste Management picked up the trash on Thursdays, and you got fined for throwing litter in the bay.

They didn't make it as far down the beach as the place where the teenagers partied, though the boy assured her that if she was looking for fun, she could find some action around the bend. Instead, they settled in the sand, and the boy told her all about himself as he rubbed her leg, how he was going to community college and planned to get his contractor's license. He asked her few questions, and soon enough his hand was under her shirt. She should have stopped him before he wiggled her out of her jeans, but she didn't, and by the time she said, "Whoa," it was too late.

It wasn't such a big a deal. She didn't even really mind, not at first. She was lonely, and besides that, she'd had sex before, at least fifty times, maybe sixty, but he was no gentleman, and when she tried to push him away, he rolled her over and came at her from behind, his thick hand shoving her head toward the ground, and she thought her neck might pop and she might lose consciousness, and she thought it might be better. He slipped out, but slammed back in gritty, and she had sand up her nose and sand in one of her eyes. She couldn't blink it out, couldn't wipe it. She squinted shut her eyes and hoped the tears would wash the sand away. She had no magic shoes, no chicken in Mason jars, no big sister, with or without a Black husband, to help her out of the mess she was in.

Afterward she got sick. She threw up beer and what remained of her Kids Meal, and she was crying when the guy left her there, saying, "You're just a little drunk. You'll be alright in a minute." He waved good-bye and said, "You sure you don't want me to drop you off in town somewhere? I don't mind." She said no, waved back, and he said, "I'll see you around, then."

When he was gone, she rinsed herself off in the bay, and then settled up near the dunes for a while, catching her breath, watching the stars. If she had magic flip-flops, could they spring her to the stars? The stars were probably already posted with "No Trespassing" signs.

Even if she had magic shoes, even if they could take her anywhere, she wasn't sure where she'd go.

14

She'd been in bounce houses at carnivals before, where you could leap and throw yourself against the blown-up rubber walls, only to spring back and land on the soft floor. But you could hurt yourself that way, in spite of the cushioning. Somebody's knee against your nose, or even your *own* knee, and you were stunned and bleeding.

She'd gotten a pair of moon shoes once for Christmas, with coils in the soles that made her taller. But when she put them on, she'd been surprised by the wobble. They weren't a good design, and the hard plastic straps hurt her feet. You couldn't tell from the catalog that you'd have to work so hard just to keep from falling over when you wore them.

She closed her eyes and imagined the kid named Randy, tiny as a newborn, curled up in his momma's belly, completely naked except for that pair of flip-flops. In her vision, she gave those shoes rhinestones, even though most boys wouldn't go for bling. She imagined him turning somersaults, tiny feet sparkling.

If she had magic flip-flops, she'd leap into another time, not this lifetime at all. She'd spring out of her body and into a different body, a different life.

In a while, she began the dark walk back toward Randy's cave, but she was sore and chafed between her legs, and the rest of her was sunburned. She stopped from time to time to give the stinging a chance to lessen. She tried to think of somewhere to go, but no place came to mind. Even if she found her sister, what would she say?

Then she heard voices—a group of boys laughing and calling— and she heard the voice of the boy she'd been with before: "Hey, Happy Meal! You still down here?"

Quickly she hurried from the voices. It was very dark, and she hoped they wouldn't spot her, but somebody had a flashlight.

"Is that her?" a different boy said. "Hey, Happy Meal, is that you? Come party with us!"

She ran out into the water, splashed into the bay, and dove under.

The water wasn't deep enough. She grazed the bottom with

her knees, even clawed herself out deeper with her hands until there was enough water to swim, trying not to kick. She stayed under as much as she could, hoping they wouldn't see her head pop up in the dark to steal a breath.

She swam toward the fallen-in ferry dock. It took a long time to get there, and when she reached the pilings, she stayed out among the deeper ones, where Randy's dad had done his crabbing the day before.

She surfaced near the place where clusters of pilings were bound together at their tops by great wire ropes. Quickly she wiggled between two posts, cutting her arm and tearing her clothes on sharp barnacles. Standing up between those posts, encircled by them, she tried to be as still and as silent as a post. Her heartbeat was the loudest thing around.

Blue crabs skirmished against her soggy jeans, climbing the pilings around her. Underwater grasses teased at her ankles and gave her the jitters, but she tried not to move.

"Where'd you go?" one of the boys shouted. "We brought you some French fries." They heckled and laughed, and somebody swam past her and out toward the channel. Then someone else followed, and they whooped and splashed, played Marco Polo in the dark, and speculated about whether or not she had drowned.

She closed her eyes and tried not to touch the pilings, tried not to move the water or make a shadow. She told herself she was strong, strong enough for a barge to bump into and not knock over, and when a crab pinched, she didn't whimper beyond the inhale of her gasp.

It was a bad night because even after the boys were gone she was too scared to leave, afraid one of them might be sitting up on the rocks of the jetty just waiting for her to emerge. She knew bacteria from the water might creep into her cuts, even the raw places she felt between her legs, and infect her. She peed there in the water, and it stung but warmed her legs. Afterward, she got cold, and she didn't understand how a summer night could bring on such a chill. As the tide fell, and more and more of her body was out of the water, she grew stiffer and colder and shivered.

Her toes cramped. Her legs cramped. Her butt muscles knotted up on themselves. Her neck cramped, her jaw cramped, her head throbbed, and in that shape she couldn't help thinking about that other boy, the one from school that they'd all teased so mercilessly.

Owen Howe, the "fag du jour" the kids from French class called him. She didn't take French, so she just called him "homo." The way he wore his pants, the way he held his ass up high and prissed around the school, everybody teased him, not just Dori and her boyfriend. When the English teacher wasn't looking, they'd throw things at his head—pens or a copy of *Crime and Punishment*, even a pocket stapler once. Sometimes he took it. Sometimes he'd cry, "Quit it!" in his high-pitched homo voice, and the teacher would ask, "What's going on?" But no one admitted to anything.

Dori waited out the falling tide, trembling, holding her breath. The water slapped softly against the pilings: *shush, shush, shush.*

Maybe this was her punishment for what she had done three days ago to Owen Howe.

Some of the teachers thought Owen deserved it. When kids beat him up in the bathroom and stuck his head in the toilet, some of them said, "If he didn't act so gay, they'd leave him alone."

Maybe she deserved what she was getting too.

Finally the sky began to lighten, and she could see that no boys waited. It was Tuesday then. Dori was mad.

On the beach, she found an empty fast-food bag with nothing inside it except packets of ketchup. She kept the ketchup and threw the bag into the bay, just to watch it get soggy and float around. She sat on the rocks and tried to decide what to do next.

Seagulls and pelicans stood sentinel from the tops of pilings, claiming their spaces. It looked so peaceful out there on the water, but it wasn't. At any moment, a bigger gull might steal the throne of a smaller one. Then the smaller gull would flap over to the next post, and bully the bird perched there. They might as well be yanking the chair out from someone in the lunchroom, just to watch him fall on his ass and spill his pizza in his lap.

Sometimes two small birds roosted on the same piling, but that didn't keep the larger bird away. The larger bird would descend right on top of them until they were forced to give up their territory. Out there on the bay it was every bird for himself. The best you could hope for was to be born big and powerful.

But there were herons, too, and they didn't play that game. They kept some space around them. She wished she'd been more of a heron where Owen Howe was concerned.

That morning, while her clothes dried, she rested in Randy's cave, trying to come up with a plan. She didn't have much money left. She'd spent most of the cash her mom had given her just to get that far. Her so-called sister seemed as unreal as a pair of magic flip-flops left behind in someone's pregnant belly—and about as useful. She wondered if she really had an older half sister named Teresa King at all, or if it was just another story her mom had made up.

Her mom made up all kinds of things: visions of the Virgin Mary, encounters with movie stars on far-away vacations, even medical conditions she didn't really have. Her mom was insane. Dori couldn't count on her mom. All her mom's stories were tattered; moths had eaten holes in them. You could fall right through.

So why did she miss her mom so bad? It made Dori crazy, how she hated her and still wished she could crawl into her lap.

She wanted to die. She wished she'd died back on that bus, so she could finally stop struggling all the time. She should have thrown herself in front of the Greyhound as it pulled away. At least the Greyhound had decent tires.

But suicide was the unforgivable sin. Her dad had called it "a one-way ticket to the Great Lake of Fire," and though she hadn't read *The Inferno* the year before when her teacher assigned it, she'd listened in class to the descriptions of that lowest circle of Hell, where Satan gnawed forever on the flesh of Judas Iscariot. And if anybody had good reason to off himself, it was Judas.

She couldn't commit suicide, no matter how much she wanted to.

As she dozed in the cave, the church bells counted out the hours, and in a while she remembered that it was Tuesday, when Randy's granny went to the physical therapist at eleven.

So she followed the water, climbed up the bank, and cut through a field of dried hay to a place where some hedges and trees made her less conspicuous. Randy's granny kept chickens, and they ran up to her, clucking as she got close, probably hoping she had corn in her pockets. She shooed them away and crouched behind their coop.

There, she tried on stories in case she got caught: she was doing a 4-H project on poultry and didn't mean to trespass. Or her car had broken down and she needed to use the phone. Or she was looking for work, odd jobs. Or she was dehydrated and sick.

In a while, Randy's mom drove up in a green Ford and blew the horn. Then Randy himself hopped out and banged on the door yelling, "Granny!" He ushered the old lady down the steps and into the car, and they all drove away.

Dori forced herself to count to a hundred slowly in case the granny had forgotten something essential. In her mind, she recited the pledge of allegiance and also a poem she'd memorized for Spanish class before she hurried to the back door, hoping it wasn't locked.

When it was, she kicked at the door, but nothing happened. She kicked it again, hard, remembering the previous night, remembering those boys, remembering karate lessons from back in sixth grade. She kicked up high, near the lock, remembering video games she'd played with her boyfriend, remembering Owen Howe and how easy it turned out to be to crack his ribs.

At last, the door gave.

Inside, she filled a plastic grocery bag with pills. The old lady's prescriptions were right out on the counter, and she took them all. She found more pills in the bathroom, and a jar full of quarters up on a shelf.

She found a little revolver in the nightstand and five twenty-dollar bills in an envelope on top of the dresser.

She found antiseptic wipes and cleaned away her fingerprints as she went. She didn't ransack the place or make a mess. She closed drawers and left things neat. When she'd finished gathering all that she needed, she ate a jarful of chicken and even rinsed the jar. She took peanut butter, saltines, and a cold Coca-Cola, and as she left she pulled the door shut behind her.

Dori's eyes were full of clouds, or it seemed that way, like she was too tired to see through them. She might have grown cataracts. She might have a fever so high it had fogged up her pupils. She was so tired that as soon as she made it thirty miles up the shore on the transit van, she paid cash for a motel room and went directly to sleep.

She slept through that night, woke up, ate peanut butter and crackers, and slept again. Her eyes were full of clouds, and when she closed them, she leaned backward, did a backbend through the clouds, and found Owen Howe waiting for her there.

"Why?" he asked her. He was upside down, too, and bleeding out of his nose and mouth and eye sockets. "How come you hate me so much?"

"Because you're a fag," she said, like it was obvious. Wasn't it obvious?

He didn't even deny it. "What difference does that make?" asked Owen.

She didn't have an answer. She didn't really care, to tell the truth. There were gay people everywhere on TV, gay singers, gay talk show hosts. But they didn't go to her high school.

It wasn't even personal, what they did to Owen. It wasn't even *about* him. He was just a boy in her classes, the easiest target they had. In high school, everybody needed someone to punch and kick and taunt and hate.

But Dori couldn't tell him that, because he'd sieved down through the clouds again. Or else she had.

All afternoon she hung out by a gas station, watching folks come and go, asking occasional questions of itchy, strung out-looking boys putting air in their tires or heaving bags of ice out of the machine, and in a while she sold the pills to a skinny guy with fever blisters who met her behind the Dollar General across the highway.

But he ripped her off.

She understood that the cholesterol medication and blood pressure pills weren't hot items on the street, but this old lady had Percocet, too. Those were worth ten dollars apiece, maybe more. She'd kept back some for herself. She knew what they were worth.

The guy behind Dollar General gave her ninety bucks for the lot. "Take it or leave it," he said. "But I wouldn't leave it if I were you."

From his tone, she knew he might turn her in. If she didn't take it, it could all be over—and it wasn't like she had a clean record. She'd already been in juvenile detention for shoplifting, and now this thing with Owen.

"I tell you what," said the guy. "Next time, I'll give you a better price." He sucked at his upper lip until one of his blisters broke and began to bleed. He dabbed at the blood with his tongue. "You bring me some more, and everything checks out, I'll be fair with you."

She decided to keep the handgun. If he turned her in, she might need it.

She bought a few things at the dollar store: some toiletries, mascara, underwear, flip-flops, a too-big T-shirt to sleep in, and a tote bag with a sunflower embossed on the front to carry it all around in.

She spent another night at that motel, ordered pizza, took showers, watched movies on TV. She found a phone number for a Teresa King in the directory, but when she called the number, the answering machine clicked on, so she hung up. She wrote down the street address—a different address—in case she ever decided to track down her older half sister, who might or might not be real.

When she couldn't stand it anymore, she called her mom.

"Darling, are you out of your mind?" her mom scolded. "You ought to have better sense than to call here."

"Don't hang up!" Dori said. "Mom, wait!"

"Don't tell me where you're at!" said her mom. "I don't even want to know. They've probably tapped this phone by now, so wherever you are, you better be somewhere else shortly."

"Okay," Dori said. She heard the lighter click and her mom's heavy drag on a cigarette. In the background, Dori could hear somebody spinning the wheel on *The Price Is Right*, and she wished she were back home on the couch, with nothing to do but watch soap operas all afternoon.

"That boy is in a coma," her mom whispered. "They've arrested Cane and charged him as an adult, and now they're looking for you. So you stay away, you hear?"

"I don't know what to do," Dori said. "I don't have anywhere to go."

"You're a smart girl," said her mom. "You'll figure it out."

As Dori gathered her things, she chided herself for being such an idiot—and not just an idiot, but an ugly, despicable person. She was the ugliest person she'd ever laid eyes on, with her sunburn peeling off in nasty, soggy strips. She tried to powder her nose, but it did no good. The makeup just clotted against ruffles of loose skin. She looked like a freak. Why would her half sister take her in when she looked like such a freak?

There before the mirror, she glared into her own eyes and said, "Ugly."

Her eyes looked back at her just as accusingly.

"Ugly, disgusting bitch," she declared. "You deserve to die." She watched her eyes fill up and squeezed them shut, but when she opened them again, she just looked uglier. So she wiped her face, reapplied her mascara, grabbed her bag, and headed for the mini-mart where the transit van made its regular stops.

The van drove her back the way she'd come, heading south down the flat four-lane highway, past falling-in barns, a building supply; past woods and more woods, an occasional church or cluster of houses, past a field where seagulls followed in the wake of a plowing tractor; past a Mexican restaurant, its gravel lot jam-packed with trucks; past the traffic light where you turned to find the town where her half sister supposedly lived.

It was late afternoon by the time she checked into a motel just south of that town, a run-down place that catered to fishermen, and there she swallowed more of the old lady's drugs and climbed into bed and prayed to die. First she prayed to Jesus: "Our kind and gracious Heavenly Father, take me from this world and make a place for me in your holy Kingdom." That's how her mom or dad would have prayed if either of them had ever prayed to die. But Jesus wouldn't listen to that kind of prayer. He was a "Thy will be done" kind of guy.

She cranked up the AC, covered up in the blanket, and tried it again: "Prince of Darkness, if you're listening, I'm yours. Come and get me," but it terrified her to have said such a thing, and she immediately repented, begged Jesus for forgiveness, and tried to rock herself into a permanent and total sleep.

When she was little, she thought Akoma was a place where people went for vacation. She'd heard people talk about it: "Douglas Smith is in Akoma, and he ain't never coming back," and she'd wondered how Mr. Smith could afford such a fine holiday, when everybody else had to save up just to get to Gatlinburg. When she was little, she pictured Akoma with sliding boards everywhere, with monkey bars sticking up out of the ocean, so you could climb to the top and see all the way to Japan, then backflip from the highest bar and land on a dolphin that would cruise you through the waves.

She wished she could go back in time and be that girl, and not be wanted for questioning in the attempted murder of Owen Howe, who was having a helluva time in Akoma.

According to her mom, Owen Howe was kept alive by nothing but a machine. In a way, she felt terrible about it. In another way, she was jealous. At least he had somebody taking care of him.

In spite of all the pills, she woke again. She remembered where she was, and why, and cried into a cheap and musty pillow until her tears ran out. Then, even though she was groggy and hungover, she took herself to the lobby for the free continental breakfast. She'd paid for it, after all. Waiting for her waffle, she overheard some fishermen talking about a state park down the road, and so, without a better plan and low on money, she hitched a ride.

She walked along that beach for a time, past people sunning, people out in the shallows floating on their rafts, past dogs chasing sticks, dogs chasing birds, dog owners chasing dogs. She'd never had so much time with herself, so much time to think, to mope and feel guilty, and she didn't like it. For long stretches, she'd see no one at all, and then she'd pass around a point and find a paddleboarder sweeping the bay. She'd see a kayaker, a kite-boarder, a fishing boat. One woman even stopped to show her an arrowhead she'd picked up, and Dori wished she could be that woman's daughter, walk home with her and find that it was where she'd always belonged, in a house full of arrowheads, decorated with driftwood and feathers, and that everything before had been a dream.

Though she hadn't died, as she had hoped, she moved along in a kind of conscious coma, keeping herself as empty of thoughts as she could. She knew she was walking in the direction of town, and if she followed the beach long enough, tracked around or through its creeks, she'd arrive eventually at the harbor, then the pier, then the public beach, then the fallen-in ferry dock and the place where she had a raft and green potato chips and Superman pajama bottoms waiting. Whenever thoughts of Owen or thoughts of going to jail came to mind, she hurled them into the bay and drowned them quick.

She still had the revolver if she got desperate.

Late that morning, she discovered a dead turtle washed up on some rocks. At first she mistook it for just another rock, but as she got closer, she noticed the subtle mosaic of the shell, grooves as perfect as brand-new tires.

The smell was enough to repel her until she remembered the gallery and the artist who painted on sand dollars. A turtle shell had to be worth more than sand dollars, maybe worth hundreds. The turtle's head and flippers had blackened and mummified in the sun, but the shell itself, about the size of a serving platter, was flawless.

"Look at you," she said. "You poor old thing," and she laughed at herself for talking to a dead turtle. She knew she was lonely, but geez.

She picked up the turtle by its edges, held it as far from her body as she could, and continued down the beach. But it wasn't long before the stench made her stop. She rinsed the turtle at the water's edge, but it didn't help. Even her hands stunk. So she found an oyster shell, and she used it as a knife to try and pry away the reeking meat in the hopes that if she could separate the turtle from its shell, she could make enough money to spend more nights in motels (assuming her half sister refused her, assuming she found her half sister at all).

In a way, she admired the turtle. For one thing, it was already dead and didn't have to put up with anybody's shit. The turtle didn't care if she mauled it. It didn't feel a thing. Even in death that turtle was tough. She'd like to be that tough. She wasn't tough at all—and look at how far she'd fallen, there on a strange beach, alone, unknown, and unloved.

But the meat was as stubborn as jerky, and though it stretched, it wouldn't give. In the end, she found a plastic grocery bag washed up behind some driftwood, and she used it to wrap the turtle. The bag had holes, but it helped, and she made her way up the shore with her smelly half-wrapped parcel.

It was afternoon before she came to the harbor where there were plenty of water hoses for her to borrow, a water station between every two boat slips along the docks. She chose a faucet on land, attached to the side of the harbormaster's office and surrounded by a good hedge of roses that she hoped would block her from the eyes of recreational boaters and fishermen. But the guy working the gas pumps noticed her and called out, "What you got there, gal?"

He finished fueling up a skiff, put his long gas hose away, and sauntered over to Dori, looking official with his clipboard beneath his arm.

"I said what you got there, gal?"

"Dead turtle," Dori told him, without looking his way.

"Smells like it," he replied.

"Found it on the beach."

"Did you now?" said the man. "Hey, Eric," he called over his shoulder, "come take a look at this!" Then to Dori he said, "You're in luck—or maybe not—'cause Eric's here. He's the waterkeeper, you know."

Dori just wanted to be left alone. She'd never heard of a waterkeeper and didn't want to meet one. She wasn't counting on show-and-tell, but suddenly she had fishermen all around her. It seemed obscene, the way they watched her.

The guy named Eric jogged over, lugging a cooler, and said, "Wow. That's a Kemp's Ridley," and like she needed a lecture, he said, "It's the rarest of the sea turtles around here and also an endangered species." He took it right out of her hands, not even caring about the smell, flipping it over and examining the underside. "This one's not very old either," he added. "Where'd you find it?"

"Down there." She pointed. "On some rocks. I didn't kill it. It was already dead."

"I wonder what happened," he said. "We just released some of these last year. I'll have to call the rescue team to see if they can identify it." He put the turtle into his cooler. "Thanks," he said.

"Wait," said Dori. "You can't take it."

"You can't keep it," he said. "Sorry, but I thought you knew that."

"What are you talking about? I found it on the beach, just dead there." After all the work she'd done, she wasn't about to give it up. She lunged for the cooler, and the guy named Eric pulled the cooler away.

So she kicked him, hard, in the shins, and she started swinging with both arms, and then somebody grabbed her, held her from behind and said, "Get the chief."

It all happened so fast—before she had a chance to take a deep breath and calm herself down. If she'd taken the time to think, she wouldn't have kicked the bejesus out of the man who was holding her or spit at the guy named Eric, who seemed completely surprised by her reaction. She didn't even have a chance to regret it until somebody forced her down onto the crushed-up clamshell pavement, her arms behind her back, her tote bag lumpy beneath her abdomen. She could feel the revolver press against her hipbone, and she hoped it wouldn't discharge by accident.

It wasn't long before a policeman was there.

He led her over to a picnic table and made her sit. "You got any kind of ID on you?"

Dori shook her head and hoped he wouldn't search her bag. The gun wasn't even her biggest problem. If he found her driver's license, stashed in her wallet along with what was left of her money, it'd only be minutes before he discovered she was wanted for questioning. Why hadn't she shredded her license back when she'd had the chance?

"Who do you belong to, girl?" asked the cop, but she didn't answer. "You can't go around assaulting people for no reason," he added.

As if that jerk hadn't stolen her turtle.

"It's called self-defense," she hissed. She caught herself before she finished the thought—*you fucker*—and didn't actually call him that name, but her tone must have conveyed it because the cop replied, "Whoa now, missy. That ain't no way to make friends. You want me to lock you up?"

"No, sir," she said.

The guy named Eric sat next to the policeman astraddle the picnic table bench, dabbing at the scratches on his face with a dirty bandanna. He kept trying to explain that taking the turtle wasn't personal, that it was all about conservation and preservation, and he told her that the shell would eventually be on display at the Barrier Island Center, like that would do her any good.

Even though Dori had left him streaked and bleeding, he turned to the chief and said, "I'm not pressing charges. It's just a misunderstanding."

"Suit yourself," said the chief. To Dori, he added, "I can still arrest you for resisting an officer, but I'm gonna give you one last chance. Tell me where you live so I can take you home. Otherwise, I'm hauling your sassy ass to jail."

So Dori took a leap of faith—like most leaps, a desperate one—and gave the chief of police her older half sister's name.

II.

Teresa paused at the end of the pier, took her phone from her pocket and scrolled through her playlists, looking for music to pump her up, something peppy enough to transform her leisurely morning beach walk into a full-blown exercise routine. But she hit a button by mistake and, instead of Lady Gaga, out came the voice of Sperm Donor #8466, their runner-up. Apparently, the last time she synced her phone, she had transferred the donor interviews along with her new music.

Donor #8466 was an entrepreneur, an easygoing, laughing guy and a winemaker with plans to one day purchase his own vineyard. Both she and Jen had liked him a lot—much better than the donor who came in third, a doctor with a scratchy voice who couldn't even think of a favorite childhood memory to share. They'd downloaded audio interviews for their top three baby-daddy contenders, but even though the doctor was the closest physical match to Jen, they'd eliminated him right away once they heard him speak.

In the end, they'd chosen Donor #9721, a lawyer, and they'd gone through six rounds of inseminations at the fertility clinic across the bay, paying extra for their lawyer's graduate degrees. But they still weren't pregnant.

Teresa stopped along the shoreline to flip over a horseshoe crab. Mating season was a complicated business for them, too. On June nights, when the tide was high and the moon was full or new, the horseshoe crabs crawled out of the bay and onto the beach to breed, large females tailed by smaller males. Inevitably some of the males got stranded on their return trip, flipped onto their backs by competitors or by the tide and left exposed and desperate as the sun came up.

Teresa tickled the legs of the crab to make sure it was still alive. When it kicked back, she lifted the edges of its shell, carried it to the water, and watched it slowly drag itself out into the bay.

Listening to the entrepreneur's interview felt a little like cheating, given that they'd already committed to the lawyer, so she scanned her phone and found *his* interview. As she made her way down the beach, flipping one horseshoe crab after the next, she noticed something troubling in the lawyer's voice. He was a whiner. Everything he said came out as a low-grade complaint. Why hadn't they detected that before? He liked law, but really wanted to be a writer. He'd done some writing, but just textbooks for law students.

No wonder they hadn't gotten pregnant. Even his sperm was ambivalent.

Jen had been a big fan of the lawyer from the start. She hadn't finished college and was impressed by his credentials. More than that, she liked him because he was a reader and subscribed to the symphony. She wanted a kid who'd be artistic and soulful and smart.

But if they were trying to match the donor with Jen, the entrepreneur was obviously the better choice. He raced go-karts as a kid. He was brave and playful. Why had he come in second? They should have gone with the entrepreneur. He'd never worn braces or glasses and had no known allergies, his only injury a broken arm from when he flipped off his trampoline, the little daredevil.

Daredevil sperm cells were sure to be more potent than the sperm of any poor, complaining, sad-sack attorney.

Some of the horseshoe crabs Teresa found along the shoreline were already dead. Those she left on their backs for the seagulls to peck clean. But she was able to rescue seven or eight, give them another chance, another day to spray their seed.

30

It seemed like sperm was all she could think about. That month, for the first time, she and Jen planned to inseminate at home, both to cut down on the expense and on their stress. Their friend Eric, who had secretly agreed to serve as a sperm donor, had been on call for the past week. But though Teresa was due to ovulate, though she'd dutifully peed on sticks each morning to check her hormone levels, she hadn't yet made the single line transform into a double. It was becoming embarrassing, how little power she had to pass a simple pee test.

She'd hoped that exercising would help her stop obsessing about it, but even when she went for power walks, she found herself distracted by thoughts of sperm donors.

If Eric's goods did the trick, they might not even need to order more vials from the cryobank at nearly a thousand dollars a pop. But if she didn't conceive this go-around, she'd insist on the entrepreneurial sperm. They could place their order in plenty of time for next month's ovulation.

That afternoon, as Teresa watered the cucumbers she'd planted along the city strip—a kind of community garden she'd hoped the community would help take care of—she barely noticed the police cruiser pull up and park beneath a tree. People parked there all the time and walked the last block to the pier, hauling coolers, lugging beach chairs and floats, tugging children by the arm.

In a daze, she sprayed just above the plants so that the water would rain down on their leaves, and she considered for the hundredth time whether it was finally time to put down Sugar Britches, her cat.

When she'd first dug up that ground in the spring, replacing crabgrass and dandelion with organic humus and topsoil, Sugar Britches had crouched near, stalking the robins that stalked the worms in that newly turned soil. When the seeds were barely sprouted, she'd had to run him from the garden, which he'd claimed by then as a litter box, scratching up the tiny greens.

31

Only a couple of months later, and he didn't have the energy to follow her outside.

So when she heard the chief of police call out, "Hey, Teresa!" and looked to see that he'd stepped from his car, was facing her, she startled. She almost sprayed him with her hose. In the same instant, a skinny teenage girl she didn't recognize charged in her direction. The girl was clearly in some kind of trouble. Before Teresa knew what was happening, the girl had practically wedged beneath her arm into an awkward, protective hug.

The chief stood there in full uniform in the scant shade of a crepe myrtle, legs spread, and said, "Teresa, if this gal weren't staying with you and Jen, I'd be hauling her in. When she gets mad, she fights like a wet setting hen."

"I said I was sorry," snapped the girl.

Teresa tried to place her. Her wavy brown hair was bobbed off just below her ears—different from the style most girls her age wore. Was she a former student? One of the kids who'd helped Jen last summer at the deli? She was raggedy-looking: green eyes smudged with mascara, a peeling nose and forehead, a sharp chin with a fresh and bleeding cut, and long legs in rolled-up jeans, wet halfway up her thighs.

"I didn't even know you *had* a little sister," said the chief. "She's got an attitude on her, don't she?"

Just that fast, Teresa's brain did the spins, like somebody had wound her up tight and let loose. She nodded and smiled at the chief, who whirled in her vision, a swarm of himself.

The spray of the water made a hint of a rainbow between him and the cucumber plants, and she wondered if she might be hallucinating. She'd been up most all night, obsessing about ovulation, had worked all day, and she'd skipped lunch. But could you hallucinate smells? Something smelled gamy, even rotten, and she realized the stink was coming from the girl, like she'd been dragged back from the grave at the last possible minute.

The girl took the hose right out of Teresa's hand. "Let me help," she offered, and she turned her back to the cop and began watering the squash plants that Teresa hadn't yet reached. She sprayed the ground around them so hard that the dirt jumped up and splattered the leaves.

"Thank you, Chief," said Teresa. She wasn't sure if she should say anything else, if she should invite him in, offer him something to drink. She'd served with him on the library board, two terms, but if they went inside, he might find out she didn't know this sister she was suddenly protecting.

Her mouth worked separately from her mind, and she heard herself asking, "Any leads yet on the break-in at Miss Betty's?"

"Still working it," said the chief. "Most considerate criminal you've ever seen, I'll warrant you that. Gotta be somebody that knows her."

"Huh," said Teresa.

"Business okay?" he asked, nodding toward the old motel they'd spent the last year—and most of their savings—renovating.

"Coming along," Teresa said. "We've got the west side done and the east side done. Just working on the middle now." Most of the motel could be considered middle.

"Good to hear," said the chief. "You keep your kid sister outta trouble, all right? Tell Jen I said hey."

He climbed into his police car and left.

Before he'd rounded the corner, the girl began to cry. "Oh my God," she said. "Oh my fucking god! Thank you." She doubled over like she'd just finished a marathon, hands on her knees, panting. She dropped the water hose right onto the sidewalk and let it run.

"You're welcome, I guess," Teresa said. She took measured breaths, steadying herself, and hoped she wouldn't pass out. She picked up the hose and turned the sprayer off.

"That wasn't how I pictured us meeting," the girl admitted.

"You're Dorothy Ann then?" asked Teresa.

"Dori," said the girl. She wiped her nose, but her tears kept rolling. "I don't know what Mom was thinking when she named me that. I'm gonna change it to just Dori as soon as I turn eighteen."

The last Teresa had heard, her mom had joined up with a Jesus-militia and was on a crusade to win souls for Christ in the mountains of Tennessee. She hadn't spoken with her in years. "Is she dead?" Teresa asked. The question popped out before the thought had even fully formed. She didn't know what answer she expected. Or wanted.

"Mom?" Dori replied. "No," she said. "She's okay. We had a fight, so I took off. She's fucking crazy, you know?"

Teresa *did* know, but she didn't tolerate foul-mouthed teenagers. She taught high school—US history—and filled out detention slips lickety-split for anyone who used that kind of language.

"So I thought maybe I'd come stay with you for a while?" Dori shrugged and smiled, and Teresa saw that one of her front teeth was broken off at a sideways angle. A lot of tooth was missing there, a whole triangle. It looked like it must hurt. She saw bruises and bug bites and remnants of hickeys on the side of Dori's neck. She saw darting eyes.

She recognized those eyes: fern-green with heavy lids that made them look perpetually sleepy, lids that would probably need lifting one day. Like hers. They had the same eyes.

"Come on in," she said.

But she took her time with the hose before ushering Dori into the apartment, coiling it evenly and hanging it on its hook, in its rightful place beside the spigot.

In the small kitchen, the stench grew even more pungent. It was a graceless start—telling Dori she stunk—but so be it. "I don't know what you've gotten into," she said, "but you really need a shower."

Dori blushed. "I picked up a rotten turtle," she explained. "I think it's up under my fingernails."

"Huh," said Teresa, because what could you possibly say to that? "Okay then. Just give me a second." In the bathroom she stashed her ovulation test kit and pee cup in the cabinet. She grabbed the trash can with its used test sticks on the way out. "All yours," she said. "I've put a fresh towel and washcloth on the toilet."

Dori passed her reeking clothes through a crack in the bathroom door, and Teresa used a potholder to pick them up. Jeans size four, top size small, cheap made-in-China fabric, thong underwear. Who *was* this girl? She doused Dori's clothes with vinegar—a whole bottle—hoping it would neutralize the smell, threw in the potholder, too, added detergent to the washing machine, and punched in the code for the sanitizing cycle, along with an extra rinse.

It was bizarre—beyond bizarre—to wash a stranger's thong underwear, a stranger who was also her half-baby sister.

She'd known that her mother had started another family years after leaving her first family behind. Teresa had just turned twenty-three when she received the birth announcement and a picture of an infant with a pink elastic headband stretched around her bald head. But she'd never seen another picture of Dori, and she'd had no contact with her mother at all since she'd sent her the invitation to her and Jen's commitment ceremony a full twelve years before.

Her mom had never even acknowledged it.

Dori would have been five by then. She could've been a flower girl. By the time same-sex marriage had become legal in Virginia and she and Jen had upgraded, Dori would have been old enough to serve as a junior bridesmaid, if they'd had a traditional wedding, which they didn't.

Since Teresa had never seen Dori in the flesh and only knew her name to be Dorothy, she always pictured her as Dorothy from *The Wizard of Oz*, decked out in a gingham dress, low ponytails in her hair, walking the streets of east Tennessee with her dog in a basket, knocking on doors and handing out fliers about the End of Times and John 3:16.

But there was nothing wholesome or innocent about her.

Teresa tried to call Jen but couldn't get through. Jen was out on the bay where you couldn't always get a signal, so she left her a text: *Urgent. We have company. Hurry if you can.*

Teresa was every bit as tall as Dori, but probably sixty pounds heavier. Since none of her own clothes would fit, she raided Jen's drawers, borrowing exercise shorts and a T-shirt. She hung them on the knob outside the bathroom door.

Dori's shower continued a long while more. It was a wonder the hot water lasted. While she waited, Teresa carefully lifted Sugar Britches from his bed and carried him over to his food bowl. Sugar had once been so fat his jiggling belly swept the grass. Now he was all bones—except for the tumor on his haunch, large and firm as a plum.

"Come on, baby," she said as he rejected first his kibble, then his wet food.

She'd had him since he was a kitten, a little stray that had showed up beneath the porch. He was mostly black with some small white streaks on his face and chest. But his most distinctive marking was his rear end, which was entirely white. He looked as if his back legs had been dipped in paint, or maybe powdered sugar—hence, his name.

Now, at fourteen, he wanted nothing to do with his food. Teresa managed to tempt him with the tiniest bit of baby food licked from her finger, but when the bathroom door finally opened and a cleaned-up Dori emerged, Sugar startled and crept away.

Sitting there at the table, drinking orange juice and gobbling down a ham sandwich, Dori admitted between bites that her mom didn't like her boyfriend. "She grounded me when I didn't deserve it," Dori claimed. "I'd run up the phone bill, but that was a total accident, because she changed the text plan without telling me. So I snuck out and spent the night with my boyfriend, and Mom got pissed."

Teresa remembered how difficult her mom could be, but of course Dori would be grounded for running up the phone bill. There was nothing unreasonable about that. And what kind of mother wouldn't get pissed off when her teenage daughter spent the night with a boy? She'd be pissed, too.

And what made *any* teenager think it was okay to talk so openly about spending the night with a boyfriend or girlfriend, whether it was true or not? "Wait a minute," Teresa said. "Don't you have a job or something?"

"I used to," said Dori. "At Pizza Hut."

"So if you're old enough to stay out all night with your boyfriend, why aren't you old enough to pay for your own cell phone plan?"

Dori rolled her eyes. "I contribute," she said. "I pay more of the bill than she does, actually."

"Go ahead," said Teresa. "How did you end up running away?"

"I *didn't* run away," Dori claimed. "She kicked me out."

It wasn't a good start, this friction between them, but Teresa hadn't been expecting a little sister to show up with zero notice. If she'd given half a thought to what her sister might be like, she'd have imagined her so different, considering her upbringing— obedient, meek—not this bristly, abrasive thing.

"Don't you get it?" Dori said. "Mom doesn't want me anymore. I didn't know what else to do." She sighed and pressed her forehead into her hands. Mustard stains rimmed her chewed-down nails.

Teresa couldn't tell if she was crying or not. But if there was one thing she understood, it was that feeling of not being wanted and the long-term damage it could cause. In a way, she wished she'd left her mom before her mom had a chance to leave *her*. "You have to call and tell her you're safe," Teresa insisted. "She's probably worried to death."

"She doesn't want to hear from me," Dori mumbled. "Trust me."

෨ ෨ ෨

The motel, a single-story cinderblock structure in the shape of an L, was set back off the street far enough that ten cars could park out front, a car for every room. In spite of the prime location— only a block and a half to the bayside beach—the bank had foreclosed on the property five years earlier. No one had made an offer for a long time because the place needed so much work.

Teresa and Jen had lived just down the street, and on evenings as they walked past on their way to the pier to watch the sunset, they dreamed up all the things they might do if they owned it: convert it into a skating rink, a bowling alley, a pasta-making plant.

Jen liked the idea of running an old-fashioned motel, and the town certainly needed more lodging for all the folks who came through. There were fishing tournaments for rockfish or black drum or flounder throughout the season. But every school year wiped Teresa out, and she couldn't imagine spending her already-too-short summer breaks dealing with vacationers who just wanted to get drunk with their buddies and forget their troubles. Even the thought of keeping up with the vacancy sign felt like too much work.

Still, they peeked in the windows, wandered the perimeter, and one day Jen brought along a measuring tape and took down the dimensions of the office apartment itself. That space alone was nearly as large as their little bungalow.

And so they made an offer, with the agreement from the town planning commission that instead of renovating as a motel, they'd lease blocks of rooms to independent businesses. They got the dual-use permit, sold their house, and moved into the office apartment at one end of the structure. Jen relocated her deli to the other end, where they knocked out a wall between two of the rooms so there'd be ample space for tables, in addition to the kitchen and counter.

Dori's tour of the place started at that end, where they'd done the most work, and it showed. "So this is Jen's Deli," she said. Teresa walked her through the small entry, past the glass cases with their hefty hams and turkey breasts and beef roasts and cheeses. At that time of day, there weren't many customers, and the manager was busy going over paperwork with a delivery driver. So Teresa pointed out their renovations, the checkerboard tile floor they'd spent too much on, the glass doors out back, the pergola they'd added just last year so that honeysuckle could twine around the trellises, creating shade and a sweet aroma for the customers who whispered to one another at small tables.

"Nice," Dori said, but it was clear she was just being polite.

As they left, Teresa caught herself babbling, providing too much information about the barber who'd rented the room next door to the deli, but who worked only three days a week—like Dori cared. Why would she care?

Next door to the barber, a title company handled real estate closings, and next door to the title company, a flower shop doubled as a tailor. At least they had an interesting window display—flowers arranged artfully around an antique Singer sewing machine. "It's kind of cool, really," Teresa said. "You can pick out fresh-cut flowers or six-packs of pansies while you get your dress pants hemmed." She knew it seemed strange, but it was quaint, one of her favorite businesses on the shore. "Do you need anything hemmed?" she joked.

"I don't have any clothes," said Dori. "Somebody stole my backpack."

They couldn't even get the tone right.

"Bummer," said Teresa.

What else was there to say? And why did everything have to be so awkward? But it couldn't be easy for Dori either. They'd been together less than an hour, and already it felt like a month of Sundays.

"So basically you live in a strip mall?" Dori said.

Heat flushed through Teresa's neck and chest. "Well, that's not how I think of it," she replied. "But I guess that's one way to see it."

There wasn't much more of the place to show: just the four rooms still unfinished. Teresa produced a key and unlocked one of the doors.

It was musty in there. "Whoa," said Dori. The walls were dingy and streaked from rain, and the floors were mismatched wood full of staples and patched with tin.

"A lot of work left to do," Teresa said. "My summer project. But it shows you how far we've come! Last week I got the carpet up, thank the goddess, and there's a new roof on the place, so all those stains on the ceiling are just left over from old leaks. It looks bad, but at this point it's mostly cosmetic."

"It's pretty disgusting," said Dori. "Why don't you hurry up and finish it?"

The way she said it, it could have been her mom—not just the criticism, but also the snotty tone.

"We plan to, but at the moment we're out of money—or at least out of money to spend on *this* project. You didn't think I was your *rich* long-lost half sister, did you?"

She led Dori along the outer corridor and to the last room before the apartment: Room 2. "And this is the guest quarters, where you can stay tonight. Beyond that—well, we'll talk."

Teresa handed her the room key and said, "Make yourself comfortable. I've got some stuff to do." It was a lie, but she'd had enough. Between Dori's attitude, Sugar Britches' decline, and her never-ending obsession with her own impending ovulation, she needed a good distraction. Nothing sounded better right then than crawling into bed with a book, though she wished she was reading something a little lighter. She was halfway through *Up from Slavery*, the autobiography of Booker T. Washington, which she planned to assign her Honors 11 students in the fall.

Dori stared at the key without putting it in the lock. She looked as confused as Teresa felt.

"Go on in," Teresa urged. "Take a nap or watch TV or something. We'll have dinner when Jen gets back. It won't be long. An hour or two, max."

"Who's Jen again?" asked Dori.

"My partner," Teresa replied.

"Oh, okay," Dori said. Tentatively, she entered the room and closed the door. Teresa heard her turn the deadbolt, then flip the security latch.

Dori was scared.

And why wouldn't she be?

Teresa scrubbed the bathtub, then ran a bath for herself and settled in with her book. But she couldn't concentrate. For the first time, she realized how complicated and tricky it must have been for former slaves after the Emancipation Proclamation, when they finally had a chance to track down long-lost relatives. In spite of the celebrations, at the end of the day those people were still strangers, with completely different histories and completely different lives.

Yet nothing was more important than reuniting.

In the summers, when counter help was plentiful, Jen left her manager and a team of college students to run the deli's storefront while she delivered sandwiches and drinks from her skiff. Charter cruises, fishing vessels, and vacationers boating by the sandbar all relied on her floating sandwich shop for their gourmet goods. But today Jen didn't even stop by to check on the afternoon's sales or drop off the cash box from the boat before she dashed into the apartment, leaving her soggy, sandy Tevas on the welcome mat.

"I got here as fast as I could!" she announced. "Do I have time to get a shower?"

"Huh?" Teresa replied.

"Is he here?"

"Who?" She was trying again to get Sugar Britches to eat, but he'd turned his head.

"Eric!" said Jen. "You said we had company?"

"Oh," Teresa replied. "Oh honey, I didn't mean Eric. I'm sorry."

She left the food next to Sugar Britches' bed, got up off the floor, and pulled Jen into a hug. "I didn't mean to trick you. It's my *sister*," she said. "I mean, my half sister—in Room 2."

"You're kidding," said Jen.

"I'm not. She wants to stay with us awhile."

"Wow."

"Give me your hand," Teresa said, and she pressed Jen's palm against her own racing heart and held it there until her heart quieted down.

When Jen had showered and counted her till and they'd both gotten ready for dinner, they knocked at the door to Room 2. No one answered. Teresa called Dori's name again and again. It felt funny in her mouth and funny to think that she had a half sister named Dori at all.

"I swear," said Teresa. "Do you think she took off without telling me? She doesn't even have her clothes!" Her clothes, freshly washed, were folded up in Teresa's arms. They circled the motel and even got the spare key to Room 2 to check inside, but there was no sign of Dori.

Then Teresa spotted her in the distance, strolling back from the pier like she owned it, like she owned the whole town. It was hard to reconcile the image of that cocky girl with the image of the child on the sidewalk, crying as the police chief drove away.

"Hey," Teresa called when she was closer. "You scared me. You could have told me before you just left like that."

Dori shrugged and said, "I didn't go far." It wasn't an apology.

"This is Jen," Teresa said.

Jen offered her hand, and Dori stared at it a second before she shook it. Maybe she'd never shaken hands with a woman. "Good to meet you," said Jen. "Let's eat."

"You wanna change first?" Teresa asked. "I washed your clothes. I left them in the room."

"Do I need to?" asked Dori. She'd tucked in the T-shirt and rolled over the waistband of Jen's exercise shorts so she could wear them up high, showing off long, lean thighs, along with plenty of scratches, scrapes and bruises.

"We're just going to the pub," said Jen. "You're fine." They began

42

the walk down the uneven sidewalks, past crepe myrtle trees out-growing their bark but not yet in bloom. Dori and Jen walked side by side; Teresa fell in step behind them.

"So you're business partners?" asked Dori.

"*Life* partners," said Teresa. She heard herself and wished she could change the way she said it. How could the way you said *one word* come out so defensive?

Dori looked back at her and raised her eyebrows. Teresa didn't know how to read the gesture.

"Didn't your mom tell you that?" Teresa asked.

"She left out that little detail," said Dori.

They hadn't walked more than a few steps in silence before Jen deflated the drama: "Well, let's just get that cleared up right away then!" she said and laughed. "Your big sister's a big lesbian, and so is her wife!" She sounded delighted about it. She practically yelled it. "Now, we're not in the business of converting people," she teased, "but we do rock out to a lot of music by Melissa Etheridge and the Indigo Girls. You don't have a problem with that, do you?"

Dori shrugged and shook her head. "To each his own," she muttered.

"*Her* own," Teresa replied.

Dori was silent the rest of the walk and looked a little stricken as they were seated. She flipped through the menu and then excused herself to the bathroom. She stayed gone a while, and when she came back, she busied herself with a wooden peg game, jumping from hole to hole and trying to leave a solo peg in the middle.

Maybe it helped that all around them neighbors and friends made small talk. The waiter knew their drink order without asking. From the bar, a waterman placed a sandwich order for his crew for the next day, and Jen wrote it down in her phone. Obviously, everybody else in the pub dealt with their relationship just fine.

While they waited for their food, Jen invited Dori to play darts, and to Teresa's surprise, Dori agreed. It wasn't long before she was talking a little, even cheering when she landed a dart close to the bull's-eye. Jen introduced her to the bartender and patrons as Teresa's long-lost baby sister. She made it seem like everybody should have one, and a visit was cause for a grand celebration. When the food arrived, she put her hand right on Dori's shoulder and guided her back to the table. If Dori flinched, Jen didn't acknowledge it, and maybe a steady hand was what Dori needed anyway. Watching them, Teresa wished she could be more like Jen, more at peace with the world and all its surprises.

As friends came by to speak and share news, they picked up bits of Dori's story: her favorite subject in school was biology; her older sister lived in a perfect place to explore marine environments. When asked where she wanted to go to college, she said she was keeping her options open. When asked how she'd gotten such a sunburn, she claimed she'd fallen asleep in the hammock.

Again and again, people kept saying to Teresa, "I didn't know you had a little sister," and over and over she replied, "I'll tell you the story sometime when you have half a day to spare."

Dori warmed up. She wasn't bad at handling conversations with strangers. In fact, she was pretty good at it. Sitting there watching her in action, Teresa suspected she shouldn't be trusted. Her mom had been the same way, able to talk a blue streak. She could talk the judge out of jail time, talk the preacher right out of communion, but you couldn't believe a third of what she told you.

"Okay," said Jen, when they were alone again. "We need to get the facts straight. Can't have the townies knowing more about you than we do. What grade?"

"Eleventh," said Dori. "I should be a senior, but I missed a year when we moved."

"That's extreme," said Jen.

"No kidding," said Dori. "So was our move."

"And you've come to us from Tennessee?" Teresa asked.

44

"Mississippi," she said. "We left Tennessee after Mom got out of the nuthouse and finally sprung me out of foster care."

"Whoa," said Teresa. "Foster care?"

"How long ago was that?" Jen asked.

Dori shrugged. "Couple of years."

"Okay," said Jen. "And how's your mom doing now?"

"She's a psycho," said Dori. She looked hard at Teresa, held her eyes without blinking. "And she always has been, hasn't she?"

She needed affirmation, connection, but Teresa couldn't provide it. Who knew what Dori was after? "She's always had her problems. That's for sure," she said. "But I wouldn't call her a psycho exactly."

"Clearly you haven't hung out with her lately," Dori spit.

In all the years she'd been out of touch with her mother, Teresa hadn't let herself think about things like psychiatric hospitals or foster care. From her earliest memories, her parents fought, usually because of her mom's antics. Like the time she took Teresa to sit on the roof during a thunderstorm, rain pelting down, smoky clouds shrouding the sky until lightning flashed through spectacularly. Teresa and her mom had clapped and cheered for every lightning strike until her dad got home and found them there. "Get in this house," he demanded, but her mom refused. Finally, he climbed up to the roof himself, took Teresa beneath his arm and carefully guided her down the slippery ladder and back inside. The storm looked a lot scarier from indoors. She kept running out back and into the rain, calling to her mom who had scooted to the far reaches of the shingles by then.

Until she was older, she didn't understand that all mothers didn't throw oranges from the fruit bowl when they got frustrated or rush out of the house sobbing and disappear into the woods for hours at a time.

And other mothers certainly didn't get hurt as often. The hospital emergency room formed the backdrop for so many of Teresa's earliest recollections, as her mom was prone to stepping on nails or tripping over extension cords and splitting open her head. Dangers seemed to lurk wherever she went.

It took a while for Teresa to notice that most of her mom's accidents happened whenever she or her dad had other things planned. When she was in the finals for the regional spelling bee, her mom had an attack of pancreatitis, and both parents missed hearing her spell *malevolent* and *schism,* though she got kicked out anyway on "parliament." What did it mean that she could still remember, still *held onto* those words?

When Teresa landed the part of Mrs. Van Daan in the junior high production of *The Diary of Anne Frank,* her mom fell down the auditorium stairs on opening night.

And then when she was in eleventh grade, her mom had run off with the Baptist preacher—a married man, no less—leaving Teresa and her father to face that blistering scandal.

The next year, a letter addressed to Teresa arrived, her mom's loopy cursive flowering across the pages from a yellow legal pad in smudgy, blue ink. The letter proclaimed how good God had been! How she was living with her sisters and brothers-in-Christ on a farm where they grew their own food and celebrated every Sonrise and Sonset! She invited Teresa to visit and even join them there, but her father was sick with emphysema by then. It took him nearly three years to finally choke to death. Her mom didn't show up for his funeral or help Teresa resolve any of the family affairs.

She had dropped out of college that semester, but went back the next. Some semesters she could only take a couple of classes; some semesters she took six at once. When she graduated with a degree in secondary education, she sent an announcement to her mom's last known address.

Her mom wrote back from a different location. She was traveling around the South by then, spreading the Good News of Christ's impending return. She congratulated Teresa and even sent a gift: a book of devotions for her desk drawer at school, so that when those students got the best of her, she could center herself in God's love. She'd put sticky notes between the pages to share favorite passages. Inside the front cover, she included advice: *Handling the boys will be especially hard, for they won't respect a woman. But there's a man to help you, a man you can call on: Jesus Christ. Invite him into your classroom, and you'll do fine.*

Teresa found a job teaching history two states away and moved from her hometown and all those complicated losses. But she did her best to keep in touch. She even tried to visit once after her mom called from a pay phone, crying. Teresa got a last-minute substitute to fill in at school and drove two hundred miles to a diner where they'd arranged to meet. But her mom stood her up. Later, in a letter, she said that it was just bad timing and that she'd finally gotten off "those terrible pills" (as if Teresa had known she was *on* pills), and now her psychiatric medications could finally do their work.

Sometimes there'd be months of silence. Then, just when Teresa would think she must have died, she'd receive a note—and that one time, the birth announcement for Dorothy Ann, no letter attached, only a rural route box number for a return address.

It blew her mind that her unstable mother would bring another child into the world. Her mom was over forty by then. Teresa herself was old enough to be a mother, but she had better sense.

She bought the baby a sweater and mailed it, hoping it would be big enough. And that was the last thing she sent until she invited her mom to their commitment ceremony and reception.

It was a risky thing to do.

Teresa often wondered if her mom had suspected she was gay. She'd been a tomboy, more interested in playing in the creek than playing dress-up, but that was no good indicator, and her mom had run off with the preacher long before Teresa began to date. Even after she started seeing women, there was no occasion to come out to her mom, and anyway she didn't need another reason to be rejected.

Then Jen came along.

With Jen, she fell in love, and all the clichés about love seemed true: she was over the moon, brought to her knees. As silly as it seemed, she wanted her mom to share her happiness. As unlikely as it seemed, she wanted her blessing.

At the very least, she decided she should give her mom a chance to know and love Jen. What did she have to lose?

She anguished over the letter she included in the envelope with the invitation to their commitment ceremony. She could still remember how her belly cramped as she waited in line at the post office to be sure she'd included enough postage.

But all that anxiety was wasted. There was never a reply.

"She can't help it," Jen tried to console. "If she's as evangelical as you claim, she probably can't say anything without condemning your lifestyle. You know the old saying: if you can't say something nice, don't say anything at all."

And her mom didn't.

Over the years, Teresa's hurt and anger dissolved into numbness, and when same-sex marriage became legal in Virginia and she and Jen tied the knot again, it didn't even occur to her to share the news.

In fact, her mother's absence became no more noticeable than a pepper shaker missing from the table. Most of the time, it made no difference, though every now and then a little more spice would have improved on an already fine recipe.

By the time the chief of police escorted Dori to her door, Teresa had seriously believed she was "over" her mother. But there in the pub with Jen and Dori, she could hardly swallow her fish and chips for the guilt. Maybe there'd been a reply lost in the mail. Or maybe her mom had never received her letter and invitation in the first place. She might have moved to a different address by then. Why hadn't Teresa given her the benefit of the doubt?

And how could she ever expect to be a good mother if she hadn't even been a good daughter and sister? She'd given in way too easily. With the Internet, she could have found her mom. If they'd been in touch, she and Jen could have provided a home for Dori, instead of abandoning her to the foster care system. No wonder Teresa hadn't been able to get pregnant. She had to work a lot harder to connect.

"When I was little," Teresa told Dori, "I used to beg Mom to play with me. We lived way out in the country where there were no other kids, so I didn't have anybody to play with. But the only game she'd play was orphanage."

"That's weird," Dori said.

"We'd line up my paper dolls in a row, and she'd dream up these awful stories about their dead daddies. She'd have them clawed to death by bears or blown up with dynamite."

Dori laughed. "Sounds just like her."

"Or she'd make up stories about their mothers who burned up in house fires or drove off cliffs, sometimes killing the children riding along in the car. She'd hold up a paper doll with bent arms or a loose neck and say, 'This one here's the only one who survived, and she'll never be normal again.'"

Jen put her hand on Teresa's thigh and squeezed. "Yikes," she said. "Not very nurturing, was she?"

Dori chimed in, "She's *still* not."

"I wanted to play school," Teresa continued. "Big surprise there. I even agreed to let the paper dolls have a mean teacher who paddled them for not knowing their state capitals, as long as at the end of the day, all the kids could go home and eat fried chicken and macaroni. But Mom would say, 'Gruel! They're starving to death with nothing to eat but gruel.'"

Dori laughed again, her face softening. "I can totally see that," she said.

"One time I found my favorite paper doll dangling from the leaves of the dragon tree we kept in the livingroom. She had a yarn noose around her neck and her head flopped over. She looked so pitiful, wearing nothing but her drawn-on underpants. I called Mom, and she came and sat with me there on the living-room floor, and we cried together as we watched her blowing in the wind from the heater vent. Mom said, 'Poor little thing. They hung her for treason.'"

Teresa hadn't known that word yet: *treason*. She'd had to look it up.

෴ ෴ ෴

49

They finished their blackberry crumble and paid the check. But on the way out of the pub they passed a table where Teresa's friend Cassidy and her family were having dinner. Cassidy jumped up, her mouth still working on a forkful of salad, and threw both arms around Teresa. "I can't stand summers!" she said. "I never get to see you anymore."

"I miss you, too," Teresa admitted. "But I love summers!" Cassidy had once been her best friend and sidekick at the high school, but she'd gone down to part-time when her kids were little and had then become the release-time teacher. So she worked only ten hours a week. Summers weren't as necessary for teachers with that kind of schedule.

Cassidy hugged Jen and whispered, "These kids are driving me batty. I'd never survive as a stay-at-home mom." She smiled at Dori and asked, "Who's this?"

When Jen introduced her as Teresa's little sister, Cassidy screeched and then immediately turned to Dori and asked, "Do you babysit?" Of Teresa she asked, "What other secrets have you been keeping from me? We gotta go out for a glass of vino, pronto. No, make that a *bottle!*"

As Teresa tried to explain the sibling thing in the fewest possible words, Jen waved good-bye and led Dori toward the exit.

"We'll catch up soon," said Teresa. "It's Dori's first night in town, so I really need to go."

But Cassidy wouldn't be deterred. She walked with Teresa along the tables and past the dartboard. "Seriously," she whispered. "I've got something I need your advice about. What are you doing on Thursday? Will you go with me to the Motor-World Thrill Park? *Please?* I've promised the little monsters a trip to the park, but I don't want to spend the whole day by myself."

There were a lot of reasons for Teresa to hesitate. She didn't know if Dori would still be around. She wasn't sure how Sugar Britches would be, or if she'd still be on ovulation alert.

"I'll buy your tickets," said Cassidy, following Teresa right out the door, where Jen and Dori waited next to the bike rack. "We can do the bungee jump together."

"Not a chance," Teresa replied.

"I'll pick you up at nine, okay?" said Cassidy. "On Thursday morning. Be ready!"

Teresa nodded and hurried to catch up.

They agreed that night that Dori could stay for a few days. Dori reassured them that she'd leave whenever they wanted. She wasn't intending to take advantage. She just needed a place to get her head straight and figure out what to do next. But in the next breath she hardened her jaw and swore she'd never go back home to her fucking crazy mom, no matter what.

Teresa had been around too many passive-aggressive types not to understand the manipulation, but Jen didn't grow up like that. Jen was wide open and sometimes downright gullible. She even offered to take Dori with her on the boat the next morning, and they made plans to meet for breakfast beforehand.

As they dropped her off at Room 2, Teresa asked, "Do you have everything you need?"

Dori nodded.

"Okay then," Teresa said. "We'll see you in the morning."

But Jen wasn't as eager to be rid of her. "Are you sure you're okay staying in here by yourself?" she asked. "Because we could put a blow-up mattress in the living room if you'd be more comfortable."

She looked to Teresa for approval, but Teresa just said, "Honey, she's practically an adult—and besides that, she hardly knows us! I'm sure she'd prefer a room of her own."

"I'm cool," Dori said. She tucked her hair behind her ear and added, "Thanks for everything." She didn't hug them goodnight—but her disposition had definitely improved.

As they went into the apartment, Jen said, "She brings out your mean streak, T."

"I know it," Teresa replied.

∽   ∽   ∽

51

It had been an otherworldly day, and long after Jen fell asleep Teresa replayed the scenes: Dori running from the cop car toward her, like a kid playing tag and rushing to the safety of home base. Dori strutting down the street, hipbones first, making exercise shorts look seductive. And after she found out Teresa was gay, Dori refusing to meet her eyes, refusing to *give her* her eyes. It felt punishing, withholding. Like Dori was channeling their mom.

Why was Dori there, and what did she really want?

It had taken years, but Teresa'd finally succeeded in walling off her mom. Then along came Dori, blowing up everything. Suddenly Teresa could hear her mom's voice again, that Southern drawl she hadn't heard in so long. Her mom had a sweet, placating tone that sometimes didn't match the terrible things she said. "Treesa," she'd called her, with a long *E*. "Treeeesa." It was a beautiful sound, but a dangerous sound.

Teresa let herself remember the song of the sound as she tried to quiet her mind and cross into dreams. In that half-sleep space, she replayed images of her favorite paper doll dangling from the dragon tree.

"They hung her for *treason*," her mom had said, and Teresa heard her own name. Except for that "n" on the end, it could have been her name.

It hadn't seemed right or possible that a person (or a paper doll) could be punished (even put to death) just for being herself.

But that's how it happened sometimes.

And Dori—was she more like their mom? Would she slip the noose around Teresa's neck and then cry to see her suffer? Or was she more like the doll: lynched, the ultimate victim, head pinched off from her heart?

Back on the day of that paper doll execution, Teresa had snipped the yarn from around the girl's limp neck, placed her gently on the floor, and covered her broken body with a Kleenex. "We'll need to have a funeral," she'd announced somberly.

"I'll make the coffin myself," her mom had volunteered.

III.

Room 2 looked a lot like a motel room—a queen-sized bed and nightstand; a dresser with a TV propped on top; a small bathroom off to the side—but the walls had been painted golden yellow. There were bright blue curtains on the window and a bright blue bedspread, four cushy red pillows, and silky-feeling lime-green sheets. Dori hadn't thought of putting those colors together before. She liked the combination, but were they lesbian colors?

She checked out the chest of drawers and found extra sheets and blankets stowed there, even napkins and a tablecloth. In the bottom drawer, she found folded tapestries in Indian designs. Those definitely looked lesbian. She searched the drawer of the bedside table, but instead of a Gideon Bible, which she would have welcomed but wasn't really expecting, she found sticks of incense, a lighter, and a book of Buddhist meditations.

Since Buddhists were almost as terrifying as lesbians, she closed that drawer.

Could she sleep in the guest room of Buddhist lesbians, even if one of them was her sister? They were nice enough, but the thought of them touching each other grossed her out. She wasn't a prude. She'd even kissed a girl once, at her boyfriend Cane's urging, but she wasn't gay. She hoped she hadn't inherited that gene, or even half the gene, if being gay had anything to do with genetics.

According to her parents, being gay was a wrong and terrible choice. She knew the scriptures—Leviticus 20:13: "If a man also lie with mankind, as he lieth with a woman, both of them have committed an abomination: they shall surely be put to death; their blood shall be upon them." It was one of the passages from Bible drills. She'd always been good at Bible drills.

But since Teresa and Jen weren't men, maybe it wasn't quite as bad.

She turned out the light and closed her eyes, but she couldn't fall asleep. Maybe her mom had left Teresa behind and started a new family *because* she was gay. Maybe that was why she'd kept her a secret all those years.

But if that was true, then Dori had Teresa to thank for being born. If her mom had stayed with her first family, then Dori wouldn't even exist.

On the other hand, wouldn't it be better if she didn't exist? Maybe she had Teresa to *blame* for being born.

She tried to imagine what her mom would be doing at that exact moment. Praying, probably. Begging God for the peace that passeth understanding, or maybe sending up pleas for a whole new family, now that Dori was out of the picture.

Could she seem as horrible to her mom now as Teresa must be?

As crazy as it seemed, Dori missed her mom. It choked her up, thinking she couldn't even call her anymore, couldn't even hear her voice.

When Dori was little, her mom got a tattoo of Jesus carrying his cross up the hill to Golgotha. Jesus himself stood just ten inches tall. He popped out of the top of her mom's jeans shorts and stretched more than halfway up her back. He was wearing one of those draping robes, like he wore in most pictures from the Bible, but he was crouched over, because the cross was so heavy, and his face was turned down so you couldn't see much of his expression.

The cross jutted out from behind his shoulder blade and extended another four inches or so toward the sky. It looked almost like the cross might be tipping over. Jesus might be about to drop his cross, but he was doing his best to balance it there, poor guy. All that summer Dori's mom wore cut-off shorts and her bikini top, so the tattoo could heal in the air. She'd only gotten the outline for it, and some of the outline had scabbed and then blurred. It looked like a page from a coloring book, but it was definitely Jesus. All around him, and around his cross, the tattoo artist had etched in lines like sunrays shooting out, like Jesus would be glowing if you could see the thing in color.

"Nobody'll be able to admire it beneath your Sunday dress," Dori lamented.

"That's okay," said her mom. "Nobody else needs to see it, 'cept for you and your daddy. And Jesus, of course. Jesus can see right through your clothes, so he knows it's there."

At her next tattoo appointment, rather than have the artist fill it in, she asked him to add the words *Only God Can Judge Me* in big, thick, cursive letters across the top.

And then her mom ran out of money and never went back to have Jesus colored in. But there were times over the next few years that she'd take off her top and stretch out on the carpet, and Dori would plop down with her magic markers beside her and color Jesus.

It was her favorite thing to do. Sometimes she'd make Jesus into a teenage mutant ninja turtle, and her mom didn't even care when she painted him green and gave him a mask. Sometimes she'd make Jesus into a woman and give him great big boobs. She'd transform the cross into butterfly wings, huge ones that took up the rest of her mom's back, and she'd draw all kinds of designs inside those wings, swirls and paisleys, so Jesus wasn't suffering a bit. He could fly off to Timbuktu if he felt like it.

She'd make Jesus into a blue fairy. She'd give him high-heeled shoes. She'd turn Jesus into a ladybug. She'd let him smoke a cigarette or a pipe.

Sometimes she'd draw bricks around him so that the cross disappeared, and it looked like he was kneeling against a wall instead. She'd give him some marbles and imagine he was the greatest marble shooter in history.

Sometimes she'd draw structures around Jesus, houses or tee-pees. She made him into an Indian chief. She sketched a bicycle between his legs, gave him a dog and even a monkey that tap-danced on his cross.

Always she gave Jesus a great big smile.

But at the end of each coloring session, they'd scrub off her mom's back, sometimes until it turned shiny and red. They had to get rid of all traces of magic marker. If soap wouldn't work, they used Crisco and then soaped it again. "Your daddy'll throw a hissy fit if he sees it," her mom would say. "You know how he feels about the Lord."

It was Dori's favorite game she ever played with her mom. It sounded a whole lot better than Teresa's stupid orphanage game.

They lived then in an apartment building at the edge of a nowhere Tennessee town. It was a place her daddy rented, but he was only there sometimes. He drove a big truck, delivering things as far away as Ohio or Florida, but he was almost always home by Sunday.

He had a small but dedicated congregation that met in a room inside an industrial building. Dori and her mom had to get there early each week and take folding chairs out of a closet and set them up in rows for the service. Sometimes the whole congregation would be there, waiting in metal chairs, and they'd listen for the big rig's brakes. Her daddy would blow the horn and then come strutting through the door already preaching.

"Of course I'm filthy," he'd say. "My hands are dirty with oil and sweat. My clothes sour, my skin unwashed, and I could probably run off Satan himself using only my breath as a weapon! But Hal-lelujah, my Savior can take a man stained with sin and baptize him and bring him up white as snow. Hal-le-lu-jah, my Savior doesn't care what I look like on the outside!"

All the people would be singing "Amen," crying out "Preach it, Brother," and Dori's daddy would captivate them with sermons he'd made up on the road. He'd tell them about people he met at truck stops and signs he saw along the highway, and then he'd tie those stories into the scripture somehow, until he had the whole room crying and confessing. He was a poor man's preacher. The poor, the hungry, even the drunk were welcomed at his church. And his congregation loved him. They brought food to share, took up love offerings, and stayed after services to volunteer to go witnessing door-to-door. Each week new people came.

Dori thought her dad must be a great man for so many people to love him. When he was home, young men and women came over to the apartment constantly, giving him reports of souls they'd led to Christ. He had prayer meetings right on their living room floor. He'd call for pizza, and they'd eat it off of paper towels and worship there together.

But there were also times when he'd order her mom to go get in the truck. She'd say, "I can't leave Dori," and he'd say, "The Lord'll take care of Dori. We won't be gone long. I got a special need," and off they'd go.

Sometimes Dori read all her *Junie B. Jones* books and they still weren't back. She went to bed and woke up and ate and watched TV and slept again. Once there was a storm, and the lights went out, and she sat there in the dark and went crazy and gnawed all the skin off the insides of her lips. Another time, they were gone for three days, and she was scared to leave the house, so she didn't even catch the school bus. When her third-grade teacher called, she said she had a virus.

They always came back, eventually, and they always brought her presents: a stuffed cat with rhinestones for eyes, and once even a Monster High doll, which she'd put on her Christmas wish list the year before. They'd refused then, on the grounds that the doll might be satanic, so Dori knew they felt guilty when they returned with Frankie Stein. They always acted like nothing was the matter, like their eyes didn't have that voodoo glimmer beneath the surface that told Dori they'd been on some kind of binge. She knew about drugs. She knew she wasn't supposed to ever use them. She knew that when you took drugs, you got that under-glimmer in your eyes that made you forget the Bible and what it said was right and wrong.

57

For a while Dori was afraid, and then she just got mad.

One night, for a reason she never understood, they packed up in the big truck and drove away. They drove to the far side of the state and started over, living first out of the truck, then attending a church, meeting a preacher, and camping in his driveway. From there, they moved into a single-wide trailer. They called themselves Baxters then, though technically they were still Williamsons. Dori imagined they were in the witness protection program, but she wasn't sure what they'd witnessed or what they were being protected from. She didn't go to school, but her mom made her copy scriptures and fill in pages from math workbooks. Her daddy built up a new congregation while her mom led the army of soul-winners for Christ.

But sometimes, after walking the streets and knocking on doors and praying with sinners or walking the streets and having doors slammed in their faces, one of Dori's toys would disappear—a stuffed clown or a doll—and later she'd find it in her mom's closet, mutilated, dead flies or bees glued over the eyes and mouth.

"What'd you do?" Dori would protest.

"I'm sorry, baby," her mom would reply. "But you're too old to play with that anyway. I haven't seen you play with that in ages, and I'm using it for God's glory."

And Dori would get even madder. "How is this for God's glory?" she had yelled, but her mom would send her to her room to sulk by herself.

She knew her daddy took speed on the highway to stay up late and drive. Sometimes he took it when he wasn't even on the road. He confessed it at church, but used the "I'm a sinner, too" line to make his congregants turn toward him, not away. "I'm a flawed man," he'd say. Big tears would roll down his stubbly cheeks as he paced up and down the aisle of the little church. "I'm a flawed and broken man. But I know somebody who can take me as I am, forgive me for my wrongs, and set me right again. He'll take me JUST AS I AM."

Then everybody would sing the hymn and cry with Dori's daddy. They'd flock down to the altar and lay hands on him to pray for his deliverance. They kept right on following him and doing whatever he said in the name of the Lord.

They had picketed outside an abortion clinic. They had driven a hundred miles to block the parking lot of a gay dance club. All night, they'd stood there with their signs, shouting at the fags, who shouted right back. It was fun. As the sun came up, they'd gone out for pancakes, then driven back home and slept all afternoon.

But it didn't add up, how her dad had condemned some sinners but seemed so eager to forgive others. Always it seemed like he was most willing to forgive the crimes he committed himself.

"I've got an addiction," he'd said after he got caught on a security camera in the parking lot of a discount superstore with his hand in his pants. He took speed, watched the ladies, and jerked off, then told the congregation that if Christ could walk on water, if He could turn water to wine, then He could surely help out a poor sinner with an unholy addiction. While some people moved their membership to another church, at least half of them stood behind her daddy. There were even new members who came to hear the sermons of an acting, practicing sinner. Who could understand them better?

So it didn't make much sense to Dori when she'd gotten in so much trouble for stealing. She'd lifted a pus-eyed kitten, of all things, from a pet store at the mall. She had made it out of the store, but a clerk came running after her. He caught her near the food court with the wiggling kitten tucked inside her jacket, beneath her arm. Mall security delivered her to the police station, where they'd made her wait for her parents.

When they got home, she'd said to her dad, "I'm a sinner, too," and he backhanded her and then whipped her with his belt. It was in the Bible, the whole thing about sparing the rod and spoiling the child.

After that she hated him completely and for good.

That same year—she'd just turned thirteen—her parents began a building fund for a new church building. They wanted to make a Christian school, and not just any Christian school, but one governed by the Ten Commandments and not by the laws of man. They'd taken donations, held bake sales and car washes, stood at the intersections of traffic lights in nearby cities asking drivers to contribute to their new Christian school. They'd raised thousands of dollars when it all began to fall apart.

A girl from their church, barely eighteen years old, confessed to her parents that she'd had sexual relations with Preacher Baxter. He denied it, but most of the church turned against him anyway. He was from out of town, and that girl and her family had lived there for generations.

Dori's mom hadn't believed it. "Your daddy's being persecuted," she'd hissed. "Just like Jesus. All great leaders get persecuted. They're tested and tried by Satan and his army, but in the end, righteousness transcends."

"I swear it," said her daddy. "I swear it on a stack of Bibles high as my head that I never touched that gal."

"I thought swearing was a sin," Dori had smarted off.

And then her mom had turned on her: "You ought to bow your head and ask forgiveness," she'd hollered. "You don't know how lucky you are. You ought to be thanking the Lord you have parents committed to staying together through the trials and tribulations."

But they didn't stick together much longer. In another month, Dori's dad had taken the money from the building fund and disappeared with that girl in his eighteen-wheeler. A few members of the church had tried to help Dori and her mom then, saying they knew it wasn't their fault. But when the gas company cut off their propane that winter, nobody loaned them the money to have it turned back on. Dori's mom sent her to a deacon's house to ask for assistance with the bill, and though they were kind to her there, invited her in, fed her some supper, they claimed they didn't have any money left to give.

Those people were lucky she hadn't come back and burned their house to the ground.

60

The shame was unbearable, so Dori hardened her jaw, locked eyes with anybody who looked her way, clenched her fists, and prepared to fight. When nobody fought back, she took it out on herself. She tried to break her own leg with the hammer, beating it against her shin until she couldn't stand it. But all she did was make a mottled bruise. She tried to break her hand, and then her mom saw it and said, "What have you done?" and Dori told her, and her mom took the hammer away and locked herself in her room with more of Dori's old toys and all the nails.

Dori stole things for the sake of stealing, things she didn't even need, ridiculous things like the big container of napkins next to the cash register at the fast-food place. Most times she got away with it, too.

When they were evicted, nobody offered them a spare room.

"Just like the Virgin Mary," said her mom. "Forced to give birth in a stable. Can you imagine that, Dorothy Ann?"

"No," Dori said. But she hated her mom for making her stay at a shelter on a bunk bed with a stained and stinky mattress, and she *really* hated her mom for what she had done next: wandering the streets, holding out her hands toward strangers, crying and praying, wild-eyed, wild-haired, strands of thick spit stringy between her lips.

"Come *on*," Dori had begged, but she wouldn't follow. She didn't. They had taken her mom to the hospital and Dori to a cinderblock building where she'd waited on a bench all day long for some social worker to place her in a home with complete strangers.

Now she was in a home with strangers again, but this time she had a whole room to herself, a bathroom to herself, an AC unit to herself that she could turn up or down as she liked, a TV she didn't have to share, though after she stretched out on the bed, she discovered she was too tired to even roll over and reach for the remote. Her arms tingled and her legs felt like logs. It had been such a long day since she'd hitched that ride to the state park beach, and found the stinky turtle, and kicked the water-keeper, and taken a ride with the asshole cop who'd brought her to her sister's strip-mall guest room, where she rested on a perfect, feathery pillow.

Thinking back on it, Dori decided it wasn't really so bad, spending the night in a lesbian house. At that moment, it beat every alternative she could imagine.

IV.

In all the excitement around Dori's arrival Teresa had forgotten to watch how much she drank. She'd let the waiter at the pub refill her water glass three times, maybe four, and though she peed before she went to sleep, she woke in the middle of the night and badly needed to go again.

Until she reached the toilet, she forgot she was testing for ovulation. The lid was down, as she'd deliberately left it, with the ovulation test kit sitting right on top of the seat to remind her.

It was a strategy they used to keep her from peeing by accident. Too many nights she'd taken herself to the bathroom without waking up completely. But she had to hold her urine to test for the LH surge. The hormones needed time to steep so she could see if a second coveted line appeared next to the first, control line, and so she'd know whether to call the clinic or, in this case, their friend Eric.

She went back to bed, stretched out on her back, and tried to find the best position for her bladder. She crossed her ankles, squeezed her thighs together, and took deep breaths. She tilted her pelvic bones up, a trick that sometimes worked, but still she couldn't rest.

She was miserable, and to make matters worse, Jen was snoring, the little guttural throat-clicks that drove her crazy. To make things worse *still*, Sugar Britches wasn't there beside her.

All his life, he'd slept above her pillow, waking her each morning by pulling a single hair from her head, or sometimes, if that didn't work, tapping her with his paw, or else migrating to the foot of the bed and nipping at her toes. But for the past month, he'd stopped coming into the bedroom, remaining instead on his cushion by the sliding glass door. She missed him.

So she got up and went to where he slept, put her pillow down next to him, stretched out on the floor on her side, and stroked him.

He didn't purr, but he didn't flinch or move away either, so she rested there, fingers grazing his side gently, down and around his tumor, until she felt something sticky and wet. She turned on the lamp and saw that his tumor had started to leak. A trickle of bloody fluid ran from the bald center, where he'd licked away his hair, to the edge of the bulge and around. Not good.

She blotted it with a wet paper towel, then turned off the light and gently massaged Sugar Britches behind the ears. She let her tears roll onto her pillow without wiping them, and she dozed there, off and on, until she couldn't hold her pee a second more.

There was no double line. There was the one purple stripe, indicating that the test itself was working, and there might have been the tiniest hint of a second line—depending on the light. Teresa didn't know if that meant she wasn't ovulating at all, or whether she was *about* to ovulate and had caught the hormones at the very earliest point, or whether she simply hadn't held her urine long enough to tell. It was a familiar conundrum, one she found herself in most mornings when she tested. It seemed like she was always testing and always second-guessing the results. The anticipation of ovulation became a loop in her brain, and she went around and around, beyond dizzy. She felt like one of those gymnasts on the uneven parallel bars, afraid to let go.

"Do you think we should call Eric anyway?" she asked Jen that next morning. "Would it be awful to ask him to jerk off again tomorrow, if today's not really the day?"

Jen shrugged. "I don't think guys mind it that much, but it could be kind of awkward. Do you really think it might be happening?"

She was already eight days overdue. She'd been keeping charts for months. She'd made notes about the texture of her discharge, had a record book on the nightstand with the ups and downs of her basal body temperature. None of it helped.

"I don't *know*," said Teresa. "I'm scared we're going to miss it. We should wait, I guess."

"It's okay if we miss it," said Jen. "We can try again next month. We've got time."

It pissed her off for Jen to be so cavalier about it. They didn't have that much time. Not in the big picture. Teresa was already forty. Jen was only thirty-seven, but she'd had endometriosis and an early hysterectomy—so it was Teresa's job to carry the baby, even though Jen was physically in better shape. Jen could eat anything she wanted and not go over a hundred and thirty pounds. She was everything a mother should be—strong, active, loving, happy—and she was laid-back enough that if she just had viable, working parts, she wouldn't ruin every cycle with the kind of anxiety that made Teresa's ovaries tremble and freeze up.

They'd gone back and forth for *years* about whether to have a child, with Jen ever eager and Teresa afraid to pass on her genes. "What are you talking about?" Jen teased. "You've got great genes. Look at you. Best genes I've ever seen." But it had taken a lot of work to convince Teresa.

Once they decided to do it, they'd spent months selecting the donor, reading through medical records, sending in pictures of Jen to have donors physically matched: olive skin, compact build, dark eyes, dark brown hair. They'd ordered baby pictures along with the audio interviews before finally settling on Donor #9721, the lawyer, who, in his baby picture, was dressed as a miniature cowboy.

But after six inseminations, and all the tension and excitement that came with each trip across the bay to have the long catheter inserted through her cervix, and after six disappointments when her period continued to arrive, Teresa doubted both the potency and rightness of their cowboy-turned-lawyer.

Of course, they could always order more sperm, most likely from the entrepreneur, or they could start their donor search all over again. But they'd already spent many thousands of dollars, even dipping into their home equity line, and Teresa felt more fractious than she'd felt in years. Why should they spend all that money on sperm if she couldn't even figure out whether she was ovulating?

Though he looked nothing like Jen, Eric was a good compromise.

"I really can't stand to miss it," Teresa admitted. "It's making me crazy."

Jen gave her a squeeze and poured her a cup of coffee.

"Don't let me drink more than just one cup," said Teresa. "I'll test again when I get back from the vet."

In her highest fake opera voice, Jen sang out, "Ob-sessss-sive."

When Sugar Britches was a kitten, he had loved going on car rides. He'd draped himself around Teresa's neck and meowed at the cars passing by on the highway. Now he curled up on the passenger seat and paid no notice to traffic. All the way up the road, Teresa kept one hand on the wheel and one hand on Sugar Britches. They already knew that the tumor was incurable; it was so high up on his haunch and embedded so deeply that even amputation wasn't an option. According to the last set of tests they'd done, it had metastasized. All the way to the vet she cried behind her sunglasses.

The receptionist led her into a room right away, probably to keep her from upsetting the others in the waiting area, but the vet, a tattooed woman in purple scrubs, reassured her. Sugar didn't appear to be in pain. He was curious when the vet came in and bumped his head against her hand before she examined him. He was still eating a little—Teresa exaggerated the amount—and using his litter box, too. They could give him more prednisone and a spray for the place where the tumor had opened and bled.

"We both know how this is gonna end," the vet said. "But you don't have to make the hard decision today. Just watch for infections or signs that he's in pain. You'll know when it's time."

Teresa thanked her, sniffling, and gratefully took Sugar back home.

She needed to pee but aimed to hold it as long as she possibly could. So she cleaned the kitchen and put away the dishes, trying to figure out how they'd know. Would Sugar start howling if they waited too long? Should they spare him any potential pain by putting him to sleep before pain arrived?

And wasn't there still a teeny-tiny, infinitesimal chance he might recover? She let herself imagine it only for a moment before chiding herself for that lapse.

She vacuumed the living-room rug, working through scenarios in her mind. The animal clinic was closed on Sundays. If Sugar had a turn for the worse on Sunday, they'd have to take him to the emergency clinic across the bay. It was a long drive, but doable.

A lot of people put their pets down early because they couldn't stand to watch them deteriorate. At least she wouldn't be one of those people.

She found the Swiffer wet wipes and cleaned the linoleum in the foyer and kitchen, as well as the tile in the bathroom, peeling off dirty wipes like diapers, replacing them with clean white ones, only to dirty them up again. As she worked, she tried to shift her thinking to things that made her happy.

Like Jen.

Jen was everything no one else had ever been. Teresa'd met her at the deli, where Jen suggested Havarti over cheddar on her turkey sub. That sandwich changed her life. It came alive on her tongue. It was everything she could do not to go back and order a second one, just for the sensation of eating it. The next day, Jen had offered a taste of a creamy homemade French dressing for Teresa's salad. Even though Teresa ordinarily stuck with vinaigrette, she'd ordered it. Instead of slices of lemon in the water, Jen had dropped in slices of cucumber. Thick, round slices with their deep green rims. Intrigued, Teresa had watched her as she worked. She came back day after day. She tried half the menu before Jen invited her out on her boat.

Teresa had said yes. She didn't mention that open water made her queasy. She climbed aboard and became first mate. When Jen had suggested they hop out in the middle of the bay for a swim, Teresa jumped in beside her. Even as the boat had floated off, even as she panicked, she didn't let on. She'd have rather drowned than missed the chance to kiss Jen beneath that blue, blue sky.

And everything had worked out fine. Jen had swum out and retrieved the boat and they'd been together ever since.

Before Jen, Teresa'd never had much of a love life, not the kind people describe in poems or brag about to friends. She didn't really even *like* sex until Jen came along. But with Jen, every vertebra in her spine transformed into a beautiful, colored bead. Somehow, Jen spun those beads, one by one, bottom to top, until the energy from the deepest parts of her surged up and shot through.

When she wasn't with Jen, she looked for the exact color of her eyes in freshly roasted coffee beans, in the bark of the oak tree after rain, in the shading of the sunlight on the mulch around the hibiscus.

And Jen wanted a baby. Teresa intended to give her one.

In her mind, she practiced for the coming insemination. She'd read everything there was about in-home inseminations. Turkey basters were impractical—too big for the job. There were smaller basters, the kind you use to give babies medicine, but syringes made the most sense, and they'd invested in several different sizes. Jen had even modified a couple to enlarge the suction holes. She'd choose her syringe when she saw the size of Eric's contribution.

Teresa had always pictured Eric going into Room 2 to do his business, but with Dori in town that became impossible. Now he'd have to use their bathroom, which was right next to their bedroom. She'd be waiting just behind the door for him to finish, for Jen to deliver the sperm.

In a way, it seemed silly—all the steps they were taking to pretend the baby belonged to her and to Jen. The simplest, most efficient delivery would be sex with Eric—but that'd be embarrassing, and it would definitely disrupt the fantasy.

They really needed that fantasy.

She dusted the end tables and the bookshelf, wondering if the chemicals in cleaning solutions could inhibit ovulation, and she decided that maybe she should just quit testing and try again next month. Dori would surely be gone by then.

Sugar Britches would probably be gone by then, too.

The thought of losing Sugar choked her up. She checked on him and discovered that while part of the tumor had scabbed, it had started bleeding from a different location. It was like something inside the tumor was trying to hatch. It looked and felt a lot like an egg—a bloody, firm, cracking egg. As she dabbed at the mass with a wet cloth, she started sobbing again, the kind of wracking sobs that made her bladder threaten to give. She hurried to the bathroom and tested. The line remained as solitary as ever.

Late that afternoon, Jen and Dori returned from the water with an armload of surf shorts and T-shirts and even a bathing suit top. They'd raided the lost and found at both the harbor and the marina.

"My new wardrobe," Dori announced proudly. She laughed and helped herself to the laundry detergent.

"Are you kidding?" said Teresa. "What if somebody comes looking for those clothes?"

Jen brushed it off. "Nobody ever picks that stuff up. Some of it's been there for years." She reached into her pocket and pulled out a pair of plastic sunshades with the name of a golf club printed on the side. "Look what I brought you."

Teresa laughed and tried on the glasses.

"Check out my boat shoes," said Dori. They were a men's size 8—way too big for her feet. "Cute, aren't they? They just curl up a little at the toes." She did a dance to show them off.

"You should have seen the dolphins today, T," Jen said. "We saw what? Twenty or thirty?"

"At least!" Dori said. "They weren't five feet from the boat. One of them even swam by on his back!"

She seemed so energetic and normal. Almost like a kid. Almost like *their* kid.

"And they have blowholes," she continued. "I thought only whales had blowholes."

"Sounds like a fun trip," Teresa replied.

"We got lots of tips, too!" Jen added. She high-fived Dori, and Dori just smiled, that broken front tooth so prominent. "Especially from that family from Maryland with all the teenage boys. I think Dori worked a number on them. They bought every last ham and cheese on the boat."

Later, when Jen told Teresa that she'd hired Dori to help her out on the floating deli, Teresa didn't protest. But she asked, "For how long?"

"As long as she's here, I guess," said Jen. "It'll give her something to do. She's a lot stronger than she looks. She was a big help loading the coolers."

"Okay," said Teresa. "But she's underage, and that makes us liable."

That evening, when Dori came back for dinner, they told her she had to call her mom. "You don't have to tell her where you are," Teresa said. "But you have to let her know you're safe."

Dori scowled.

Jen added, "And have her send your social security card so I can get you on the payroll."

"Then she'll know where I am," Dori complained. "Can't you just pay me under the table?"

"I don't want to get in trouble with the tax man," Jen explained. "I'll pay you cash until your social security card gets here. Then we'll do a W-2."

Dori nodded, but Teresa knew she had no intention of calling her mom. And *she* certainly had no intention of following up.

Though Teresa spent half her life with teenagers, trying to convince them that the past was always alive and spinning inside the present moment and that studying the past could help them shape their futures, she had no idea what to do with Dori. What did you *do* with a seventeen-year-old sister who shared your mother but none of your personal history? So she pulled out Yahtzee.

"Yahtzee?" Dori said. "Seriously? Don't you have a Nintendo Switch or something?"

"No," said Teresa.

"Why *don't* we have a Nintendo Switch?" Jen asked.

Teresa ignored her and turned on the TV, and the three of them took turns rolling the dice and taking their chances at full houses or straights.

They played game after game, glancing occasionally at whatever crime show was on, and for a while things went fine—until Sugar Britches crept over and stretched out next to Dori's feet on the carpet. His tumor had started oozing again, and when Dori saw it, she squealed, "Ugh. That's gnarly!" and shifted her chair away, startling poor Sugar.

"Have a little compassion, would you?" Teresa said. She put down her score pad and gathered up Sugar and held him next to her collar, scratching behind his ears and down his neck, his little shoulder blades pronounced and sharp. He weighed almost nothing.

"It's not personal," Dori defended. "It's just nasty. And unsanitary," she added. She pulled up her feet, like even the floor where Sugar had walked might be contaminated.

"Your turn," Jen said. "Can you just go?" and Dori did. She rolled four sixes on the first try and got a Yahtzee on the second, and in her excitement and her almost certain win of that round, she forgot about Sugar.

At some point, Teresa put him back down on the floor, and a little later he moved within reach of Dori's foot again. Teresa kept an eye on things, thinking Dori might kick him away, but instead she kneaded beneath his neck with her toes, bright pink nail polish half flaked off.

That night, as Teresa and Jen were getting ready for bed, they heard someone knocking. When Jen answered the door, she discovered the caller wasn't at their door at all, but rather at Dori's. It was one of the boys who'd been on the sandbar that day, a college student from Maryland on vacation with his folks. He'd asked for packets of spicy mustard to go with his sandwich and a side of the kettle chips.

"We're just going for a walk," Dori explained.

"Oh," Jen said. "Okay, but it's late. Don't stay out long."

Teresa and Jen watched TV in bed, only half paying attention and half listening for Dori's return. "Do you think we should wait up?" Jen asked.

"I don't know," said Teresa. "Maybe we should've given her a curfew. I have no idea."

"She was on her own before she got here," Jen said. "So I guess she can take care of herself."

"Don't forget that it was the chief of police who dropped her off," said Teresa. "And that story about the turtle shell and planning to sell it? Something about that doesn't add up."

"You're way too suspicious," Jen said.

"Of course I'm suspicious. *We don't know her*, and something just feels off. I go back and forth between wanting to help her and thinking we should put her butt on the road."

"We can't do that," said Jen.

"I know," Teresa relented. But in a minute, she wondered, "What if she's not even my sister? She could be posing."

"Why would she do that?"

"She could be *anybody*."

"Don't be paranoid," said Jen.

"Oh, fuck off," said Teresa, but it was a lukewarm insult, at best. She rolled over and pouted into her pillow.

She hoped she wasn't becoming *literally* paranoid. All her life, she'd worked at staying sane. She'd been disciplined and deliberate about not letting fears or compulsions take over her life. As a child, she hadn't understood what was wrong with her mom, but as an adult, she knew plenty of names that might fit: bipolar, borderline, narcissistic personality. Maybe all three at once. She didn't want to be any of those things. She wanted to do whatever it took. But sometimes, when stresses and worries puddled all around her, she knew she must have the capacity to slip, as fast as you might slip on black ice, or even on just a little water spilled on the floor. Genetically speaking, how could she be that different?

And since they'd started the inseminations, she'd been plagued by a new symptom. Sometimes when she didn't intend to, she pictured the people she encountered as unborn babies. It was weird and *not* something she wanted happening in her brain.

Sometimes when she stopped by the coffee shop, the girl behind the counter became this crinkly, primitive-looking fetus, soft-boned, her features all smeared, handing her a cappuccino with flippers instead of fingers. Teresa would blink hard, and the image would disappear.

Occasionally, sitting in her classroom, she'd look out at her students taking a test, and for just a second they'd all be unborn, covered in fluid and clabber, nibbling not pencil tips but thumbs.

She'd even seen her principal as a fetus once, right in the middle of a faculty meeting. He was standing at a dry-erase board, holding up a marker, and all of a sudden, it wasn't a marker in his hand, but his own umbilical cord. He'd looked so milky-murky, so unformed and vulnerable that she instantly forgave him for making them stay all afternoon on an in-service day when the students weren't even there. It had made her want to cuddle him, nurse him. But you can't just breast-feed your boss—or at least, you shouldn't.

The TV program changed over to the nightly news, and Teresa sat back up and listened with Jen to the weather. Dori still hadn't returned. Their bedroom shared a wall with Room 2, so they expected to hear when she came in.

"I know I should get in touch with my mom," Teresa admitted. "But I feel like I'd be opening Pandora's box."

"Oh, honey, I've got news for you," Jen said and yawned. "That box is *open*." She clicked off the lamp on her nightstand, but before she could get settled Teresa had turned on her bedside lamp.

"God, Jen, it sucked so bad when she left us," Teresa confessed. "I can't even tell you. But in hindsight, I can see that it was for the best. My life's been so much easier without her in it. Poor Dori. I can't even imagine—"

"Sounds like you can," Jen said. Then she asked, "Do you even have a phone number for her?"

Teresa shook her head. For probably the hundredth time that day, she began to sniffle.

"What's the matter now?" Jen asked.

"I'm just sad," said Teresa, "and tired and worried and confused. I feel like I might be going crazy."

Jen spooned up against her. "Everything's gonna be okay."

"Not Sugar Britches," said Teresa.

"No," Jen admitted. "I guess not."

They fell asleep but woke again when they heard the bed bumping in the next room, a hard and steady percussion. Then the moans began.

"No," Teresa whispered. She put the pillow over her head, but then pulled it right back off and listened.

"I'm afraid so," muttered Jen.

"Oh shit," said Teresa. "What should we do?"

"Nothing," Jen replied. "It's her life."

Teresa sat upright. "But it's *our* house," she said. "God! You'd think she'd have more respect!"

Jen patted the mattress beside her. "Come on. Lie back down. Just try to go to sleep. She doesn't know we can hear."

"Baloney," said Teresa at full volume. "She grew up with my mom. She's had a lifelong education in manipulating people. She *wants* us to hear."

As if on cue, Dori let out a song of a moan, and the melody grew higher and higher and became, at the end, the kind of yipping you'd hear from a small, demanding dog.

"Holy shit," said Teresa. "You don't think she's being raped, do you?"

"Sounds to me like she's enjoying herself," Jen said. She laughed a little, into her pillow, and then Teresa also started laughing—the kind of horrified laughing that gets funnier as it goes. Teresa buried her face into Jen's back and shook with laughter.

"She's probably just asserting her heterosexuality," Jen continued. "Staying with two lesbians that she didn't even *know* were lesbians—she probably really needs a stiff cock."

The next morning was Sunday, and though Teresa wasn't a hundred percent sure, she was fairly confident that the urine test showed the start of a second purple line. The second line wasn't as deeply colored as the first, but that probably meant her LH surge was beginning. With the second line about to show up, she'd almost certainly have to ovulate within twenty-four hours. "Yes!" Teresa yelled from the bathroom, and Jen wasted no time phoning Eric.

He couldn't meet them until the afternoon, though. He'd agreed to go to church with his new girlfriend whose nephew was being christened. Afterward they were going out to lunch. He said he'd be there as soon as he could, but probably not before three.

The whole time he was on the phone he whispered. His girlfriend didn't know he was donating sperm to his two closest lesbian pals. He hadn't been dating her for very long and hadn't worked up his nerve to tell her yet.

"He should tell her," Jen said. "I thought he was going to tell her."

"He can tell her later," Teresa argued. "After he gives up the goods."

"It's ethically wrong not to tell her," said Jen. "What if they have kids one day? She deserves to know their kid has a half-sibling right here in town."

"It's none of her business," said Teresa. "Not at this point. We don't even know if we'll get pregnant. If we do, and if they become serious, he'll tell her."

They'd both known Eric a long time, Jen the longest—because she'd grown up there on the shore and had ridden the same school bus, though he was a few grades behind her. She'd gone to his Little League games when their team made the playoffs for the state championships and remembered the time he got hit in the head by a line drive and was airlifted to the children's hospital across the bay.

He was just out of high school when Teresa met him. She'd taken a job teaching for the county and had recently bought her first house. She'd found Eric's business card on the bulletin board in the teacher's workroom and had called him up to get an estimate on refinishing the floors.

Eric was a historian of flooring. He'd told her how back in the '50s and '60s, the ladies would buy a nine-by-twelve piece of linoleum each year and tack it down in the middle of the room, then paint the wooden boards around it to match. That's why her floors had such odd combinations of discoloration and nail holes.

"You weren't even alive then," Teresa had said. "How do you know all this?"

It turned out that his favorite uncle had a business refinishing floors, and Eric had begun an apprenticeship with him when he was just thirteen. He had worked summers and weekends by his side, and when the uncle had dropped dead of a heart attack, Eric took over the business, even though he still had a few weeks of high school left.

Teresa had hired him without checking any of his competitors' prices, and he sanded and varnished and polished the floors in that house and in the next one that she bought with Jen. But by the time they'd bought the old motel, flooring had done a number on his back. At his chiropractor's advice, he'd shifted to a new line of work, serving as waterkeeper for the county: retrieving lost crab pots, restoring eel grasses, removing trash from the bay, and responding to neglected or sinking watercraft.

Because Jen also worked the water, they bumped into each other in the marshes and sat out storms beneath the shed at the crab picking plant. On hot afternoons, they had beers at the pub, where Teresa would sometimes join them. Teresa and Jen weighed in on all the women Eric dated, giving him advice and consoling him when things went south. He was a good guy, but he went through women quicker than discount light bulbs.

It was pure coincidence that he had come for dinner—solo—on the night after they inseminated for the very first time. Being so new to the process, so excited and certain it would work, they had gone ahead and told him they were having a baby, if not in the next nine months, probably within the next ten or eleven.

Uncle Eric was elated. The very next day he had dropped off a stuffed octopus.

And when the inseminations didn't succeed, time after time, he became the only person in town who knew what they were going through.

One night, when they'd all had a little too much to drink, he offered to "help them out" if they ever wanted to try a different donor. That time had finally arrived.

But they didn't know what to do about Dori. How would they pull off an insemination just one wall away?

The college boy from Maryland solved that problem. He stayed there all night in Room 2. After they woke up, which wasn't until eleven-thirty, Dori brought him over for breakfast. Teresa couldn't believe it. Dori acted like it was the most natural thing in the world, inviting a strange boy with bedhead and crusty eyes into their kitchen to have cereal with berries on top. Did her mom allow that kind of behavior?

"Today's Warren's last day of vacation," Dori said. "So I'm spending it with him until his family leaves. We're going to the beach to play volleyball."

Teresa cut her eyes at Jen, who was trying again to get Sugar Britches to eat. Without speaking, Jen mouthed the words: *Let. It. Go.*

That afternoon, when they knew that Eric was on his way, they left the door unlocked and slipped off to the bedroom. In preparation, they'd scrubbed out a roasted red pepper jar, boiled both the jar and the lid, and placed it next to the bathroom sink on top of a clean, white towel, alongside a *Playboy* magazine they'd ordered online. Now all he had to do was make his deposit, knock on their bedroom door, and leave the jar on the floor just outside.

They'd discussed and arranged all the details beforehand. Jen wanted it to be as seamless and as natural as possible, and so according to the plan, she and Teresa would make love while Eric did his thing. Ideally, Eric would gift them with the sperm around the same time that Teresa was reaching orgasm.

But it was naïve to even hope for that kind of synchronicity.

"I can't do this," Teresa said and laughed.

"Why not?" asked Jen. She lifted her face from between Teresa's thighs. "Just relax. It's the same thing we do every Sunday."

Teresa tried to get into the spirit. She flexed and released her hips, but it was impossible. It was too much pressure. "You gotta stop," she said. "Really."

"Okay," said Jen. "Okay." She moved back up, snuggled in, and began to kiss Teresa's neck. Teresa nuzzled into Jen's hair. She took a deep breath and reminded herself that she was exactly where she wanted to be, with the person she loved most in the world. How many people still felt that way after so many years together?

And then she heard the door open and shut.

"Shit," she said. "I hope it's not Dori."

"Shhh," said Jen and hushed her with a kiss. "You know who it is."

Heavy footsteps clomped down the hall, and in a very chipper baritone voice—falsely chipper, falsely baritone—Eric said, "Hi, ladies. It's just me," and closed the bathroom door.

He wasn't supposed to talk. That hadn't been in the directions. "I'm too uptight to do this," Teresa whispered.

"You're fine," said Jen.

"There's no way I'll ever be able to come on command. You know it doesn't work like that."

"Shhh," said Jen. "You don't have to." She reached beneath the bed and pulled out the vibrator.

"What if he hears?" Teresa asked.

"So what?" said Jen. "Just turn it on." She kissed Teresa's nipple, tugging it lightly with her teeth. She skimmed her fingers over Teresa's soft round belly, making tiny circles around her navel, figure eights feathering her abdomen, pulling on her nipple and then sliding her fingers down and teasing her as Teresa massaged herself with the vibrator.

Teresa didn't want to go too fast—because she still hoped she might climax when Jen shot the sperm inside her. That way, the contractions would pull it in as far as possible, as deep as possible. At the same time, she didn't want to go too slow, because if she wasn't ready, if she wasn't right there on the brink of it, she'd get too freaked out about what they were doing to let her body release.

If she could just stop thinking—stop trying so hard—she might actually relax enough to conceive. But she was tight all over, and her thoughts kept turning to Eric, wondering how he was doing in the bathroom, if he was watching himself in the mirror, if he was sitting on the edge of the bathtub conjuring images of his girlfriend as he jerked off in a roasted red pepper jar.

Would it have been better to give him an oyster container?

In a little while, the bathroom door opened. "Okay, ladies," Eric called. "The deed is done! I'm outta here."

"Thanks," they both replied.

"We'll see you later," Jen added, because in a ridiculous and innocent attempt to normalize things, as if that were even possible, they'd invited him back for supper in just a few hours.

Teresa sat up and pushed Jen toward the door. "Hurry," she said, "before it loses too much heat."

"I'm naked," said Jen. "Let the man get out the door." But she rushed out to collect the sperm and raced right back to bed.

Teresa had propped up her butt on pillows, and she was still stimulating herself, although it seemed beyond crazy to bother. "Come on," she said.

"Please stop giving me directions," Jen snapped. "I'm doing the best that I can."

Like a scientist, Jen scrutinized her equipment. There were four sizes of syringes lined up on the night table next to the bed. Jen took a medium-sized syringe and stuck it into the small jar.

"Be careful not to suck up air," said Teresa. "You'll give me an embolism."

"I'm being careful," said Jen, but then there was that awful slurping sound as bubbles got into the syringe. "Oops," she said. "Just a little air."

"You can't put it in me with air in there," said Teresa, still masturbating. "You have to get the bubbles out."

"Okay," said Jen. "Let's try this again," and she blew out the sperm to start over.

"Oh shit," she said.

"What?"

"I made sperm froth," Jen admitted. "Yuck."

Teresa snatched the jar out of her hand and studied the foamy lather. She knew what a disaster it was. By the time those bubbles dispersed, all the swimmers would be dead. "How could you do that?" she asked.

"Cut me some slack, would you? I've never done this before." Gently, Jen tipped the jar to the side, trying to separate the bubbly sperm from the non-agitated stuff. "It's okay," she said. "I can still get some of it."

But Teresa rolled away, her legs tight together. "I can't believe it!" she said. She was so upset that her words would hardly come out. Her words hunkered down in her throat. She couldn't even yell. "You have one little job to do," she whispered. "One little job, and you screw it up!"

She sounded like her mom.

She was crying, but Jen was done coddling. "Just shut up and spread your legs," Jen said, so Teresa did.

At last Jen pulled the sperm into the syringe and slid it between Teresa's thighs, emptying it inside her, air and all. "There!" she said. "Don't die on me!"

But by then Teresa was *boo-hooing*, and with each sob a little bit of sperm blooped right back out.

V.

After volleyball and swimming and a walk on the pier, Dori took Warren to the fallen-in ferry dock to say good-bye.

She told him the story of the ferries that used to load there, then cross to Little Creek—but she added in a Category 5 hurricane to demolish the dock, and she invented a family that washed out to sea, their bodies never recovered. She told him the place was haunted, that spirits crouched inside each of those hollowed-out pilings, and that if you stayed out there all night, you could hear them bickering, blaming one another for every indignity.

"You ever stayed out here all night?" he asked.

She nodded.

"What'd the ghosts say?" he teased.

"You wouldn't believe me if I told you," she replied.

She showed him Randy's little cave, and they retrieved the blue raft so they could sit side by side and watch the sailboats and waverunners pass.

Before Warren left, he asked for her phone number, and it was tricky to explain that she didn't have one. Everybody her age had a phone. She made up a story about dropping hers in a mud puddle. It sounded so dumb. "I'll text you when I get my new phone," she promised.

He wanted to find her on Instagram and Facebook, and she said okay, but gave him a fake last name. It was sad it had to be that way. She'd have liked to have seen him again. But she couldn't have new friends posting on her old wall. The police were probably watching for activity on it. She reminded herself not to check it.

He invited her to come up to Maryland for a visit. Maryland sounded so far away, but apparently the state line was only an hour to the north, though where he lived—Baltimore—would take another couple of hours. She'd never been to Baltimore, and sitting there with Warren it started to seem like Baltimore might be the place where she could really start over: change her name, change her story.

When it was time for him to leave, Warren got up, brushed himself off, and said, "I'll see you next summer, I guess, if not before?"

Dori pouted out her bottom lip and nodded.

He squeezed her hand and left her sitting by herself. Soon the tide ate his footprints. She dug her bare toes into the hot sand to cool them, tunneling to damper ground.

She closed her eyes and felt the sun on her head and face, the sun on her shoulders, and it felt good, but she wished she were like a whelk and could dig down into the cooler wet dirt, all the way under except for just a tiny hole for breathing. If she were a whelk, she wouldn't come up for a long time. She'd stay under until next summer. By then she'd be forgotten, along with the Owen Howe incident, and she could surface again and just be Warren's girlfriend. No drama. No problem.

Wiggling her toes in the sand, she remembered Randy's magic sandals and pretended that when she pulled her feet out, she'd miraculously have on shoes that could spring her directly to Baltimore.

If she had magic sandals, she'd make damn sure they had straps on the back.

She kicked her feet free and set out to make a plan. First up: buying a burner phone. Those weren't as expensive as the ones that came with contracts. But making just over minimum wage at Jen's floating deli, it'd take a while. Maybe in a week she could ask for a raise or find odd jobs to supplement her income. She didn't know how long she'd be able to stay with Teresa and Jen anyway. If they called her mom, if they found out she was in trouble, they wouldn't let her stay. *No way* would they let her stay if they ever found out about Owen Howe.

For all she knew, it could be on the news.

She wished she'd never laid eyes on Owen—or on her boyfriend, Cane, for that matter, although she'd liked him well enough before everything went to hell, before they bumped into Owen at the 7-Eleven and came up with their stupid scheme to fuck with his head.

Dori turned the blue raft long-ways, flopped back on it, and closed her eyes. Out there by the bay, so far away, it seemed like another lifetime. But in reality, it had been just over a week— nine days—since they met up with Owen next to the Slurpee machine. They were already high and already angry. Dori'd snuck out of her bedroom window since she was grounded, so she had no curfew to worry about. Cane didn't have a curfew at all. His dad drank Lord Calvert all day and was always passed out by nine.

Owen had been drunk that night, too, completely shit-faced. Otherwise he'd have had better sense than to climb into the passenger seat of Cane's truck when they invited him to a party at the river. She hoped he was drunk enough to have blacked out before they got there. Maybe, if he ever woke up from his coma, he wouldn't remember a thing.

There hadn't been a party, not really. A couple of Cane's cousins had an old RV by the river, and they went there sometimes to get stoned by the fire and just hang out. They had parked in a clearing, but pushed through bushes and trees to get to the camper, where the cousins were playing cards and smoking a joint.

"Hey," Cane had said. "Look who we brought!"

"Dude," said one of the boys, palming his doobie. "You're kidding me! Why?"

"Owen's cool," Cane had said. "Somebody fix him a drink. You got any of that white lightning left? Let's see him chug *that.*"

The offended cousin had left in a huff, but the other one stayed and cheered on Owen as he took shots of the moonshine that you could pour into a saucer and light on fire. Dori'd watched it burn plenty of times. She'd tasted it herself. It felt like drinking gasoline.

Dori had gone inside and fallen asleep on the couch, and when she woke up later, no one was around except Cane and Owen. Owen was tied up in a wooden chair, a dishrag in his mouth, and Cane had a pocketknife pointed at him.

"Hey, Baby," called Cane. "Get up. We're gonna play that game I told you about."

She sat upright. "What are you doing?" She nodded toward the knife. "Put that thing down," and Cane had laughed, tossed the knife onto the couch cushion, and sat down beside her. He pulled her onto his lap and began sucking on her earlobe. She hated when he did that. It gave her the willies.

"See if you can get his dick hard, Dori," he coaxed.

"No!" she said. "Gross!" But he had tickled her until she couldn't help laughing, even though she didn't really want to. He'd held her down and given her kisses on the neck until she got chill bumps and that slow throbbing between her legs.

He'd said, "Just show him your boobies and see if that'll do it. I wanna see how queer he is." Cane reached up under her shirt and tweaked her nipple, making her knees weak, and soon he had her camisole off, his mouth on her breasts, his hands up under her skirt, and even though Owen was right there watching, she could feel herself getting turned on, and she could definitely feel Cane stiffening inside his jeans.

"How big of a queer are you anyway?" he asked Owen, who was wiggling around in his chair not three feet from the couch. "A lot or just a little bit?"

Owen's eyes were so glassy.

"Open his pants, Dori," Cane said. "Give our buddy some relief."

Dori had hesitated. Cane nudged her toward Owen, and so

she unbuttoned his pants and opened up his zipper. She didn't have to touch his dick. He wasn't wearing underwear, and it sprung right out.

"Oh my Lord, would you look at that?" said Cane. He gestured with both arms, and then turned on the overhead light to point out Owen's boner. "You're just a part-time queer. Looks like a little boobie gets you all hot and bothered."

Owen couldn't answer, of course.

"You like nookie, too?"

In an instant, Cane pushed up Dori's skirt, yanked down her panties, bent her over the side of the couch, and plowed her good.

"You watch," he said. "You might learn something. You like that, don't you, buddy? We just need to get you into rehab, get the gay worked out of you." He slapped against Dori's backside with his hips.

He went on and on. It seemed like he went on an hour, but he didn't come.

All the blood running into Dori's brain made her mad. In a while, she lifted her head, shook her hair out of her eyes, and glared at Owen. Owen was the *reason* Cane was acting that way. If he weren't there, they'd be watching a movie or asleep already—not out in the woods in the middle of nowhere, fucking for an audience. She felt like she was in a porn flick.

Cane kept grunting and thrusting, and as he did, Dori got more and more pissed. She was nothing but a chance to prove a point. Cane had snorted too much meth—clearly. She'd get another infection if he kept going.

"Quit it," she said finally and shoved him off and wiggled around to escape him. He caught her by the wrist, but she yanked away again, pushed down her skirt, kicked off her panties, and went to the cooler to get a beer.

"Get back over here," he yelled. His dick looked pathetic, swollen and shiny and bruised.

"Take me home," she said.

"Get over here, I said."

If anger could make you insane, then Dori had gone insane. Her brain had turned to embers and ignited. Everything she saw was tinged with fire. She hated them *both*. She wanted to kill them *both*.

"Fuck you," said Dori. "You're just putting on a show for Owen. You're a bigger freak than he is."

They had both looked at Owen then. Owen's gaze was fixed on Cane's junk.

She was sure Cane was going to hit her, but instead he turned to Owen and said, "Didn't you ever hear about Sodom and Gomorrah? Didn't you?" Then he backhanded Owen, knocking over the chair he was tied to. It cracked as it hit the linoleum. Dori picked up a different chair, a ladder-back, and swung it at Cane, breaking it over his head.

It stunned him for a minute. It stunned Dori, too. Her hands and forearms zinged from the impact, like she'd been shocked. She was shocked that she'd done it, shocked that it zinged so much.

"Bitch," he said. "You've got the worst damned aim I've ever seen." He was bleeding then from the nose and neck, but he looked at Dori and laughed at her, and something about it struck her silly.

He actually thought she'd intended to hit Owen Howe and missed. He was wearing an old wooden chair around his shoulders like a frame, and his pants were still down.

"Fucking fag," said Cane, and he stomped hard on Owen's mouth with the heel of his boot, and Dori joined in and didn't discriminate as she punched and kicked them both.

Sunning there by the fallen-in ferry dock, she couldn't even *believe* it, really. It was all so pointless and had gotten so out of hand. It seemed like something that happened on TV, not in real life. If Teresa and Jen knew half of what she'd done, they'd never speak to her again. She hoped they never found out.

"Shit, shit, *shit*," she said. She sat up on the blue raft and yelled as loud as she could, "SHIT," and a seagull with a black head squawked back.

There was nothing to do except wait. She didn't know if Cane would rat her out or not. Maybe he'd ratted her out already. But he'd been so fucked up, she wasn't sure he'd even remember all that had happened. Did *she*?

Cane had gotten sick. That's what stopped everything. He threw up on the floor right next to Owen's head. Owen had passed out by then, and Cane staggered back, looked around, and said, "Damn, we made a mess." He crashed out on the couch right across from where Owen lay, still tied to a chair and bleeding on the floor. In a panic, Dori had put on her shirt, grabbed Cane's keys and driven his truck back to his house. She had parked in his yard, left the keys in the ignition, and run the two miles home in the moonlight.

As she stood there in the shower, her mom rubbing off the blood, saying "Oh, Dear Lord Jesus," she had confessed everything.

"We got to pray," her mom had said. "We got to pray for that boy right now."

For the first time in years, Dori had kneeled down beside her, heart pounding, skin crawling, and bowed her sorry head.

But even her mom didn't know where she'd gone. Her mom had taken her to the bus station, had given her the saved-up rent money and sent her on her way. But her mom had no idea that Dori knew Teresa's address. Dori'd been carrying around that address since she was seven years old and had stolen, out of a desk drawer, an old mailing label her mom had saved. For a long time, she'd stashed it in her pencil box, and when she got older, she moved it to her wallet. Sometimes when things were hard with her mom, she'd pull it out. Just looking at Teresa's address made her feel safer, knowing she had a sister out there somewhere.

Now that she'd found her, she didn't want to ruin that, too.

Maybe she'd get away with it. Maybe Teresa and Jen would never know, and everything that had happened nine days earlier would pass like a bad thunderstorm and one day even *she* wouldn't remember. Or maybe somebody would invent a forgetfulness potion, like they had in the movies, and she'd guzzle a quart of it and finally be free.

In a little while, some people climbed over rocks off to her right, rounded the point and came closer: a short person and a tall person, the short person yakking and waving his arms around, the tall person just walking along and nodding.

It was Randy and his dad.

Randy ran up when he saw her. "Hey! You're back," he said. "Yep," said Dori.

"You been crying?" Randy asked. "Your eyes are all swoll up."

"Allergies," said Dori.

Randy gave her a sad pouty face, leaned over, and kissed her right on the top of the head, a gesture that made Dori want to squeeze him. She couldn't remember anybody ever kissing the top of her head like that. Even after his lips were gone, she could still feel it.

Randy's dad nodded her way, said, "Afternoon, Miss."

"Hi," she said.

He nodded toward Randy and said, "If he gets to bothering you, just holler. He's kinda different," and in a half whisper, he confided, "He ain't quite right, but he does real good in school."

Randy stomped in place, splattering up sand and surf. "*You* ain't quite right," he yelled. "I'll show *you* who ain't quite right!" Then he charged his dad and tried to tackle him, but the dad flipped him by his middle, threw him over his shoulder, and tickled him until Randy squirmed away laughing. "Don't you devil-hack that lady, now," the dad warned, and then he waded out into the water, white rubber boots midway up his calves to keep the crabs from nipping where they shouldn't.

"I got something to show you," Randy said. He'd brought along a rusty metal bucket, and deep inside it, all along the bottom, were slimy-looking deep red gizzards and livers, flopped and folded over one another.

"Yuck," said Dori.

Randy grinned and stuck his hand into the bucket, hauling up a palm full of jiggling organ meat.

"What's it for?" she asked.

"Bait," he said. He nodded toward his daddy out among the posts. "We went to the locker plant yesterday to get some meat, and the butcher gave me all these for free." He took a sniff into the bucket and wrinkled his nose. "You gotta be real gentle with 'em," he said. "Wanna feel?"

"No," said Dori.

"I love how they feel," said Randy. "So soft and silky. But you can't smush 'em. Crabs won't bite if you smush 'em."

"I hope you don't turn out to be a serial killer," said Dori.

Randy cocked his head back and laughed straight up at the sky. "Me?" he asked. "No. This is how you practice for getting biddies. Before you can get biddies, you have to tote around a bucket full of gizzards and livers, and if you haven't smushed 'em up at the end of the week, that means you won't smush a biddy to death either."

"In this kind of heat, they'll be raunchy by tomorrow," Dori said.

"Biddies get to stinking sometimes, too," said Randy. "And they poop all over each other." He laughed and added, "You sure can't squish 'em to death just 'cause they smell bad."

"Huh," said Dori.

"You can't judge their potential by how they look on one single day," Randy explained. "A shitty little biddy could grow up to be the Rooster King, you know?"

"You've got a point," Dori said. "But how'd we get to talking about shitty biddies?"

"You think that's bad; I know a song about shitty biddy *titties*," Randy replied, and he sang a little bit, making it up as he went. "If you got a phone, you can make a video and put me up on Instagram," he offered.

"No phone," Dori said, and shrugged.

"I don't have one either, but I'm getting one when I turn eight," Randy claimed. He knelt beside her, stuck both hands into his bucket and sloshed around. It made terrible noises.

"A serial killer couldn't handle this," Randy said. "A serial killer would just squish it right though his fingers." He pulled up a gizzard in his palm, then squeezed really hard until bits of meat dribbled between his knuckles. "Like this!" he said. Then he laughed like hell. "Scared you, didn't I?"

"You're one creepy kid," said Dori.

Randy washed his hands at the edge of the bay. "You ever held a biddy?" he asked.

"No," she said. "But I've held a newborn kitten."

"Biddies are littler," said Randy. "They got the teensiest bones. My granny gets biddies sometimes and raises them in the brooder, but now they've all growed to pullets. Watch this," he said, and he pulled out a single liver, shook it off, and threw it into the water. "Just wait," he said. "A crab'll come grab it. Maybe two will fight over it and we can watch 'em."

They watched the water a little while, but no crabs came.

"How's your granny doing?" Dori asked.

"Somebody busted down her door," Randy said. "Stole everything she had, the sorry bastard."

"That's awful," said Dori.

"Yeah," said Randy. "Some old drug addict, after her pills."

"That's too bad," said Dori. "Maybe she needs an alarm system."

"That's what my momma thought," said Randy. "But the police said it wouldn't do no good. 'Cause them old drug addicts just run right in, grab the pills, and run right back out the door before the cops can even get there."

"Huh," said Dori.

"And besides that, Granny can't work the buttons on an alarm keypad 'cause her fingers have arthritis. She can't hardly call you on the telephone. She don't want no alarm system. Said it'd be going off all the time and scaring her to death if she had one."

"Y'all should think about moving her to the nursing home," Dori suggested.

"She ain't going nowhere," said Randy. "She's gonna stay right there and rot."

"Did they catch the guy who did it?" Dori asked.

"Not yet," said Randy. "But they're working some leads."

She played with Randy for a little while, wading out with him and holding the blue raft while he tried to stand atop it and surf. He fell in each time, and each time she helped him back up.

He wanted to pull her around on the raft, and so she let him. She stretched out on her belly, and he grabbed the rope and maneuvered her between the pilings, weaving in and out. He talked nonstop about gizzards and livers and shitty biddy titties and cops and drug addicts and more, and she just nodded and said "yeah" and "okay," only half listening. There in the sunshine, she played back all her worries and wishes through her mind. If she'd had a little brother to keep her busy all her life, maybe she wouldn't have turned out to be such a criminal.

"I gotta go," she told him in a while. "You keep the raft in your cave, and we can share it."

"Really?" said Randy. He gave her a high five. "See you next Sunday?" he asked.

"Maybe," she said.

When she got back to Teresa and Jen's that evening, they acted surprised to see her. She walked in without knocking and startled them both in the kitchen, where Jen chopped onions with a butcher knife and Teresa studied a recipe book at the counter. They both looked at her in a way that made her think she should have knocked.

"Should I have knocked?" she asked, and Jen said, "It's okay. We just didn't know you were coming," but snitty-snit Teresa peered down over her reading glasses and said, "From now on, please do."

"Sorry," said Dori.

She sat down on a stool at the counter next to Teresa and watched them. Teresa went back to her recipe. Jen took tiny sips of wine ever so often as she sliced the onions into the thinnest purple strips, then cut them again sideways to make them even smaller.

"Don't you have one of those chopper things?" Dori asked.

"You mean a food processor?" Jen asked.

Dori shrugged.

"Yeah," Jen said. "But I like to chop onions."

It made no sense, but at least Jen acknowledged her. Teresa ignored her completely. She went scavenging through the pantry, pulling out this ingredient and that one, checking expiration dates. Dori coughed a couple of times, kicked her feet against the counter, but still Teresa wouldn't look at her.

Her mom did that, too, sometimes when she was mad, gave her the silent treatment. It was hard to believe Teresa could be her mom's other daughter. When her mom was on her medications, she always fixed up, used foundation and eye shadow and hot rollers on her hair. Teresa didn't even shape her bushy eyebrows. Her mom watched her figure, too, kept everything in proportion. Teresa was built like a railroad tie. Dori wouldn't want to get in a fistfight with Teresa. Her arms were as thick as Dori's legs.

It worried her that Teresa wouldn't look at her. Maybe they'd found out about Owen Howe. When the phone rang, Dori's heart sucked in on itself until it was no bigger than a flea with the heebie-jeebies, going crazy inside her chest. She was sure that her mom was on the other end of the line, or maybe the gay patrol alerting them that their own family was the enemy.

But the caller turned out to be a dinner guest running late.

"He'll be here by seven-thirty," Teresa said to Jen.

"We need the extra time anyway," said Jen, and she scraped her onions from the cutting board directly into the frying pan, where the melted butter sizzled.

Teresa added spices, then turned to her at last and said, "We have a friend coming for dinner."

"Cool," said Dori. At the table, there were three place settings, and it dawned on her gradually that the third bowl wasn't for her. For some reason it hurt her feelings to be purposefully left out, and then she was surprised by the disappointment.

Jen must have read her face, because she asked, "Did you want to stay?"

"That's okay," said Dori. "I'll just have some cereal."

"It's okay if you want to stay," said Teresa. "We assumed you were with your boyfriend."

"He's not my boyfriend really," said Dori. "And anyway he left this afternoon."

"Oh," said Jen. "That's too bad."

Dori didn't know if it was "too bad" because now they had to deal with her or if they felt sorry for her because she was obviously sad and moping around. "I'll just have some cereal and go," she offered. She wondered if they begrudged her even that.

But what was she supposed to do? She didn't have any money of her own to buy food. Did they expect her to buy her own food?

She had visions of going into Room 2, taking the revolver out of her tote bag, and shooting herself in the head, the gun barrel positioned directly beneath her chin so that when she pulled the trigger, her brains would splatter straight up onto the ceiling panels. It'd serve them right to have to clean up that mess. She'd wait until their guest was there, maybe until dessert.

On the other hand, she didn't really feel like dying yet.

Teresa let out a big, exaggerated sigh. "I guess you can tell I'm annoyed," she finally admitted. "That's because we had to listen to you fucking some kid you just met for half the night. A kid who's not even your boyfriend apparently. That has to *stop*," she said. "No more guys in your room. If you want to bring a guy home, you'll have to visit with him in here with us. Not in your bedroom. Understand?"

Dori didn't mean to smile, but it was such a relief. The problem was *Warren*. Not her. Not news of Owen Howe. Plus, she had a *bedroom*. Plus, her uptight sister just said, "fuck."

"You think that's funny?" Teresa asked. Red splotches spread all across her neck. "Because it wasn't very funny last night when we couldn't sleep for all your moaning. It was completely disrespectful."

"Sorry," said Dori.

"Look me in the eyes," said Teresa.

Dori glanced her way and then looked down.

"In the *eyes*," Teresa repeated, so Dori did. Her eyes were intense and green and flashing. "No more guys in the bedroom."

"Got it," said Dori. Then, because she was afraid she'd smile, even though she didn't mean to, she added, "I don't think it's funny. I just have a problem sometimes with inappropriate affect."

Both Jen and Teresa looked puzzled.

"I've been to therapy," said Dori. "I know about inappropriate affect. When your behavior doesn't match your emotions?"

Neither of them spoke, and she worried then that she'd said too much. Maybe they wouldn't want her around, knowing she'd been in therapy. Maybe they'd think she was as crazy as her mom, or maybe they'd even think she'd been institutionalized, like a serial killer.

"Does it scare you that I've been to therapy?" she asked. She didn't seem to be able to shut up.

Jen said, "Of course not" at the same time that Teresa asked, "Should it?"

"No," said Dori. "I got raped, that's all. I had to go to therapy after that."

Teresa let out another huge sigh and turned back to the skillet, and Jen said, "God, Dori, I'm sorry that happened to you."

It wasn't the truth, though. Dori'd been court-ordered to therapy, but not for being raped. The first time she was caught shoplifting, she was sent to therapy. The second time, she went to juvie. She hadn't meant to say the thing about rape. She hadn't even *been* raped, not technically, but she kind of knew what it felt like. The rape thing just slipped out, the way all her lies slipped out: almost unconsciously, and she didn't really know if that was a habit or a problem.

Jen handed her a vegetable peeler and showed her how to scrape some strange, pale squash, so Dori went to work, shivering off small strips. This squash had the most impossible skin ever. She looked up at some point and saw that Teresa was crying into her spices. Teresa turned down the burner, wiped her wet cheek on her shoulder, said, "I'm going to get changed," and left the room.

"What's up with her?" asked Dori.

"It's okay," said Jen. "It just upsets her. It upsets *me*, knowing you've been through that. That really sucks."

"I'm fine now," said Dori. "I'm totally over it." She tried to be cheerful and added, "That's why I went to therapy!" but it came out wrong.

She finished one of the squashes, and Jen split it down the middle, scooped out the seeds, and chopped it into chunks. "You should stay for dinner," she said.

"I don't think Teresa wants me to," said Dori. "I'm pretty sure she hates me."

"She doesn't hate you," said Jen. "She's just going through some stuff. It's not all about you."

"I should go to my room and watch TV," said Dori.

"You should stay," said Jen. "It's just our friend Eric. You'll love him. He's a hoot."

She recognized Eric right away as the guy who'd stolen her turtle. As soon as she saw him, she wanted to head-butt him, knock him flat on his back, and stick steak knives in him.

But at the same time, if events had gone differently, she wouldn't have found Jen and Teresa, and she wouldn't have met Warren. She might still be sleeping in Randy's cave, or if Eric had pressed charges, she might be in jail.

She smiled and said, "Nice to meet you," like she'd been born a lady, and in return, he gave her a knowing half-bow. "Hi," he said, and the night went better than she expected. Dori didn't mention the turtle; Eric didn't mention that she'd clawed his face. He still had scabbed-over scratches, and when Jen asked what had happened, he claimed he'd gotten caught on the wrong side of a crab pot and winked Dori's way.

Dori couldn't believe they served soup for dinner. Who liked soup? And this soup didn't even have meat in it. It was some strange, stinky, spicy orange stuff that she was almost afraid to try. Luckily they had put a lot of butter in it, and they also had bread and a salad.

Eric wasn't bad looking. He was kind of goofy: bald, but with a full beard; short, but not too short; and he wore little round glasses that grew on Dori as the night went along. She sat there at the table trying to force down the curried butternut squash soup, a dish only a lesbian could like, and imagined how she might get Eric to take her out in his waterkeeper boat to look for turtles.

But he didn't pay her much attention. In fact, if she hadn't known better, she'd have thought that Eric was making a move on Teresa. He watched Teresa constantly. At one point, he got up to refill her water glass—and twice he asked her how she felt. But Jen didn't seem to mind. What was up with *that*?

Jen kept reaching for Teresa, squeezing her shoulder or running her hand across her back as she got up to get more bread, and it didn't make sense. Teresa was the least lovable sister Dori could have imagined. All those years, she'd fantasized about meeting Teresa, imagining they'd go shopping and get pedicures and take trips to the Bahamas. In her fantasies, Teresa had understood her, listened and colluded with her. In real life, everything she said came out bitchy. The way she held her face, you'd think the whole world smelled like a turd. She could be cute if she tried, if she spent some time on the elliptical machine. She had pretty green eyes and pretty full lips, but her hair looked like it hadn't been trimmed in ten years, and all she ever did was wear it in a braid down the middle of her back. If she combed it out, she might notice all those split ends.

Eric was sopping up the last of his soup with bread when he said, "So that's just wild that you two have the same mom. What does she think of your reunion?"

"She doesn't know," Teresa admitted.

"She wouldn't like it," Dori said. "She likes to keep the different parts of her life separate. She didn't even tell me about her other family until I found some pictures in a box in her closet."

"Really?" Teresa asked. "What kinds of pictures?"

"All kinds," said Dori. "I remember one of you wearing a diaper and picking strawberries, and one of you in a baby pool. I thought at first they were *Mom's* baby pictures—because the cameras back then sucked. The pictures were all grainy and faded. But then they had dates and captions on them: *Teresa, 8 months* or *Teresa and Stan at the tractor pull.* And I was like, '*Who* are Teresa and Stan?'"

She was talking a lot, but she couldn't seem to stop. "Then I found this family portrait. It freaked me out to see Mom there in her '80s up-do with you and some dude with a curly perm mullet."

"Uh, that'd be my Dad," said Teresa.

"I figured," said Dori. "What happened to *him?*"

"He's been dead a long time," said Teresa. "What happened to *your* dad? Is he still around?"

"Don't even get me started," Dori replied.

Eric turned to Dori and asked, "Well, what's your mom like?"

"She's a pain in the ass," said Dori. "But she's okay sometimes. She's an artist. She does folk art, mostly, out of stuff she buys from yard sales."

"Oh, Lord, is she still into yard sales?" Teresa asked.

"Yep," said Dori. "She collects all kinds of stuff, and then glues or wires it together. All her pieces are Biblically inspired. She writes different Bible verses on each sculpture, and people at craft shows think she's some kind of prophet. She's got a big reputation on the craft show circuit. Haven't you seen her work?"

Teresa shook her head.

"You can buy it in galleries and stuff," Dori said.

"Seriously?" Teresa asked.

Dori nodded. "I'm surprised you haven't seen it. There's a gallery in Tennessee with some pieces. Maybe Virginia, too."

"That's pretty far-out," said Eric.

Teresa agreed, awkwardly, and laughed. "I had no idea. Come to think of it, she used to love to make hospital beds out of shoeboxes for all my dolls."

"Let me guess," joked Jen. "The dolls had advanced cancer."

"Or leprosy," said Teresa, and everybody laughed.

"She's pretty good, though," Dori said. She poked around in her partly eaten salad with her fork, spreading it out so it wouldn't seem like she'd left so much on her plate. "If I'd known you didn't have one of her sculptures, I'd have brought you one," she said and smiled. "As a hostess gift."

After dinner, Eric and Jen decided to look up Teresa and Dori's mother on the Internet. It made Dori more than a little nervous, thinking that if they typed in her mom's name, something about her own disappearance might show up. Plus, if they read her bio, they might find out that she didn't live in Mississippi at all—but in North Carolina. Dori didn't want them knowing where to look.

"She's probably not a big enough artist to be on the Internet," she claimed.

"If she's in a gallery, she must be," said Eric.

"It's just a little backwoods gallery," said Dori.

"Where's the laptop?" Eric asked.

Air latched up in Dori's throat and refused to go down to her lungs. She needed to get out of there. She was an idiot. Why had she instigated an Internet search? Her stomach felt heavy from all the curry, and she couldn't get enough air, so she said, "I think I'm going to bed now. See you guys later."

"Wait," Jen called. "We're having dessert in a few minutes."

"I'm not feeling that great," Dori replied.

But Teresa, that bitch, wouldn't allow her to leave until she'd helped with the dishes. Dori hurried to clear the table while Eric fiddled with cords on the router to get a wireless signal, and Jen looked for the folder with the password in it. The power had gone out the day before, and they'd lost the Internet connection.

Dori rinsed orange residue from the dishes, stacked them in the dishwasher, and was about to sneak away when Teresa walked in holding Sugar Britches. His coat looked greasy, and he held his head at a funny, unnatural angle.

"Can you stay long enough to help me feed him?" she asked. "We've got to get him to eat something. He hasn't eaten all day."

"I guess," said Dori. His tumor had crusted over, black and scabby and nasty-looking. He kept trying to clean it, and it made Dori gag just thinking about it. "He's probably nauseated from trying to lick it," she speculated.

"If he doesn't start eating soon, he won't make it," Teresa said.

There was another term Dori had learned in therapy: magical thinking. She was pretty sure Teresa was guilty of it. It didn't look like Sugar Britches was going to make it whether he ate or not. They offered him his dinner both in a bowl and in a saucer. Teresa tried warming the food, but he wasn't interested. She even opened a can of tuna and drained the juice into a bowl. Still, Sugar turned his head.

"I've got an idea," Teresa said. "Wait here. Don't let him leave." She picked up Sugar and thrust him into Dori's arms, and so Dori held him. He weighed so little it felt like he must be hollow, like a chocolate bunny. She stroked his fur, scratched gently under his chin, but avoided touching the tumor.

When Teresa came back, she brought along a towel and a syringe. "You want to hold or feed?" she asked.

Dori shrugged.

"I'll hold," Teresa said. "You feed."

Sugar didn't even struggle when Teresa swaddled him in a towel. She crouched on the kitchen floor and plopped onto her rear end, shaking the spices in the spice rack when she landed. Dori settled there beside her with the wet food mixed with water and the syringe.

101

"Come on, baby," Teresa said. "Open up."

"I've never done this before," Dori admitted. She sucked up some food, and at Teresa's instructions inserted the syringe to the very back corner of Sugar Britches' mouth. Then gently, slowly, steadily, she pushed the plunger.

Liquid cat food dripped all over them, off Sugar's whiskers and chin, off Teresa's hands. It splattered all over the towel, all over Dori's arms, Teresa's legs. Dori concentrated on shooting it in steady but slow, so he wouldn't choke. "It's okay, Sugar," she whispered. "We're just trying to help you."

"Don't get any air in it," Teresa warned. "It'll give him a stomachache." So Dori was careful, so careful.

They kept taking breaks so Sugar could swallow. Whenever he tensed up, they took breaks.

"I'm sorry he's so sick," Dori finally said. She had a wet cloth, and she was wiping the food that had dribbled down his neck. "I'm sorry you're so sad."

Without lifting her eyes from Sugar, Teresa whispered, "Thanks."

He must have hated it, being force-fed like that, but when they were done, when they'd wiped him off, Sugar walked calmly back into the living room where Jen and Eric had found a few images of their mom's sculptures on the laptop.

"Check this out!" Eric said. He resized the image until they could clearly see the sculpture: a naked doll with magic marker scribbles all over it, upside down, its head smashed into a melon-sized piece of rock. The doll had one eye open, one eye flattened against the stone, hair shaved off unevenly, like a Holocaust victim, arms and legs askew. There were pieces of granite embedded in the doll's flesh, some so small they looked like freckles, some larger, protruding. The piece was titled "Happy Shall He Be."

A different image showed the Bible verse scribbled across the doll's rear end and back: *Happy shall he be, that taketh and dasheth thy little ones against the stones.*

"Yikes," Jen said. "That's not in the Bible!"

"Psalms 137:9," Dori replied. "Check for yourself." But they didn't have a Bible, or at least one that she'd seen.

Another of her sculptures was a small, brightly painted wheelbarrow, made of something like papier-mâché, and inside it little Fisher-Price figures in a line on their backs, with their heads all muddied. Then the inscription: *Behold, I will corrupt your seed, and spread dung upon your faces.*

"That's from Malachi," Dori told them. "I can't remember which verse."

"That's just creepy," said Jen.

"Please tell me she didn't use real shit," Teresa added.

Dori laughed and said no, that it was cocoa.

"What does she do?" asked Eric. "Go around looking for the worst Bible verses she can find?"

"Maybe," said Dori. There wasn't a picture of her best one, the one about "If your eye causes you to sin, gouge it out and throw it away." Her mom had made a model of Dori's hand for that one. It had taken a long time, but she'd loved the feeling of her mom rubbing her hand as she shaped the plaster-coated cheesecloth around the back of Dori's hands and fingers, then the palm. She hadn't even minded redoing it when it didn't dry at the angle her mom wanted. Then her mom wedged a great bloody eyeball made of clay into the space between the thumb and index finger. The eyeball with its dangling, splayed nerves made the whole thing disgusting, but the job of art wasn't to comfort or placate. That's what her mom said. The job of art was to disturb and unsettle. Seeing the images of her sculptures made Dori miss her mom. "We went there," she said. "To that gallery. They had an opening reception for Mom, and a lot of important people came."

They clicked on pictures of her mom, long frizzy gray-blond hair, big glasses, the plastic frames out of style. Even Dori knew she looked like she'd been haunting houses. "She only makes the sculptures when she's off her meds," she said. "When she's on them, she's like a different person."

There were no pictures of Dori at that website. No references to her at all, even though she'd driven her mom to the opening reception, had passed out pieces of Xanax like candy to her mom so she could get through it. But she hadn't been outed by Google, not yet.

"Can I borrow your computer to check my email?" she asked. "I haven't been online in ages."

"Sure," Jen said.

She had no intention of checking her email. She didn't want the police to track her down. But she *did* want to get Eric and Jen away from the computer and away from any more searches that included her mom's name and could potentially mention her own crimes.

So while Jen and Teresa and Eric hung out in the kitchen, scooping sorbet into glass dishes and whispering and laughing, she looked up Warren on the computer and found a reference to a mission trip he had taken to Belize. She considered looking up her name but was afraid of what she might find. She skimmed the national news, but didn't type in her town to check the local. She didn't know if she ever wanted to find out what had happened to Owen Howe.

After dessert, Sugar Britches, who'd been floor-bound a long time, jumped up onto the couch. Teresa and Jen were so ecstatic about it that they didn't even mind him getting tumor-spooge all over the cushions. While they petted him, while Eric studied his sarcoma and speculated about whether it was possible for him to recover if it fell off—because part of it had clearly died, and maybe if that part fell away, he'd be stronger, feel better, live longer—Dori erased the computer's search history and took herself to bed.

VI.

A thunderstorm at five in the morning rumbled the house and rattled all the panes in the windows. Teresa flipped her pillow to the cool side and tried to doze back off, but inside she felt like that windowpane glass, trembly and vibrating. She slipped from the covers, made coffee, and stretched out on the couch to watch the drama flash with each bolt of lightning: a million raindrops ravaged by wind as they splatted against the sliding glass door. Sugar Britches perched silently on the cushion behind her, tumor side up and airing beneath the ceiling fan.

The center of his tumor was hardening, blacking itself out from the middle. When daylight came and the thunder and lightning subsided, Teresa leaned over and studied the mass, parts bloody, parts oily, parts scabby and loose. It looked almost like a craggy ledge had formed in what was once a smooth mountain. He let her rub him all around the face and ears, even down his back and around the tumor, where his flesh changed from pliable to stone.

So strange, how flesh could change like that. She rubbed her own abdomen and imagined a baby in there, just a hint of a baby, a few cells dividing until the cell explosion created something recognizable. She hoped she'd grow a baby and not something monstrous. It was basically the same process, whether you made a tumor or a child.

She didn't feel pregnant, but it was obviously too early to tell.

Even with the most sensitive pregnancy tests, it took a week and usually longer for the fertilized egg to implant and the body to produce enough hormones to indicate conception. A week felt like forever. She had pregnancy tests stashed in the bathroom cabinet, too, right behind the ovulation kits, and she had to fight the urge to take one early, just in case.

Each time before when they'd inseminated, she'd acted like she might be pregnant already. She'd taken prenatal vitamins with the extra folic acid; she'd stopped drinking alcohol, even though her gynecologist swore a little wine wouldn't hurt. She'd gone wholeheartedly into pregnancy mode, and each time, when her period arrived, she'd gotten so blue that she had to go to bed for three days just to survive it. The sense of having so little control over her body, the defeat, was a lot worse than the clots and cramping and general mess of bleeding.

There were months when she felt soft and open to baby spirits. After their clinic visits, she and Jen would light candles and play soothing, dreamy music, and then she was sure she must be pregnant. How could any baby not want to join them in such bliss, where it would have two mothers, not just one, and two mothers who wanted a baby more than anything, who went to such lengths to get one?

Most people didn't have to work that hard.

Then there were months when all she felt was frustration and fury. Those times, after each trip to the clinic, she warred against her own uterus and ovaries and fallopian tubes, thinking of them as enemies to be conquered. A baby *would* implant there and grow there, damn it, and if it came out hating her, so be it. She'd conquer the baby too.

When her period came, she'd stay in bed and watch sad documentaries and cry until Jen finally made her get up and go do something—have lunch with Cassidy, work in the garden.

Whenever she went into department stores, it was all she could do not to shop for baby things. She priced diapers and strollers and intercom systems. She fingered the tiniest onesies, sorted through racks of overalls so small they wouldn't even fit

Sugar Britches—or at least they wouldn't have fit him before he got so sick. She knew better than to buy any of the clothes. That could jinx it. But she couldn't help looking.

She'd been mistaken for pregnant plenty of times. She had one of those builds that always confused store clerks and dressing-room attendants—broader through the abdomen and hips than the shoulders (though she was broad through the shoulders, too) and looking maybe five months pregnant all the time. She had the kind of lap that you just expected to see little kids crawling around on. Jen called it a goddess build, but that was a nice way to put it.

She refilled her coffee and went to the bedroom to turn off Jen's alarm.

"Morning," Jen mumbled.

"You can sleep," Teresa told her. "It's pouring rain."

"Bummer," said Jen, and she rolled back over. There'd be no boat deliveries in that weather.

Teresa was on high alert for abdominal twinges, but those could mean anything: implantation, miscarriage, or even just gas. Mostly she suspected what she felt was gas.

She was forty, so her chances of conceiving were already slim, her chances of miscarriage far greater. But she'd seen a specialist who'd done a complete workup and had assured her that she was still ovulating. A lot of women with difficulty conceiving used the fertility clinic for the hormone shots to induce ovulation, but Teresa didn't need those.

"I *want* them, though," she'd whined to Jen on the drive home after their first appointment.

"No, you don't," Jen replied. "You might pop out ten babies at one time, and I'm not ready to start a preschool."

If she didn't conceive soon, she could always take shots to induce ovulation, but then they'd have to pay even more.

The sperm they'd ordered had run them almost a thousand a month. They had to pay extra to have it washed, a necessary procedure if you were shooting it into the uterus instead of the vagina. That didn't count the cost of the office visit or the other expenses—all the tests and the treatment for some condition neither of them had ever heard of: *Ureaplasma urealyticum,* some kind of asymptomatic bacterial infection spread through sexual contact, even through same-sex sexual contact. They both had to take antibiotics to get rid of it.

Jen had loved that. "We share a disease!" she'd marveled. "I wonder which one of us gave it to the other? That's hilarious!"

"Hooray," Teresa joked.

"You don't understand," Jen said. "I actually get to *do* something. Finally. Give me that prescription!"

And Teresa had reassured her that she'd done a lot, that it wasn't about which of their bodies they used. They were in it fifty/fifty. They took their meds fifty/fifty, side by side.

But there was always that little fear, too, that it wasn't really fifty/fifty. Though same-sex couples had finally won the rights to marry and adopt, there could always be setbacks. With the wrong governor elected, the wrong justice appointed to the high court, anything could happen.

In a way, it was terrifying.

In another way, it was infuriating.

You could hardly even call Cassidy and her husband, Dan, a couple. They were about as disconnected as two people could possibly be, but nobody questioned their right to be parents. When it came down to it, being happy with one another, loving one another wasn't a requirement for parenthood.

When she didn't get pregnant after the first few rounds, she wondered if her body was saying no for all those reasons. She was holding in too much terror and rage to be a capable mother.

She and Jen decided that if they needed to, they'd move to a more tolerant place, where they wouldn't be the only lesbian couple in town, much less the only lesbian couple with kids. "The whole world's open," Jen said, even though it wasn't true. She kissed Teresa on the forehead and over both eyes. "Don't worry about it," she said. "We'll pack right up and go."

"But my retirement's in the state system," Teresa worried. "And your family's here."

"We'll figure it out one piece at a time," Jen reassured her.

If they stayed in Virginia, they might have to leave the shore to send the child to school. Where they lived, their kid would inevitably be a target for bullying. Even some of their friends who knew and loved them, even some people in Jen's own family pretended they were roommates and closest pals.

But things were changing for the better. A Montessori school had recently opened up, and it might be established and progressive enough by the time their child reached kindergarten age. As Jen kept reminding her, they had five years to decide. If not the Montessori school, there was a Friends school across the bay.

So they found their donor and ordered the sperm, and they got a multi-vial discount for buying in bulk. They'd used up three vials, then three more, before Teresa's latest breakdown, when she had declared that she was unfit to be a mother.

She hated the person she had turned into, the way her mind looped round and round and couldn't escape. There was even one time when she was still testing for ovulation and her period arrived—and how had that even happened?

At other points in her life, when disappointments and hard knocks had sent her reeling, she'd thrown her energy into outward things. When her mom left, and her dad, in disbelief, spent all his evenings on the front porch chain-smoking and sipping bourbon, Teresa had joined the drama club at school. She painted sets, pieced together costumes, ran the soundboard from a little room up above the balcony seats. As soon as the play was over, she volunteered to assist the gym teacher with the boys' baseball team, keeping records at every game. She didn't even like baseball but staying busy and involved in other projects got her through high school.

After her dad died, when she'd boxed up his clothes and belongings, paid the bills, signed the papers, and settled his estate, there was too much time, a chasm of time, and so she volunteered at a soup kitchen, passing out undercooked baked potatoes still wrapped in their crumpled tinfoil to addicts and others more down on their luck than she was. But suddenly, with the inseminations, she couldn't get past herself, out of her thoughts or beyond her own self-loathing.

Jen had talked her through the latest dark spell and had convinced her to continue with Eric as donor. But she wasn't winning any awards for her home-insemination behavior. If she ever conceived, she and Jen would have to start a blog or produce a YouTube video, a "Don't Do This" guide to sucking up sperm with syringes.

Teresa was in the bathroom when the knocking started up. It took her a while to get to the door. When she did, there stood Dori, crouched beneath the tiny awning and trying to avoid the downpour, fully dressed and ready for a day of floating-deli deliveries.

"Can I have breakfast?" she asked as Teresa shooed her inside, and it occurred to Teresa how confusing the knocking rule must be. If Dori was their guest, she should have access to their kitchen—or at the very least a box of cereal of her own in Room 2.

"I'll find you a key," said Teresa. She offered Dori a fresh towel to pat dry with. "And we'll make a grocery run later. Get you some things to snack on in your room." She searched the hall closet to find an extra rain jacket and tossed it to her. "We should have done that before. Sorry I didn't think of it."

"It's okay," said Dori. She poured herself a cup of coffee and fumbled around in the fridge until she found cream and then grabbed the sugar. Teresa had forgot about cream and sugar. Both she and Jen took their coffee black.

Dori seemed genuinely disappointed to learn that there'd be no work in that weather and stunned to hear that Jen hadn't yet emerged from bed.

"Is there something I can do around the deli, then?" Dori asked. "Maybe slice turkey or wash lettuce or something?"

"Jen's got plenty of people on the schedule," Teresa said. "They don't even need *her*, but I'm sure she'll go in and get in everybody's way just the same."

"Maybe I could work on one of your middle rooms, pull up nails or paint or something."

Teresa shrugged. "I thought we'd have a play day. Just you and me. We can drive up to Chincoteague. Did you ever read *Misty of Chincoteague*?"

"No," said Dori.

"It'd be good for us to get out of town," said Teresa. "Have a little adventure. Like sisters. Don't worry—all expenses paid." Then it occurred to her that Dori probably wanted to work because she needed money. "Is there something you need money for?" she asked.

"Well, yeah," said Dori.

"For what?"

"Just stuff," Dori replied, and Teresa wondered if maybe she should be giving her an allowance. When she was Dori's age, she had a job, made her own spending money, but before that, her parents gave her $20 a week to clean the house. Dori had only worked with Jen one day so far. Teresa didn't know if Jen intended to pay her by the day or by the week. What if she needed tampons? Maybe she should offer her a loan.

Jen came out of the bedroom, her hair all shaggy from sleep, wearing Tweety Bird pajamas. She plopped beside Dori at the table.

"Nice," said Dori.

"You like?" said Jen. "I've got Eeyore the Donkey, too."

While they looked up the forecast on the computer, Teresa made them all omelets with pesto and feta, perfectly symmetrical half-moons of omelets. They offered Sugar Britches a raw egg for breakfast. He used to always lick the bowl when they made scrambled eggs, but he had no appetite for eggs that morning. They offered him tiny crumbles of feta, but he didn't want cheese either.

"I need to get dressed," Teresa said. "But let's plan on leaving by ten. Can you be ready?"

"I'm ready now," Dori said. "Aren't you coming?" she asked Jen.

"Nah," Jen said. "I'll stay behind in case the weather clears."

"I can stay and help if you want," Dori offered.

Teresa rolled her eyes.

"Absolutely not," said Jen. "You go and have a good time!" She got up and scraped her plate into the trash, then scraped Teresa and Dori's plates, too. "And don't be scared of T, either," she said. She walked up behind Teresa and wrapped both arms around her. "She's only crusty when she's nervous. I think having a little sister makes her pretty nervous."

Teresa started to say something. She opened her mouth, but then stopped.

"*I* make *her* nervous?" Dori said. "That's hilarious."

"Oh yeah," said Jen. "You two need some time to get to know each other, so you can both just chill. You couldn't *pay* me to go to Chincoteague today." She winked, kissed Teresa on the side of the head, and said to Dori," Plus, she'll tell you all about the US Constitution on your drive if you let her."

"Don't scare her off," Teresa said. Then to Dori she added, "We're not talking about the Constitution today. I promise."

But they hadn't made it ten miles up the road before Teresa accidentally brought up the Fourteenth Amendment. She was trying to say something meaningful, trying to apologize, really, for having not been around when Dori was younger, when she asked her, "Have you ever done something you thought was right, only to figure out later that it was wrong?"

"Like what?" Dori asked. She'd gone through the glove compartment of the car and helped herself to an extra pair of sunglasses. She cleaned them with her T-shirt and put them on.

"Oh, I don't know—taken a side on some issue, and then later, when some time passed, realized how completely full of shit you were?"

Dori laughed. "Maybe," she said. "Probably, I guess. I don't really know what you mean."

Teresa glanced her way, but in the mirrored sunglasses, all she could see was her own distorted nose. "Like the Fourteenth

Amendment," Teresa said. "I mean, these days, it seems unthinkable that before Congress passed the Fourteenth Amendment, African Americans weren't considered citizens of the United States and weren't offered equal protection under the law. When we look at that now, we know how screwed up it was. But to a lot of people living in the South in the mid-1800s—and even in the North—it seemed outrageous to think of former slaves as citizens."

Dori put her foot up on the dashboard of the car, then asked, "Is it okay for me to put my foot up here?"

Teresa nodded, even though she hated little toe prints on her windshield. "So that's what I mean," she continued. "Sometimes you have to just keep on living and let time pass in order to figure out what's *really* right and wrong. We always *think* we know, but we have such limitations. It's like we're wearing blinders and don't even realize it."

"You mean like with Sugar Britches and deciding whether or not you should put him down?"

That floored Teresa. She wasn't thinking about Sugar at all, not just then.

"Huh," Teresa said. "Yeah, kinda, I guess." She passed a few cars before she realized she was doing eighty. Her heart felt like it was beating twice that fast. She changed lanes and slowed back down. "What I'm really trying to say is that I've been so mad at your mom and so hurt by your mom for so long that I'd just written her off."

"She's *your* mom, too," Dori said. "Why do you keep calling her *my* mom?"

"I don't know," Teresa said. "Because she abandoned me. She left me, so I left *her*, in my heart anyway. And I thought I was right, but I wasn't, because by cutting off your mom—by cutting off *Hilda*—I also cut *you* off." She paused and then decided, "I'm calling her Hilda from now on. I'm not calling her Mom anymore. She hasn't been a mom to me in ages."

"You didn't owe me anything," Dori said.

"Well, I wish I'd done that differently," said Teresa. "And I wish you hadn't been sent to foster care and could have stayed with me and Jen when your mom—when *Hilda*—was so sick."

"She's been sick my whole life," said Dori.

"Then I wish you could have stayed with me and Jen all your life."

There. She'd said it. She wasn't sure how true it was, phrased that way, but she'd said it. And maybe it was true.

But what a strange thought—that she and Jen might have had a child to raise and love so long ago.

"Wow," said Dori. "Thanks."

"And I *really* wish you hadn't been raped," Teresa continued. "Because no one should have to go through that. Ever."

"Thanks," Dori said again, but she was squirming. She was scrounging around in her sunflower tote bag for something she couldn't find, and Teresa knew she'd made her uncomfortable, but she couldn't seem to shut up.

"Like with *Brown v. Board of Education*," Teresa said. "You studied that, right? 1954? The case that finally undercut *Plessy v. Ferguson*, which allowed for state-sponsored segregation?" She might have gone on for a long time about all that history, about how sometimes things that start in one century don't get corrected until the next, except that Dori interrupted.

"Can we get something to drink?" Dori asked. "I could use a milkshake." She pointed to a fast-food place they were quickly approaching, and they had just enough time to change lanes and veer off the road.

The rain kept falling, even to the north, so it wasn't such a great day to explore Chincoteague and Assateague Islands. They had crab cake sandwiches overlooking the water and then drove out to the wildlife refuge and the ocean, where wild ponies sometimes ran along the beach and frolicked in the waves.

But there were no wild ponies that day, and the storm had stirred up the ocean from the bottom, so that it looked murky and frosted and dangerous as big waves burst over little ones.

There were more clouds in the distance, deep purple ones, and only die-hard tourists on the beach.

They walked a long way on the beach just the same, sometimes talking, sometimes not. Sometimes Teresa let Dori fall behind when she stopped to look at a shell or wade through the foamy sea edges, and it occurred to her that Dori might not even be real. She could be a ghost. She could look back and Dori could have disappeared as quickly as she'd come. She could be completely alone.

Or she could be one of *three,* if Dori stayed and a fertilized egg wiggled its way into the lining of her uterus as she passed along that rough and rain-pitted shore.

In a while, when the drizzle let up, she flopped down in the damp sand while Dori searched for devil's purses and talked with some boys who were fishing just down the beach. Teresa wormed her feet into the sand until she'd buried them. She imagined an egg in her uterus doing the exact same thing, planting itself in the soft lining, burying itself in warmth and blood.

Would her baby be a girl? Would she look like Dori? She could have been Dori's mother, but she was nobody's mother. Nobody but Sugar's. She watched the wind blowing sea foam away from the waves and across the sand in clusters of fine tight bubbles that burst and disappeared.

Down the way, a boy showed Dori how to throw a fishing line, and then Dori took his pole and cast out into the waves like a pro. Teresa got a kick out of seeing her surprise him. Dori high-fived the boy, waved good-bye, and skipped back toward her, looking as if she didn't have a care in the world.

Back in Chincoteague, they strolled in and out of shops. Dori found a hat that she liked, a gangster-style number with a feather in the brim. She cocked it down over one eye and strutted around the store looking like a Broadway dancer or a mafioso.

Teresa lifted it from her head and checked the price tag. "I'll get it for you," she offered.

"Why?" Dori asked.

Teresa shrugged.

"Because you feel sorry for me?"

Teresa smacked her in the arm with the hat and gave it back. "No, Miss Smart Ass," she said. "Because I've missed seventeen birthdays now, so I figured I'd do some catching up. Do you have a problem with that?"

"No," Dori said sheepishly.

"Good," said Teresa.

On the way back to the street where they'd left the car, they wandered through a T-shirt shop, an old hardware store, a record store, and a gift shop. Then they passed the movie theater, where there was a five-thirty showing of a movie Dori'd been dying to see. Teresa sent Jen a text, letting her know they'd be late, and she bought them tickets and popcorn, sodas and Nerds, and they sat there in the dark theater, nearly empty at that time of day.

"Too bad Jen's not here," said Dori.

"I know," Teresa said. "I'm glad you like her. I wasn't sure at first how cool you'd be with the whole lesbian thing."

Dori shrugged.

The dim lighting made it easier to talk. "Do you have any lesbian or gay friends back home?" Teresa asked.

"Not really," said Dori. "I know this one girl who's bi." She took a big swig of soda and confessed: "Sometimes I use the word *gay* to mean *stupid*—like you say something's *gay* when you don't like it. I know I shouldn't do that, but I still do—"

"Yeah," said Teresa. "My students do that too. It always hurts my feelings."

"Really?" Dori asked. "Because they're probably not talking about *you*."

"I know," said Teresa. "But it still hurts. Maybe it's good, though, to be reminded of unintentional meanness. When I was your age, we used the word *retarded* in the same way. I'm sure there were people who overheard me, whose feelings I probably hurt and didn't even know it."

"We still use *retarded*," Dori admitted. "*Retarded* and *gay* kind of mean the same thing."

116

"Huh," Teresa said. "Interesting."

"Do your students care that you're lesbian?" Dori asked.

"Most of them don't know," Teresa said. "At least I don't think they know. When students use the word *gay* around me to describe something negative, I try to correct them without coming across as too defensive—which, as you know, is hard for me."

Dori laughed.

"But I doubt my students would use the word to my face if they thought *I* was gay."

There'd been one boy, though, the year before, who'd managed to get in his digs: "Lez be honest," he'd say. Or "Lez be clear . . ."

"Maybe if they were assholes," said Dori.

"Most people aren't assholes," Teresa told her. "Most people just do asshole things from time to time."

"I'm an asshole," Dori admitted.

"Me too," said Teresa. She couldn't stop thinking about the day before and her blowup with Jen over the frothy sperm. She was at least as big an asshole as that student. "Maybe it runs in the family."

"How about the other teachers?" Dori asked. "And the principal? Do they know you're gay?"

"Some do, some don't," said Teresa. "Believe it or not, what other people think becomes a lot less important as you get older. I don't advertise it at work, but I don't hide it either."

"Do you take Jen to parties and stuff?"

"Not work parties," Teresa replied. "We don't have that many—and I try to spare her when I can."

"Are you really sparing her, though, or is that just what you tell yourself?" Dori continued. "Do you feel like a fraud when you don't take Jen?"

Teresa couldn't tell if she was genuinely curious or if she was trying to make her suffer. She felt like a spider with a broom coming after it. "I guess I do, sometimes," she answered. "It's mostly because of where we live. Who knows? If we lived in New York City, I might shave my head and wear rainbow flags."

"Seriously?" Dori asked.

117

Teresa shrugged. "Probably not. But I'd be a lot more likely to hold her hand in public. And I'd definitely take her to work parties."

The film trailer began, and then the film. Teresa watched without paying attention. Instead of the movie, she watched her breath, how shallow it was, and she worked to let the air in deeply, filling her up. The day with Dori had been so hard, and she only made it harder by depriving herself of oxygen.

And depriving her potential *baby* of oxygen. If she got pregnant, she'd have to breathe much more consciously.

She amused herself thinking that if she'd actually conceived, this movie would be the baby's very first flick. She put her hand over her stomach and imagined she was insulating the baby from noise and profanity.

The film was a romantic comedy, and she took cues from Dori on how to respond, laughing along when Dori laughed. It felt so strange to be with her little sister. Sometimes Dori seemed so coarse, but then she'd say something insightful. Teresa let her mind backtrack through all their conversations, trying to recall not just the content, but also the tenor.

And she tried to weigh out exactly what she *owed* Dori.

Did she owe her a trip to the gynecologist for birth control if she wasn't on the pill already? She definitely didn't want Dori getting pregnant—but it was hard to imagine asking a teenager she'd known for only a few days whether or not she was on the pill. Maybe she should buy her some condoms at least.

Should they enroll her in high school, let her stay the year, and then send her off to the community college? Should they pay her tuition, buy her books? Did they owe her that? Or should they ship her back home to finish out her childhood?

Dori's childhood was already gone, though—clearly. It looked like it'd been gone awhile.

Should they take her to the dentist? Get that broken tooth capped?

She couldn't stop thinking about that tooth, wondering how it happened. If it happened when Dori was raped, then it must remind her every time she brushed her teeth, every time she looked in the mirror.

Or maybe it happened in foster care. She'd had students in foster care and knew how dangerous foster care could be. It was a crapshoot, really, and girls fought every bit as bad as boys. Maybe worse. Girls could be so vicious.

Or maybe it happened before that. She imagined an altercation with Hilda, possibly when she was having the breakdown that got her locked up on the mental ward. Had she smacked Dori in the face, or done it in some more creative way?

When Teresa was a girl, there'd been another tooth incident. Instead of two front teeth, she'd grown in three. She had the regular two, but then between them, an extra, tiny third tooth descended and squeezed in sideways. Her mom took her to a dentist for children two towns away, and he said it was nothing to worry about. Teresa would need braces when she was older, and they'd pull the extra tooth then. In the meantime, they should leave it alone and let her other teeth come in.

But her mom couldn't stop worrying over Teresa's third tooth. She had called it a devil tooth and kept making Teresa let her wiggle and loosen it.

She was obsessed. When she couldn't get it loose enough to pull, she had tied dental floss around it, tight and near the gum line, to kill off the root.

Teresa had run around the house with dental floss dangling from her mouth until her dad had noticed and stopped her. Her dad and her mom got into a terrible fight about it. Even after she was in bed, she could hear them fighting, and her mom claiming it would be just like docking a lamb's tail. You just put a rubber band around the base and waited for the thing to fall off.

The tooth had throbbed all the time, and Teresa began to think that there really might be something wicked about it.

They were attending services at a hard-shell Baptist church by then. The preacher was one of those fire and brimstone-shouting preachers who talked constantly of Hell and the wages of sin and all that. Her dad thought he was a kook and stopped going to church, but her mom began reading the Bible and memorizing passages that featured the devil and the last judgment.

She had always loved the stuff that terrified her. Revelations. The Four Horsemen of the Apocalypse. But could she really have believed that Teresa was evil because of a pointy little tooth?

One afternoon when Teresa was sprawled on an area rug in the den, working on a project for social studies, her mom had kept nagging her: "Just let me feel it. Let me wiggle it a little bit."

"I'm busy," Teresa had insisted. She could still picture her project so clearly—the white poster board where she outlined the different types of governments. She'd finished the column on Monarchy, was working then on Oligarchy.

"Come on," her mom prodded. "You haven't let me feel it in a long time. That tooth is bad, Teresa," she said. "If we don't get it out soon, bad things are going to happen."

"Like what?" Teresa asked.

"Like somebody might die," she said. "Somebody you love."

"Don't say that," Teresa demanded. "That doesn't make any sense!"

"It's true," she said. "That tooth is a dark sign. Just let me feel it. I won't pull it."

So Teresa gave in. Her mom settled beside her on the floor.

"Be gentle," Teresa said and opened her mouth.

"I will," her mom promised. She wiggled Teresa's tooth just a little, then wiped her fingers on her pants to dry them. She reached back in, grabbed the tooth, and twisted. Teresa heard the roots cracking and popping, and then a tiny spray of blood landed right on the Anarchy section of her poster.

Teresa jumped up and ran to the bathroom to spit into the sink and dip her tongue into the hole and spit again. She yelled and cried for a while, screaming "You tricked me," and "I hate you," but her mom was long gone. She'd disappeared into the woods with Teresa's tooth. She didn't come back until much, much later.

When her dad had found out, her parents fought again. Teresa listened from her bedroom. Her dad put his fist through the paneling near the light switch, but her mom wasn't threatened. She claimed that she was doing God's work.

When the movie was over and they were driving home, Teresa asked Dori, "What happened to your broken tooth?"

"Got hit in the mouth with a rock," Dori said.

"Who threw it?" Teresa asked.

Dori laughed and said, "Nobody! I was riding around with this boy who had a sunroof, and a song I liked came on. I stood up so I could dance, and we passed a big truck. One of the tires threw up a rock, I guess, and it hit me right in the lip."

"And broke your tooth?" Teresa asked. She didn't know if she believed that story or not.

"Yep," said Dori. "Busted my lip, too, but I was drunk, so it didn't hurt that much." She yawned and added, "This rain is making me sleepy. Do you care if I take a little nap?"

"Be my guest," said Teresa, and Dori curled herself against the passenger door.

The rain fell hard and steady, and in the dark it was difficult to see the patches of standing water that in places turned the road into a shallow lake. Teresa took it slow. She clenched the wheel with both hands and tried not to worry about the wind, which blew the car in the direction of oncoming traffic. Sometimes she wasn't sure if the gusts she felt were outside the car or inside her arms.

But the wind and rain didn't bother Dori in the least. How could she possibly sleep? Maybe Dori didn't care if they died in a head-on collision. Or maybe Dori actually trusted her—the way Teresa had trusted Hilda, back before she realized she shouldn't.

121

Teresa had been entirely innocent when she opened her mouth to let Hilda wiggle that third front tooth, entirely vulnerable. And Hilda yanked the tooth without the least concern for what that meant.

She'd called the tooth evil to justify doing what she'd always intended to do. She'd made that tooth a problem of logic and then used her warped logic to destroy it.

To reason.

Her treason. Her way of betrayal.

Hilda had rejected Teresa in the same way she'd rejected that tooth, splitting her off completely.

VII.

By the time they got home, Sugar Britches' tumor had loosened around the edges. It reminded Dori of the way a cake pulls away from a well-greased pan when it's finished baking. Sugar's tumor was a small burned cupcake, held in place by nothing but gravity and a few hinges of scab.

It was the gnarliest-looking thing she'd ever seen. She wondered if she turned him upside down, if the center of the tumor might fall out and land there on the carpet. If so, what would be underneath?

On the floor, next to his bed by the sliding glass door, Dori combed around his neck and toward his back, distracting him as she examined the desiccated mass on his haunch. Sugar purred, and in a while she moved the comb down toward his tumor and very gently poked at the crust of darkness to see if it would give.

"Don't mess with it," Teresa said. "Just leave it alone."

"It's really loose," said Dori.

"I know," Teresa replied. "But if it comes off, it might bleed. He could bleed to death."

It was nearly bedtime. Teresa, already in her pajamas, kept yawning. Dori was ready to turn in herself, but she wanted to say goodnight to Jen, who was still at the pub with Eric.

Teresa had sent Jen a text message when they'd gotten home, and Jen had written back to say she was paying the check. But before she could leave, another big thundercloud had come up.

Since the rain was blowing away from the house, Teresa opened the sliding glass door and turned on the outside light so they could watch.

"All your AC's gonna go right out that door," Dori warned.

"Feels good to air this place out," said Teresa.

Dori nodded toward Sugar and asked, "Aren't you worried he'll go outside?"

"I wish he felt like it," Teresa said. "He used to tear all through the yard and run up to the top of that pine tree."

"Really?"

"He loved the pergola behind Jen's deli, too. He could perch up there and stalk birds for days. It hasn't even been that long," said Teresa. She went through the mail, sorting it into piles and throwing junk in the trash, and Dori continued to comb Sugar Britches and rub his ears. Every now and then, when Teresa wasn't looking, she nudged at the loose part of the tumor with the comb. It must not have hurt. She'd have stopped if it hurt, but Sugar didn't seem to mind.

Then Teresa got another text from Jen, who was still waiting out the downpour. "She ordered dessert," said Teresa. "Let's call it a night."

Teresa began typing out her reply, and for some reason Dori took the comb, hooked the edge beneath the scab, and flicked up the tumor's black, necrotic center.

Sugar Britches jumped, let out a loud, surprised yowl, and gave a little shake. When he did, the tumor unhinged. It dangled against his side like a purse. Teresa rushed toward them both, and Sugar gave a funny hop, like he was trying to get away from the new appendage, and bolted sideways out the door, tumor clinging to his side.

"Damn it!" said Teresa, "What were you thinking?" and she ran out behind him into the rain.

Dori had no idea why she'd done it. She hadn't really meant

to dislodge it. But it wasn't her fault the door was open. If the door hadn't been open, he couldn't have gotten out. He could have hidden with his tumor underneath the couch or in the pantry or something.

Teresa charged back in, grabbed a flashlight from a closet, and hurried into the storm again.

They looked for him a long time. Dori looked too, checking the area behind the deli in case he was hiding in the vines that covered the pergola. No Sugar. Rain ran down her face, between her breasts, down the channel of her spine, dripped off her arms.

She checked around the boat trailer, behind the trash cans, even in the alley. She wasn't wearing shoes, and the gravel in the alleyway poked into the soles of her feet. It hurt, but she knew she deserved it.

Teresa met her back there, beneath a streetlight. "Any sign?"

"Not yet," said Dori. Teresa's pajamas were plastered to her chest. Dori could see her nipples poking through, almost like she didn't have on a shirt at all. "I'm sorry," Dori said.

But Teresa didn't say it was okay. She just sighed and said, "Keep looking."

Soon Jen came home and joined the search, but they didn't find him. When Dori gave up and went to bed, Teresa and Jen were still out there. She could hear them just beyond her window, calling in the darkness: "Come on, baby. Come on, Sugar. Come on."

That night they left the sliding glass door cracked, and in the morning Sugar Britches was back on his bed inside the living room, dry and sleeping, a massive lumpy-looking crater the color of maggots where the bulk of the tumor had been. It wasn't bleeding, though you could see blood vessels etching the tissue. A tiny puddle of oil lined the basin of the wound.

He seemed to feel better. He even ate some breakfast. He stretched out on the couch and acted almost normal.

But Teresa and Jen were still mad.

"Why would you do that?" Jen confronted Dori. "Especially

after T asked you not to?" It was the first time she'd seen Jen mad. "Jesus, we're trying to help you out here, and you go and do something like *that*?" She threw up her hands and turned away from Dori, like she couldn't stand to look at her.

"I didn't do it on purpose," Dori said. "It's not like I tore it off!" She took her toast into the living room so she wouldn't have to eat with them and sat instead with Sugar Britches. She even apologized to him—loud enough that they could hear: "You know I'd never try to hurt you, don't you, Sugar? We're both strays, right?" And when Teresa and Jen continued to give her the cold shoulder, she said, "What's the big deal? Everything turned out fine!"

It was Tuesday, and they had boat deliveries scheduled beginning at eleven. It'd take most of an hour to load up. Dori was supposed to fill the coolers with ice and stock the drinks, but by nine-thirty she was gone.

She'd packed up her tote bag and headed to the beach. At first, she wasn't sure if she was leaving for good or just taking a walk to cool down. She made her way to the fallen-in ferry dock, getting madder and madder as she went, and she settled on the rocks to figure out what to do next.

She hadn't hurt Sugar Britches. She might have even helped him. Who knew how long it would have taken the thing to fall off on its own? There were a lot of ways you could see it, but Teresa and Jen had teamed up against her to see it in the worst possible way.

Stupid dyke bitches, both of them.

They loved their cat a lot more than they cared about her. They'd probably searched half the night for their cat, but they'd never even *thought* to look for her. All those times when her parents disappeared for days, called to witness to this congregation or that one, and left her back at the apartment with no idea when she'd see them again, with nothing in the cabinets but stale crackers and cans of baked beans. All those times when they had to pick up and move in the night, and she didn't get to say goodbye to her friends.

126

All those times when her mom went off her meds and turned into an impossible nutcase—stealing her toys and using them as "art," sticking pins and nails in her dolls, sometimes in their eyeballs and buttholes. No kid should have to put up with that. Or making her kneel and pray all night for drinking beer when her mom had *bought* her the beer, had told her it would flush out her bladder and help with a urinary tract infection, so that they wouldn't have to go to the doctor because they couldn't afford the doctor. But then she forgot that part and came after Dori with a belt, swinging it buckle-out even when she was already down on the floor, as if the first half of the episode had never happened.

Later, of course, her mom would come apologizing, crying, and promising to never, never, never do anything like that again. It was a wonder Dori wasn't cracked up herself—and where were Teresa and Jen during all those years?

Teresa and Jen didn't care.

Sugar Britches was a *cat*, for fuck's sake, and an old cat, too, and already dying. She didn't *give* him cancer. She didn't *cause* the tumor to rot in the first place. Teresa had even admitted that Sugar loved to go outside before he got so sick. Maybe he'd had a great night out in the rain, sharpening his claws on the tree bark, doing his business in the bushes instead of in a stinky litter box. Maybe it was his last hurrah.

Still, they put the blame on her.

She ought to be used to it. Teresa and Jen were no better than her mom. There was nobody in the world that she could count on. She wished she were dead.

Or better yet, she wished she were some lesbian's cat.

Every now and then she felt a little bit sorry about the whole tumor incident, but she'd apologized. What else could she do? Send them flowers? She had no money to buy flowers. She had no money to do *anything*.

Teresa could talk all she wanted about history and vision and all that happy horseshit, about the impossibility of seeing the situation you were in without the perspective time brings. But when it came right down to it, none of that mattered. That only

127

mattered when you were looking back. By then, you'd already survived.

Dori stared out at the cluster of pilings where she'd spent that terrible night just a week before. It had been an awful night, but it was over. It had happened, but it was history.

What had happened with Sugar Britches was history.

It made her cry a little to realize that her life with Teresa and Jen was also history—and so soon. They didn't exist anymore. She'd packed up her few things. She had her gun and her new hat. She had less than an hour before Randy's granny would leave for her therapy appointment to work on her broken shoulder.

And she had a plan.

Dori knew better than to try to kick in the door. Of course, they'd have reinforced the lock, installed a deadbolt or something. She hoisted herself onto an old, rusted propane tank just outside a back window. The window wasn't even completely closed or latched, but it was old and didn't want to move. She wiggled and shook, and flecks of dried white paint snowed down on her arms and hands. She got it up an inch in its frame, then hopped down and found a stick to pry it more. With some wedging and hardheaded persistence, she lifted the window enough to slip through.

She was thin enough that she didn't need a very big opening, strong enough to pull herself with her arms over the faucet, around the porcelain sink, and onto the countertop. She was limber enough to leap from the counter and land on the linoleum without knocking over the dishwashing soap or the coffeepot.

Once in the kitchen, she took the old lady's pills again, all of them, sealing them up in a resealable bag she found in one of the kitchen drawers.

This time, on a shelf in the closet, she found a jewelry box. Inside it there were rings, four of them: a wedding band and tiny diamond, a ring with a red stone—maybe a ruby—and a mother's ring with four different birthstones. Those she stashed in her pocket. Best of all, she found a Purple Heart in there. She'd never seen one, except in the movies.

She pinned the medal to her shirt and felt her heartbeat rise. She couldn't remember exactly what the Purple Heart stood for—bravery in battle or being wounded or saving somebody— but she'd been through hard things. She'd just never been recognized or honored for it.

She closed the jewelry box and put it back in its place.

She wasn't hungry a bit, but she sat down anyway at the table and ate a piece of coconut cake. It was delicious, the cake so moist, the coconut icing creamy and crunchy at the same time.

She washed her plate and fork, wiped the crumbs from the table with a paper towel, and threw them in the trash.

She looked around for anything else she might want, and on the refrigerator she saw a school picture of Randy. She lifted it and slid it in her pocket with the rings.

She made sure she hadn't left any evidence, then let herself out the door she'd broken through the week before, pulling it closed behind her. Again, she wiped her fingerprints away with disinfectant wipes she'd taken from the old lady's pantry.

From the shed behind the house, she borrowed a rake and used it to loosen the dirt around the propane tank, making wavy swirls over all her footprints.

She'd hidden her sunflower tote beneath an overgrown forsythia bush at the edge of the property, and she was on her way to collect it when she glanced down and saw the Purple Heart pinned there. She couldn't take the Purple Heart. She'd never be worthy of something like that, even if she lived for a hundred years. So she unfastened it, went back inside, and left it for the old lady on the kitchen table.

Dori made a friend on the transit van, a fellow who told her she could take the van all the way up to the county line. She stopped by the Dollar General first and found the man who'd bought her drugs the time before.

An hour later, he met her by the dumpster and paid her cash, not just for the drugs, but also for two of the rings—the ruby and the mother's ring.

The other two were broken, the golden wedding band and also the diamond. They'd been clipped across the back, maybe when the old lady's fingers swelled up, maybe after she'd injured her shoulder.

"Can't offer you a good price for damaged goods," the man claimed.

"What difference does it make?" Dori argued. "You could weld it right back together." But he wouldn't budge on his price, and she wouldn't accept it. She put the two broken rings back into her pocket.

Still, she made $200. Instead of remaining there in that town, she took the transit van north, asked around until she found a roadside motel, and checked in.

Dori'd saved some Percocet for herself. She'd earned them. While she was waiting for her pizza to be delivered, she took two and sat in the hot bathtub, letting the delicious Percocet fog descend and wrap around her. At last she could relax, and all the meanness in her could sweat right out through her pores. She was a nicer person on Percocet. If she had her own prescription, she could be the Blessed Virgin Mary.

She didn't feel angry with Teresa and Jen anymore. She didn't feel angry with her boyfriend Cane. Even if he'd ratted her out, it would only be an act of fear, a pathetic attempt to save his own hide.

And Owen Howe. Poor Owen. She hoped they were giving him plenty of Percocet in his IV drip. She closed her eyes and imagined herself in the ICU on the gurney next to Owen.

"Hey, Owen?" she called.

He didn't answer, but Dori didn't give up. He might be like Sugar Britches, right there somewhere but too scared to let anyone know.

"Hey, Owen," she said. "I know you can hear me. I walked into your future," she said. "And I wanted to tell you that things are gonna turn out alright."

It sounded silly when she said it. She snorted and quickly covered her mouth so the nurses wouldn't hear.

"Owen," she whispered. "I'm really sorry. I fucked up." Though she was high, she still meant it. Maybe she had to be high in order to even say it. "You didn't deserve that," she told him. "I'd take it back if I could."

But she couldn't take it back.

She wished he'd say something or at least acknowledge her. Sometimes she felt so invisible, and it was impossible to tell whether she was being ignored or if she'd never been seen to begin with.

"You just need to get to New York City," she told him. "Nobody'll hate you there. You can wear a rainbow flag in New York City if you want to."

In her mind, she gave Owen Howe a pair of magic flip-flops, rainbow flip-flops with big white daisies between the toes. She imagined Owen kicking off the sheet from the hospital bed, standing up, and leaping out the window and off to New York City, where things were certain to go his way from that moment on.

When the pizza man banged at her door, Dori didn't bother with putting on her clothes. She just spun herself up in a sheet, smiled at him, and gave him an enormous tip. She couldn't change what had happened with Owen, but she could change what she did forever after. She vowed to give big tips from then on.

She knew the Percocet was a temporary state, but it reminded her that there was another way available, another way to feel.

She wasn't even angry with her mom anymore. She wished her mom a happy life. She took a slice of pizza and held it up to her mom, like a toast: "Have a happy life, Mommy," she said.

That night she slept without dreaming, and the next day she

woke up feeling fine. She took another Percocet, just one, and walked over to the convenience store a quarter-mile down the highway and bought a half-gallon of strawberry ice cream.

It was the perfect breakfast. She ate it with a plastic spoon, right out back of the convenience store at a wooden picnic table. She let ice cream drip and smear all over her face, since she didn't have napkins to wipe with, and it felt good, the coldness and stickiness both. It made her feel like she was four—and she imagined she looked beautiful, childlike but sensual. If any pedophiles could see her, they wouldn't be able to stand it.

The store clerk came out for a cigarette break and said, "Whew, girl, you got trouble, don't you?"

"No," said Dori. "I'm fan-fucking-tastic." She licked her spoon and waved it in the air like a wand.

"You got anywhere to go?" the clerk asked. She was a skinny woman with two-tone hair and an infected eyebrow piercing.

"Yeah," said Dori. She laughed and spooned the melted remains from the sides into her mouth. "When I'm done with my breakfast, I'm headed to the library. I need to check my email."

"Nearest library's twenty miles south," said the clerk. "But if you'll give me a couple of whatever you're taking, I'll let you use the Internet here, long as you don't steal nothing."

Owen Howe was dead. He'd been dead three days already. Cane had been charged with murder, along with his cousin, who hadn't even been there—or at least he wasn't there when Dori left. Both of them were pleading not guilty.

According to two different news sites, she was wanted for questioning, but wasn't considered a suspect. A lot of people were worried that she'd been the victim of foul play. Rumor had it they'd found evidence at the crime scene, though in the interests of the larger investigation, police would neither confirm nor deny it. In an interview, her weeping mother speculated that maybe Dori'd been hurt that night, that those boys had killed her and thrown her body in the river.

The police department spokesman pointed out conflicting testimonies and conflicting stories. It didn't help that all the testimonies came from people whose judgments were impaired by alcohol or drugs.

Dori turned down the volume on the computer but listened to the news reports from back behind the counter, next to the lottery machine. Just down the way, on her stool, the store clerk nibbled Doritos and attended to customers. She was in her own Percocet wonderland by then.

Dori's mom put on a good show—crying, her voice trembling as she begged the police to drag that river. It made her sad to see her mom so upset. Dori kept reminding herself that her mom *knew* she was alive. She'd delivered Dori to that first Greyhound bus station.

Her mom might be a psycho, but at least she hadn't turned her in.

"Thanks," Dori said to the store clerk, and she ran all the way back to her motel room to pack.

She intended to get on the road, head north, do whatever she had to do to make it to Maryland, at least. But how long would it be before the news became national? Would it spread beyond North Carolina? Would they put her on *Dateline*?

The ice cream had upset her stomach, and she spent the next couple of hours on the toilet. When the maid tried to clean her room, she sent her away. The spasms in her colon gave her the cold sweats. They went on a long time, and she knew she deserved it for her part in killing Owen Howe.

They'd *killed* him.

Or at least he'd died. She didn't know for sure if they'd killed him. Maybe it was all the alcohol—or maybe he'd choked on his own puke. He sure couldn't have spit it out with that rag in his mouth. Or maybe something else had happened after she left the camper and drove Cane's truck back to his house.

Weren't her fingerprints all over that truck?

But if investigators checked the truck, of course they'd find her fingerprints there, her DNA. She rode around in that truck all the time. She'd had sex in the truck earlier that same night.

Maybe her boyfriend and his cousin *had* killed her. Maybe she was dead, and only her miserable, confused soul had gone roaming off to Virginia to find her long-lost sister, looking for sympathy anywhere she might get it.

She felt crazy and desperate and didn't know what to do. She pulled out the gun she'd stolen from Randy's granny the first time around. She didn't know much about guns. This one looked old-fashioned, like the ones from Westerns or gangster flicks, but it didn't have the hammer-thing to cock, so she wasn't even sure if it was real, and she wasn't sure how to shoot it. Part of her was scared to play with it, but even if it went off, what difference did it make? It wasn't like she had anything left to live for.

What good was her life? She'd *taken* a life. What if Owen was meant to be something special, like the president, and now she'd ruined it?

And how did that kid Randy understand about a shitty biddy becoming the Rooster King, and him only seven years old? He understood potential, but she hadn't seen the potential in Owen Howe, and now it was too late. What was wrong with her?

She climbed up onto the vanity and sat cross-legged in front of the mirror, watching herself play with the gun, like she was in a movie or something. If somebody made a movie of her life, would she die in that scene? Or would the filmmaker think she might have potential, too?

She fiddled with a lever on the side of the gun and released the cylinder, where she found five bullets, one in every chamber, but they looked a little corroded. She clicked the cylinder back into place and pressed the barrel against her temple, just to feel it there, and she made faces at herself: sad, pouty ones, horrified, stricken ones. She bulged her nostrils, stuck out her tongue, then put the gun down. She had bags under her eyes and a huge zit on her forehead, but she was still too cute to die right that minute.

Besides, if she died, she didn't want to look gross when the authorities found her. She was sorry, though, that she'd left Owen Howe looking gross when the authorities found him. She could imagine how humiliating that would be, and then she wanted to die again, for humiliating Owen (in addition to *killing* him), and then she took some Tramadol, because she was all out of Percocet.

But Tramadol was better than nothing.

When she reached the end of the transit line, she started hitch-hiking north. She should have known better than to get into a Volvo station wagon with a middle-aged woman driver, but as soon as the car slowed down and pulled off the asphalt, she'd run to catch up. She'd have been safer with a trucker—because this woman just wanted to drive her to the YWCA shelter. She was a feminist. She had a bumper sticker that claimed girls could do anything. But she also had a great big diamond ring on her finger. She was owned and didn't even know it.

From a young age Dori had figured out that you should never trust a woman who has her mind made up about what you need. Men might fuck you, but nine times out of ten, they had absolutely no interest in you beyond your body. The danger men posed was physical, but usually minimal. Women, on the other hand, would fuck you six ways to Sunday and expect you to say thank you when they're done. A woman's will *is* her dick.

Dori told the woman in the Volvo that she didn't need the hotline for survivors of domestic violence, and she certainly didn't need the Department of Social Services or the police. She just needed to get to her boyfriend in Baltimore—Warren, who'd recently returned from a mission trip to Belize—but the woman wouldn't shut up.

She knew people to call to help drug addicts if Dori had a problem with addiction. She shouldn't feel ashamed; she should get the help she needed *and deserved.* Her church sponsored a soup kitchen for the homeless. If Dori was hungry, if Dori needed a place to go . . .

135

"I'm not an addict," Dori proclaimed. She said it slowly, in case she might be slurring by accident. Her tongue felt dry and thick. "I'm not homeless." If she didn't get out of that car soon, she'd be somewhere she didn't intend.

The road went on and on with just trees and fields, occasional churches and lawnmower repair shops. Finally, they came to a big poultry processing plant and had to stop for a red light. Dori hopped out before the tires quit rolling. As she leaped through tall grasses along the roadside, jumped the ditch all littered with chicken feathers and trash and disappeared into trees, she could hear the woman yelling out the window for her to come back.

Dori stumbled between pines through overgrown bushes for a while, then into a clearing and out the other side to a country road. The whole world smelled like singed feathers and raw meat. The sun had dropped low, and since she wasn't sure what to do, she kept on walking.

Some older guys drove by and offered her a ride. She declined, but they kept idling along beside her, with the one guy on the passenger side asking her name, asking where she was heading and if she wanted to get stoned. Though she ignored them, they persisted until another car came up behind them. Then the driver punched the gas and sped off faster than he needed to.

It made her nervous. She worried they'd come back. And since she could see a church set back off the road, she headed there.

Even if churches were magnets for hypocrites, they seemed safer than the rest of the world. This one took the prize for the ugliest church she'd ever seen—and she'd seen some ugly ones. It clearly belonged to a poor congregation, probably the workers at the local deboning factory, and looked as though it'd been built without the help of any architect, the walls a combination of cinderblock and clapboard, the tiny windows asymmetrical and positioned too close to the roof for anybody to look out or break in. A clamshell parking lot surrounded the place, but they needed another load of shells soon because weeds of every sort had broken through. In the back, there was a small, fenced-in playground with a couple of swings and a bunch of plastic sun-faded toys. But off to one side, a giant oak tree with sprawling branches stretched up some sixty feet toward the sky. About a third of the way up, there was a tree house.

Dori let herself into the playground and climbed directly up the wooden rungs hammered into the trunk.

Someone had put old church pews up there, four of them around the edges and bolted to the platform. The seats faced in, so that if you sat down properly, you'd be worshipping the tree. It struck her as funny. The tree house was better designed than the church.

She turned long-ways on her pew, stretching her legs and using her tote bag as a backrest. She looked out beyond the church roof, with its patchwork shingles, and across the nearby fields of hay and soybeans. In the distance, little run-down houses sat here and there beneath the darkening sky, randomly speckled over the land, and she knew that inside those houses people were fighting with one another, praying, eating their supper. People were paying bills and fucking and watching TV, celebrating birthdays and considering suicide, probably thinking they lived independent lives when they were separated from one another by nothing but a little space and the flimsiest walls and doors. They all lived beneath the same clouds, got bitten by the same hungry mosquitoes.

Dori was one of them, even though she didn't know them and never would. She slapped at a mosquito on her forearm, but missed.

The bones of her spine ached from pressing against the hard pew. Her dad used to say that church pews were supposed to be uncomfortable, that they were designed that way by God to make your tailbone throb so you wouldn't doze off during the sermon.

If she was going to sleep there, she needed to get comfortable. She loosened the button on her jeans and emptied her pockets of Randy's school picture and his Granny's broken rings. She slipped the rings on her finger. They fit just fine. If she died that night up in the tree, then when somebody found her, they'd think she was a married lady. But what in the world would a respectable married lady be doing dead in an oak tree, holding a little boy's picture?

There were probably plenty of married ladies wearing wedding bands and diamonds who were just as bad as she was, who'd done things just as awful. They went on with their lives, had their families, tried to atone in whatever ways they could, volunteering at their church's soup kitchen like the lady in the Volvo.

Maybe Dori could do that, too.

But she doubted it.

She'd heard Jesus's "Sermon on the Mount" so many times she could preach it herself: the parable of the two men who built houses, one on a rock and one on the sand. She'd built her whole life on the sand. She needed to start over on a solid foundation. But how could she do that if she didn't turn herself in? Unless she turned herself in, she'd just be moving from one sandy patch to another.

Dori rolled to her side and watched a line of black ants parading down the tree, and she wondered if they were done with their workday and headed back to the colony or if they'd soldier on in the dark, collecting leaves or fungus or whatever they were after.

Her mom had told her once, "You think you're so important, but you're not. You're just like a little old ant crawling around on the floor. One day you'll get stomped and die, and the world will keep right on turning."

It had upset her back then, thinking of herself as a squashed speck of ant, but now it wasn't such a bad feeling. If she was so unimportant, then nothing she did could matter very much or for very long. What harm could one ant do in the world? Even the worst ant couldn't do that much harm.

But she'd read there were more than a million ants for every person on the planet. So even if an ant did a little bit of harm, it could add up fast.

She studied Randy's picture and pretended he was her own little boy. She hoped nothing bad would ever happen to him, like what had happened to Owen Howe. Randy was such a funny kid, with his gizzards and livers, his magic flip-flops. He reminded her of the kid she might have been, if she hadn't become the person she had become.

Randy had to be more than just a little old ant, didn't he?

And *she* had to be more than a little old ant if she'd brought down Owen Howe, another *person*—and not just another person, but a member of the National Honor Society and the Drama Club. He'd played King Lear the year before. He'd done a really good job.

Owen had to be more than a little old ant—and they'd snuffed him out for no good reason, for no good reason at all.

And what could she possibly do about it? Even if she turned herself in, it wouldn't bring him back. As porch lights came on in the distance, Dori felt darker and darker in her heart. She took off her belt and looked for a good branch to hang herself, but she couldn't go through with it. She didn't have the nerve, and her belt was too short anyway. Besides that, she was too scared to leave this life without repenting, and she didn't know *how* to repent. Saying "sorry" wasn't enough.

Up there in the tree, she cried for a long time, letting her shoulders and lungs get in on the tragedy. It was a *tragedy*, all of it.

The word *tragedy* hadn't really meant anything to her before. It was a term to memorize for an English exam. It was something that happened to Oedipus, not something that happened to regular old people. But now that Owen Howe had died, Dori understood it differently. Tragedy was deep, multifaceted, and contagious. She hadn't created the tragedy of Owen Howe. He'd been living his tragedy for years before she met him. But she recognized tragedy in him, was drawn to it, participated in it, and was infected by it. Even though Owen was dead, Dori would carry his tragedy for the rest of her life, all tangled up with her own.

She saw that her life had been a tragedy, too. It had nothing to do with what she deserved. She was born into it. Her very cells carried the guilt of her parents, the heaviness of choices that were made before even *they* were born. Denying it wouldn't help, and there was certainly no curing it. Tragedy permeated everything it touched—and it touched in ways that couldn't be seen, like fungus spreading in dark gaps beneath the bark of a stately oak.

It was intergenerational, epidemic. No wonder the Greeks loved to write about it.

But what did you *do* with it?

The cruelty she took out on Owen Howe was the same cruelty she'd been taking out on herself all her life. She'd wanted to kill Owen (and Cane, for that matter) because she'd wanted to die all her life.

It was so sad what she'd done. So sad what had been done to her.

She had no tissues to blow her nose, so she let it run and run.

The night grew darker, and a breeze came up that left her chilled. She peeked through the slats of the tree house floor down to the ground where lightning bugs flitted and flirted, blinking their green-gold glow. Little promises of light in the dark. In a while, she fell asleep up there, on a church pew high in an oak tree, wearing stolen wedding rings. Her fingers relaxed around Randy's picture, and the wind blew it out of her hand.

She dreamed that she was Sugar Britches and that a whole big part of her had died and rotted away. She was climbing, climbing, trying to escape the stinking part of herself, trying to shake it loose, be rid of it without having to touch it. She rubbed her fur against the tree trunk to scratch it off, but it held. She scurried out along limbs to places where new branches might shear it off, but still it clung to her. Finally, near the top, flanked by leaves and shadows of leaves, she unwedged the decaying mass with her own rough tongue: tasting, turning away, tasting again.

VIII.

Teresa and Jen rode their bikes up and down the streets, around the harbor, all along the beachfront, searching for any signs of Dori until it was too dark to see. The next morning, they let themselves into Room 2, fingers crossed that they'd find her returned, tangled in sheets and dreaming.

But the room was empty.

They stripped the bed and remade it with just the comforter on top. They gathered a couple of used towels and a washcloth, but that was it. Except for a few tissues and papers in the trash, a little sand in the bottom of the tub, and the too-big boat shoes she'd taken from the lost and found, it didn't look like Dori'd ever been there.

"Wherever she is, I hope she's okay," said Jen.

"What if she was lying to us all along?" Teresa asked. "Maybe Hilda didn't kick her out. For all we know, she could have been hanging 'Have You Seen This Child' posters all over Mississippi."

"Possible," Jen said, "but doubtful."

"I should have called her," said Teresa. "We could be liable."

"Liable for what? It's not like we kidnapped her."

"Can they send you to prison for harboring a minor?" Teresa pictured herself pregnant in prison, then giving birth in shackles. "I better call Hilda," she said.

Hilda's last name wasn't King anymore. It wasn't even Williamson. Williamson had been their pastor's name, the man who'd seduced Hilda with all those terrifying hellish sermons. Teresa remembered him at least. But Dori had given the name Baxter when they looked her up on the Internet a few nights before. Teresa wished she'd asked about Baxter. Whose name was that?

When they searched for *Hilda Baxter* and *Mississippi*—they didn't know the name of the town—they found a physician's assistant, a food blogger, and a post office worker who'd been bitten by a raccoon. They found a tax accountant, a real estate agent, and a donor to some political campaign.

With no better way to shorten the list, they called the art gallery where Hilda's work had been featured not quite two years before. The curator had a contact number but didn't know if it was current and refused to give it out for privacy reasons. She took down Teresa's message and promised to try to reach her.

"Tell her it's concerning Dori," she said. "Her daughter. Tell her it's urgent."

How long might it take to track her down? Teresa was scared that she'd call and scared that she wouldn't. "If she calls, what should I say?" she asked Jen.

"Tell her she was alive and well from Friday until Tuesday," Jen said. "That's all we know."

And that wasn't much. Friday until Tuesday, not even four full days, and all Teresa had to show for it was a Yahtzee score card with Dori's name written across the top. At the bottom of each column, she'd drawn either smiley faces or frowns, depending on whether she'd won that round. Teresa caught herself studying Dori's writing, the loopy back-slanted cursive of her name, the bubbly curve of her numbers, how they filled up each box on the score card almost entirely, oversized, like they'd been scribbled by a child.

❧ ❧ ❧

Teresa kept her phone closer than usual, tucking it into the pocket of her work shorts when she went out to cut the grass, placing it on the back of the toilet while she took her shower—just in case.

Late that afternoon, cell phone in her pocket, she yanked her hose out to the city strip to water the plants. It was beginning to seem like a bad idea, the community garden. She'd imagined people gathering there, visiting, pulling weeds together and sharing the produce when it came in. She'd pictured vacationers passing by on their way to the beach, picking a tomato off the vine and savoring it as they made their way to the sand. So far nothing like that had happened, and the vines of squash had started to trail over the edge of the sidewalk and into the street. One thick tendril had already been flattened by somebody's tire.

The barber who leased the space beside the deli came out to smoke. He had one of those outdoor ashtrays shaped like a long-neck gourd, maybe three feet tall and painted like a barbershop pole: red, white, and blue swirling down the long tube and around the bulbous base. Each time he worked he set the ashtray outside. It doubled as his "open" sign.

"Hey," he hollered to Teresa, "Did you hear what happened to Miss Betty?"

"What?" Teresa asked.

"That burglar broke into her house *again*. Second time in two weeks."

"You're kidding me," Teresa said. She put down the hose amid the watermelons, adjusted it so the overflow would take care of the zucchinis, and met the barber halfway to get the details. "Is she okay? Was she at home?"

"No," said the barber. "She's alright. But it'll be a fool who tries it again," he said. "I was cutting her son's hair earlier this morning, and he told me they're putting a security camera in the tree and strychnine in all her pill bottles. Don't mention that to the chief, you hear? Next time that old drug addict breaks in, he'll get the surprise of his life."

He took a last long drag on his cigarette, threw the nubbin down his barbershop pole, and went back inside.

143

It was a hot day, with temperatures in the nineties, but it was a dark day, too, overcast, the sky uncertain and menacing.

Just being uncertain can make you look menacing. In that way, the sky had a lot in common with the people walking around beneath it.

Teresa felt uncertain, too, and defensive. When Hilda called, *if* Hilda called, she'd have to work to keep her defenses down. She wouldn't ask, "Why did you leave me?" or "Why did you reject me?" She'd keep the "me" out of it and focus entirely on Dori.

She'd be like the watermelons—with their silly leaves, fat fingers of leaves creeping into the territory of the zucchinis. There was nothing defensive or mean about watermelons. She'd think of watermelons if Hilda called, those brave little baby melons taking their chances on the vines, not worrying about whether a heavy rain would pock their stripes and split their skins before they had a chance to sweeten.

It was a grimacing day, a grimacing time—with Dori gone, probably for good, with elderly ladies not safe in their homes, with baby watermelons unaware that there were thugs on the street who'd pluck them for no reason except to have something to chunk at passing cars.

How could she bring a new life into such a grim world—and why would she want to? Why would she assume she might have the chance to bring a new life into any world at all? She was still days away from a pregnancy test. It was all just wishful thinking.

And yet, there was hope . . .

And there was Sugar Britches, who'd followed her outside. He scratched in the dirt around the cucumbers and squatted to pee. Teresa didn't even stop him. If he killed the cucumbers, so be it. She'd buy them at the farmer's market, along with watermelons to replace the ones the thugs were sure to steal and throw at cars.

And there were the tomatoes, a few early ones already ripening on the vines. The tomatoes didn't know that Dori'd disappeared. The tomatoes didn't care that Miss Betty's house had been robbed a second time. They were there to mature, to do their tomato thing all their tomato lives, and they didn't worry about being at the mercy of the weather or Teresa's water hose.

Sometimes when there was no other comfort, there were tomatoes. When the water hit the leaves, it gave off a smell like spaghetti sauce, a warm, ripe smell even though most of the tomatoes themselves were still green. The possibility of ripeness was always there inside the plant, from the time it poked up through the ground. From even before.

Teresa moved the phone to the pocket of her apron and stirred tomato sauce. The wooden spoon on the bottom of the pot scraped nursery rhymes to her in a deep, soft voice: *Jack, be nimble. Jack, be quick.* She put the spoon down and chopped a few mushrooms, threw them in, and stirred again: *Little Miss Muffet sat on her tuffet.*

The tomato sauce bubbled and blurped in the pot, and Teresa scraped the bottom to be sure it wasn't sticking: *Little Boy Blue come blow your horn. Sheep's in the meadow and the cow's in the corn.*

Hilda hadn't always been a bad mother. Like everybody else, she had another side, a good side, sometimes even a wonderful side. Teresa could still remember traveling around on her hip— and how that felt, to be perched there on that spot designed especially for her. As Hilda stood before the stove, stirring her own tomato sauce, Teresa had watched the bubbles rising in the pot from her private seat.

The next best spot was the rocking chair, where Teresa crawled into Hilda's lap and looked at the picture book stretched open across both of their legs as they rocked. Hilda read poems and nursery rhymes, sang them and repeated them. Teresa wanted the rhymes to go on forever. When they reached the book's end, she begged her mom to read it again, to read it backward, to read it upside down. And sometimes Hilda did.

That night they had spaghetti with a salad for dinner, and Hilda didn't call. Not during dinner. Not during the hour of crickets, when she and Jen sipped wine on the deck, or the hour of toads, when they dozed in their chaises and woke again. Teresa moved the phone charger to the bedroom and left it plugged in on the nightstand, but the phone didn't ring until morning, and then it was Cassidy, reminding her about their trip to the Motor-World Thrill Park, which was the last place in the world Teresa wanted to be.

They claimed a picnic table in the shade of a gazebo and put down their bags. At nine and eleven, Cassidy's kids were old enough to take care of themselves inside the MotorWorld walls. Certainly they could entertain themselves. They each had a friend in tow.

"This is home base," said Cassidy. She pointed out the snack bar to their left, the bathrooms directly behind, the little kid rides just off to the right. "Meet back here by noon and we'll get lunch. Don't be late."

The children rushed away before Cassidy had finished rubbing suntan lotion on arms and cheeks, the girls headed for the dune buggies, the boys for the bumper boats.

Though Teresa had a full charge on her phone, she'd brought along her charger. She knew it was neurotic, but still she scoped out the nearest electrical source. There were sockets on the walls of the partially enclosed party room. As long as no one had a party, she could charge in there if she needed to, which she wouldn't. She kept her phone in the top of her bag so she could answer it quickly if it rang.

Cassidy turned out to be a pretty good distraction. Teresa didn't have time to think about Hilda and why she hadn't called, or about Dori or Sugar or whether or not she was pregnant. "Here's the thing," Cassidy said. "I want a divorce, but I can't figure out how to leave. I look at Dan sometimes and can't even remember what I saw in him fourteen years ago."

146

"Come on!" said Teresa. "You were wild about him. You even went to a Star Trek convention dressed up as a—what are those things called? With the ridges on their foreheads?"

"Klingons," said Cassidy. "Can you believe I did that? I can't believe you *let me* do that!"

"You were smitten," said Teresa. "When we went Christmas shopping that year, you looked everywhere until we found those Klingon language CDs. And didn't he actually listen to them?"

"He did," said Cassidy. "He's such a doofus. He still speaks Klingon sometimes."

"You used to think it was cute," said Teresa.

"I know," said Cassidy. "Now it makes me want to smack him." She shook her head. "He's a good dad, though, and the kids adore him. I know I'm lucky that way, but I just can't believe this is my *life*."

Dan was definitely a good provider. He owned the biggest construction company in the county. Teresa and Jen had visited their house plenty of times. They lived outside of town on an estate by the water. They had ten acres, a three-story brick home, a private dock and boat, expensive SUVs, a couple of horses. From the outside Cassidy's life looked ideal.

"We haven't had sex in a year," Cassidy admitted.

Teresa raised her eyebrows. "Do you still cuddle on the couch or anything?"

"No," said Cassidy. "He tries sometimes, but I don't want him to touch me. He makes me hot—and not in a good way."

"Did he cheat?"

"No. I don't think so. We just drifted apart, I guess. It happens."

"I *guess*," Teresa replied.

"We don't have anything in common anymore, except the kids. After they go to bed, all he wants to do is sit out by the dock and smoke a blunt and watch the fish jump."

All around them, car engines revved, and the midway barker called anybody who'd listen to "step right up."

"Do you and Jen still have sex?" Cassidy asked.

"Not as much as we used to," Teresa replied. "Maybe once a week, unless we're on vacation. Then we do it more."

"Seriously?"

"Sometimes if we have company, we miss a week," Teresa said. "Or if one of us gets sick."

"Well, I wasn't expecting you to do it with bronchitis, you shameless hussy."

Teresa laughed, but she wondered if it bothered Cassidy to think that two women might have a better sex life than a woman and a man. It seemed like the most obvious thing in the world that they would—but then, she was biased. "Why don't you and Dan go on a vacation without the kids?" she suggested. "See if the spark comes back."

Cassidy made an *eww* face.

"Okay, then," said Teresa. "Start smaller. Do something that he's not expecting. Send him balloons at work."

"He oughta be sending *me* balloons," Cassidy pouted.

"Well, put the idea in his head, dingbat!" It'd been a while since she'd picked up a gift for Jen—earrings, chocolates. Maybe she'd swing by the gift shop and get her a MotorWorld back-scratcher. "Then he might do something to surprise you back," she said. "You have to collect more of those sweet moments to offset the ordinary, everyday stuff."

"That's so mushy," said Cassidy.

"So be mushy!" Teresa replied. "What's wrong with mushy?" Then she added, "Have you thought about counseling?"

"I don't want to go to counseling," Cassidy said. "I can't bear the thought of getting into all that stuff. It's not worth it."

"Then I guess you *do* need a divorce."

"But we live on his salary. The money I make is just spending money. And the house is on his parents' land, so I'm pretty sure I wouldn't end up with the house."

"You could rent a place," Teresa suggested. "You could go back to teaching full time."

"Oh, hell no!" said Cassidy. "I'd rather stay married." She blew out a big sigh, like a puttering race-car motor. "Let's go check on the kids."

They found all four kids in line at the Grand Prix track, with its winding roads lined with old tires to keep rogue drivers from bouncing out of the lanes. Some of the tires had weeds growing up inside them. Some had abandoned drink cups and other assorted trash stashed in their holes.

"This place is nasty," said Cassidy. "Let's wait for them over there," and she led them to the kiddie track where the tiniest racers in Hot Wheels and Tonka cars bumped into the sides and stalled out again and again. They were too little to race, too little to even steer, but they were a hoot to watch.

"I don't know how you do it," Teresa said. "I think I'd be a good mother for really young kids, like this age, but not so much for the older ones. I'd be a nervous wreck."

"You'd adjust," Cassidy said. "You see where I'm sitting, don't you? I'm not over there just waiting to witness a head-on collision."

"Jen would be fine with older kids, but not me."

"I've learned to just turn my head," said Cassidy. "I don't want my kids to be fearful, so I don't remind them all the time that they could break their fool necks and die. Speaking of that . . ." and she went digging through her bag, found her wallet, and double-checked to be sure she had the insurance card. "Whew," she said. "For a minute there I couldn't remember if I moved it out of my regular purse." She stuffed the wallet back down. "I want the kids to be confident, so I make sure I've always got at least half a tank of gas and the insurance card, and know the way to the nearest hospital. Then I just look away."

Teresa hadn't told Cassidy about their insemination attempts. She'd intended to, back when they first started, but Cassidy worked the first hours of the school day, and Teresa's planning period wasn't until afternoon when Cassidy was gone. She'd meant to tell her when they went out for coffee one Saturday, but then one of the guidance counselors plopped down and yakked the entire time.

Teresa debated telling her there at MotorWorld, but why get someone else involved? Besides that, she hated feeling like a failure. The last thing she wanted was to have to report to someone else, month after month, that no, she wasn't pregnant.

So Cassidy didn't know. Or at least she didn't know consciously. Maybe she picked up on it in some psychic way because as they sat there watching young parents making videos of toddlers with their phones, Cassidy said, "You and Jen should have kids! You'd make great parents. You've been together longer than me and Dan, and you two still *like* each other."

"If we had kids, we probably wouldn't like each other as much," Teresa replied. It was one of the things she worried about—how a baby could come between them. Just having Dori in the house those few days had altered the dynamic. And it was so easy to picture Jen putting a baby seat in a kayak, right between her legs. She could picture herself, standing at the water's edge, yelling, "Don't you dare take that baby out on the bay!" while Jen waved and paddled off.

"Why don't y'all go over to China and get a Chinese baby?" Cassidy suggested. "They've got beaucoups of them in orphanages."

She didn't even know how many levels of offensive she could be. "It's not that easy," Teresa said. "The restrictions on the Virginia side are almost as tricky as the restrictions on the China side."

"I know it takes a long time," Cassidy offered, "but if you're willing to wait . . ."

"China won't adopt to gay or lesbian couples, so only one of us could be the parent. And even to get that far, whichever of us became 'the parent' would have to sign a document professing heterosexuality."

"That sucks," said Cassidy, "but if I were you, I'd just lie." She shrugged like it was an obvious solution.

"I don't know," said Teresa. "Knowing me, I'd spend the rest of my life worrying that if the wrong person found out, they could take my baby."

Cassidy seemed a little bored, like she didn't want to hear all the politics involved—she just wanted to believe it was doable—but Teresa continued anyway: "Even if one of us pretended to be single and straight, we'd have to go through a home study."

"Well, how hard could that be? You'd obviously pass. You own your own house. You keep it clean, for the most part."

"But only one of us could live there, Cass—at least for a while. We'd have to get an apartment or something for the other one. It's a *home study*. They look in your closets and stuff," she said. "And I don't want to live separately from Jen while I'm defrauding the Chinese government. I shouldn't have to."

"Just get a PO box," Cassidy suggested.

She meant well, but it was the typical problem of so many straight people listening to legal issues that didn't affect them. Cassidy was interested, but only superficially. She just couldn't go there.

At noon, all six of them went to the snack bar and ate hot dogs and French fries. The boys told them about this nice attendant who kept giving them extra laps and this mean attendant who threw out the red flag before their turn was up and made them go to the back of the line before they could race the stock cars again. All the while Teresa wondered what it would be like if Cassidy's kids were *her* kids. Would she let them loose inside a thrill park to terrorize and defy the attendants?

She didn't even *like* kids at that age. If she actually had a baby, it wouldn't be long before the baby was ten and probably a hellion. She'd be fifty by then. Would she be willing to take a ten-year-old hellion to MotorWorld when she was fifty?

Even if her kid turned out to be a nightmare, it'd still be her

151

job to keep it safe. How could she do that, with the world the way it was?

She thought about old Miss Betty's medications and wondered if her relatives would really put poison inside those pill bottles. Even if a drug addict was the culprit, what if he sold those pills on the street? What if he sold them to someone young and stupid, like Cassidy's kids?

Or like Dori?

Teresa kept thinking she saw Dori. Sometimes out of the side of her eye, she'd see skinny, long legs walking by, and for a second she'd hope they might be Dori's legs. One of the bumper-boat workers reminded her of Dori—the girl who stood at the edge of the pool and blew her whistle when kids didn't climb out of their boats fast enough. She was tough like Dori, clipped and decisive. It was so strange to think that if Sugar's tumor hadn't come loose, Dori might not have left.

In hindsight, Teresa wished she hadn't been so hard on her, but Dori had disobeyed—flagrantly—and her "don't blame me, everything worked out fine" attitude had made it worse.

But it was also true that Dori hadn't hurt Sugar. If Teresa hadn't gotten so outraged, Dori might still be around. She could be with them there at MotorWorld.

But would she *want* Dori there with them at MotorWorld?

Dori was defiant, a rule-breaker, and Teresa was all about rules. For the most part she followed the rules and convinced herself that doing so made her a better citizen. But that was bullshit—nothing but a story she told herself. Rules were often unfair and selectively enforced, made by people who happened to be in positions of power based on when or where or what bodies they were born into. Just ask Rosa Parks, or Malala for that matter.

It was good that Dori knew how to defend herself and take no shit.

But it was weird for Teresa to see herself as the shit-giver, when all along she'd considered herself the victim. She'd have to do better, whether she ever ended up becoming a mom or not.

They spent a few more hours in the park, playing a round of mini-golf with the kids and then giving them one last set of laps with the race cars. At last, Teresa and Cassidy found a bench in the shade, not far from the midway, and Teresa told Cassidy the entire story of Dori's unexpected arrival and departure—and the abbreviated version of her own fractured relationship with Hilda.

"The whole thing's just bizarre," said Cassidy. "I knew you didn't have contact with your mom, but I guess I thought that was your decision. Not hers."

Teresa shrugged.

"As a mother, I can't imagine *ever* giving up contact with one of my children," Cassidy said. "There's *nothing* they could do. They could assassinate the pope and I'd still go visit in prison, even if I had to fly to Italy to do it. And you know I hate to fly."

"When I was little," Teresa said, "we lived way out in the country, and we had all these guineas that roamed wild. The guinea hens were terrible mothers, the worst mothers imaginable. The keets—that's the babies—they'd follow the mothers around, but the hens kept losing them. I don't know if guineas are especially stupid or just lack maternal instinct, but it was like the hens kept forgetting they *had* babies. My mom was a lot like that."

Teresa wondered if she'd be a similar kind of mother. What if it was genetic?

When she was little, she'd sometimes hear lost keets crying in the woods, and she'd find them and catch them, packing them into a cardboard box, and return them to their clueless mother.

Was she supposed to do the same thing with Dori?

Maybe her desire to have a baby was really a desire to prove that she was different. She wasn't a guinea; she wasn't like Hilda.

She was trying to figure it all out when her phone rang. She grabbed it and hurried down the walkway for privacy, trying to make out the caller's number, which was obscured by the glare. "Hello?" she said and leaned against a mimosa tree to talk.

But it wasn't Hilda. It was her dentist's office calling to reschedule an appointment she'd canceled the month before. She knew she had a cavity, but she didn't want to have it filled if she was pregnant.

The receptionist offered her a time the following week. By then, if she was pregnant, the fertilized egg should have implanted. But novocaine couldn't be good for a zygote or for an embryo either, and what if they wanted to take x-rays?

"I don't have my calendar with me," Teresa claimed. "I'll have to call you back."

She stood there awhile and took in the view around the thrill park: children everywhere, all sizes, shapes, and shades, sunburnt, giggling, throwing fits, the juice of snow cones running down arms and purpling tongues, children sniffling and shouting. Any of those children could be hers.

But if she had them, would she want them? Would she reject them if she didn't like who they turned out to be?

The sounds around her magnified: whistles blowing, engines vrooming, parents calling, bungee jumpers howling as they whooshed through the air. Then the smells overloaded her nose and lungs: car exhaust, cotton candy, a garbage can that needed emptying. To ground herself, Teresa stared down at the old concrete walkway that led back to Cassidy. She followed years and years of spit-out bubblegum, flattened to dark, round patches, like breadcrumbs along that path.

When she got to their bench, Cassidy had shifted sideways and pulled up her feet, maybe to save the space. She'd leaned her head against the arm of the bench, and though it was hard to be sure since she was wearing her sunglasses, it looked as though she'd dozed off. Teresa sat down just past her sandals and painted pink toenails, and she watched Cassidy's breathing: steady, even. She stared at the skin on Cassidy's chest, rising with each inhalation. She could see slats of ribs beneath the skin, and she softened her focus so it seemed she could discern even individual cells vibrating there. Then Cassidy wasn't Cassidy at all, but the earliest, most nascent form of herself. Not an overworked mother in an unhappy marriage, but something more essential, primitive, not even a baby—just a gathering of potential, dividing without any sense of outcome or intent.

That night, Teresa and Jen took turns calling every phone number they could find in Mississippi for Hilda Baxter. Occasionally, someone answered, but it was always the wrong Hilda, or a member of the wrong Hilda's family. Most often they got answering machines, and in those cases, they left messages: "If you're the mother of Dori, please call back."

"She probably doesn't want to talk to me," Teresa said. "But I wish I understood *why*. I mean, even if she hates me for being gay, wouldn't her curiosity about Dori trump that?"

"Don't assume it's about you," Jen said. "We may not have called the right person yet. Or she may never have gotten the message from the woman at the gallery."

"Or maybe she got the message, but she doesn't want to talk about *Dori*," Teresa speculated. "Why are we trying to reach her again? I can't even remember."

"Because you didn't want to be liable," said Jen.

"Oh yeah," said Teresa. "I still don't."

Sugar Britches didn't eat that night, and when Teresa examined the hollow where his tumor had been, it made her queasy to see that it had gotten dirty in there, probably from the garden. Then she realized that some of the black specks were moving.

There were tiny ants in the cavity, just a peppering, crawling across that tender, boggy-looking flesh.

Maybe they were feasting on the oils that glazed the basin. Maybe they were drowning.

"Oh, no!" she said to Jen, just as Jen, still at the computer, muttered, "Oh, shit!"

"Dori lied about Mississippi," Jen said. "I think your mom's in North Carolina, T. No wonder we couldn't find her." She'd tracked down a Dori Baxter, aka Dorothy Ann Baxter, aka Dorothy Ann Williamson, through an Internet search linking her to Hilda Baxter, aka Hilda Williamson. She read Teresa the article about Owen Howe's death, about the two men indicted for murder, and about Hilda Baxter's missing daughter whom she feared had suffered bodily harm.

Teresa passed Sugar to Jen and claimed her spot behind the computer. She couldn't stop reading, clicking from one link to the next. There were pictures of Dori, her hair long and wavy, smiling without any broken teeth. And there were school pictures of the boy who'd been tied up and tortured. When she looked at his wide-eyed expression, she couldn't believe he was dead, or that his demise had been as unmerciful as the news described, or that Dori could have anything to do with it.

He had pale skin, heavy eyebrows, faint acne on his cheeks. With a small twist of geography, he could have been her student. He could have been on her team for the Model United Nations. She recognized him, even though she didn't. He had thin lips that curled up slightly and wore his dark hair a little shaggy.

She stared at his picture on the computer monitor, and he regressed there before her. She could see what he must have looked like when he was a third-grader, in a Cub Scout uniform, cap pulled down on his head. She could picture him even younger, on his belly playing with Matchbox cars, driving his little Corvette around the track. She could see him as an infant, sitting on Santa's lap, with that mouth turned down into a not-quite cry, arms reached out toward his momma.

His poor momma. *She* could have been his momma.

She could picture him still in utero, eyes not yet open, curled bean-like and safe in his warm pod.

He could be her own sweet baby, except that he was dead, and Dori, who could also be her baby, was somehow implicated.

Teresa didn't realize she was crying until the computer screen blurred so entirely that she couldn't see.

"Come on," Jen said. "Help me. We've gotta get these ants out."

Teresa swallowed down her great grief and obliged.

Once again, they used a syringe, this time filled with nothing but warm water, to gently rinse Sugar's crater. Teresa held him tight in a towel, but he didn't fidget.

"We have to put him down tomorrow," Jen whispered. "First thing."

And Teresa nodded because there were no words.

Jen dabbed the ants away, and then they sprayed him with the medicine from the vet, the stuff they used each day to keep the wound from getting infected. It wouldn't help, but it was a gesture . . .

Neither of them admitted to the other that they could smell him, but he was starting to decompose.

IX.

Dori spoke just enough Spanish to ask the driver of the migrant bus if she could hitch a ride with the farmhands to the next tomato field. So south she went, in the direction of her sins, on that hot repurposed school bus with those sweaty workers in their dirty T-shirts and jeans. They crossed the county line, and when the workers all hopped out, gathered their stakes and rakes and claimed their rows, the driver pointed Dori toward a gas station maybe half a mile away, a place where she could catch the transit van if she waited long enough; and so she walked there, and she waited.

She didn't have a plan yet—only a direction—but there was plenty of time for a plan to emerge because the transit van didn't show up. According to the mechanic, sometimes it didn't come for days. He twirled his wrench around with grimy fingers. She still had money from the rings and pills she'd sold, and so she asked if he'd call her an Uber. He laughed outright, explained they didn't have Ubers or taxicabs either one, but he'd drive her where she needed to go when he got done fixing a fuel injector. She worried she'd have to blow him, but in another hour the migrant bus pulled up and sputtered to a stop. Workers stormed the convenience store, bought sodas and chips, and a woman from that group caught her eye for a long look. When she finished at the checkout, she took Dori by the arm, said *"Vamos!"* and Dori went.

She spent that night at their trailer park, sharing watermelon slices and tamales as neighbors wandered from yard to yard, people gossiping and laughing and hanging wash on the lines. She sat on the doorstep of the woman's trailer and watched men in the next yard play music, and people sang and danced and spun beneath the moon. It felt good to be with people who didn't try to talk to her. In a while the woman who'd brought her home ushered her inside, where an older woman and three little children were preparing for bed. She pointed to the sofa where Dori would sleep.

"*Gracias*," Dori said.

Before they went to bed, Dori asked for paper and a pen: "*papel y pluma, por favor.*" But the woman couldn't find a pen that worked. She offered a pencil with a broken-off tip, and they sharpened it with a kitchen knife, tiny curls of pencil wood slivered into the garbage can with mango peels and diapers.

If she ever hoped to have a normal life, she needed to atone for what she'd done to Owen. No excuses. But she hadn't yet decided whether it'd be best to turn herself in there in Virginia or enjoy her last days of freedom as she made her way back to North Carolina. Freedom didn't feel that great anyway, sweating on a ripped-up sofa covered with a crocheted afghan. There wasn't even a fan in that room, just a screenless window propped open with a stick, but she was in no position to be picky.

She wondered if there'd be a fan in prison. There surely wouldn't be one in Hell, but maybe if she did her time, repented for her sinful ways, she could bypass Hell. She could damn sure try.

There was a candle burning on the end table next to the sofa, one of those candles inside glass cylinders, with a picture of Our Lady of Guadalupe reaching out her arms. She watched the light flickering behind the Virgin. "I'm sorry," she whispered. "Forgive me." But she'd said those words so many times before. How did you make them count?

Back when she was in juvenile detention, she'd said them, too: "Jesus, if you'll help me out of this mess, I promise to give my life to your service. Please forgive me." But as soon as she was released, she started slipping into her old habits and ways. Why would Jesus care what she said? Why would Jesus care what *anybody* said?

She pulled her T-shirt to her face to dab away the sweat. What she remembered about juvenile detention was being too cold, not too hot, and not having a blanket when she needed one. Then finally getting a blanket but needing two. And trying to sleep with the lights on all the time, the fluorescent glare penetrating even her eyelids. All her dreams were overlit, overexposed, industrial.

She couldn't go to prison.

She imagined getting lost in a migrant worker camp, finding a Pablo with a trailer of his own and making a new life there. It wouldn't be life with Warren, but it wouldn't be prison, either. She gave her Pablo a deep singing voice, a dark mustache, and a Spanish guitar. When he serenaded her, she couldn't help laughing, in spite of her bleak situation. If Cane could see her, what would he think? They'd picked on the Mexican kids, too, or at least the ones who dated whites.

Why had they been so mean?

She tried to write a letter to Teresa and Jen but couldn't figure out where to start. She kept erasing her words, and the eraser left black smudges on the page. When she tried to erase the smudges, she wore holes in the paper itself. "I made a bad mistake," she wrote, "a lot of bad mistakes, and I'm sorry. Staying with you guys was great, though. I'm so glad I got to meet you." She read it and found it completely inadequate. She erased "guys" and changed it to "girls," then hoped that didn't seem condescending. She added one last line, "I hope Sugar gets better," and since she didn't have an envelope or stamp, she folded the paper and stuffed it into her pocket next to Randy's granny's rings, which she'd returned there.

She clicked off the lamp and tried to sleep, but couldn't stop her thoughts. Owen Howe was dead, but Cane wasn't. Neither was his cousin, sitting somewhere in a jail cell, accused of a murder he didn't commit. She had to tell somebody the cousin wasn't involved. It was one good thing she could still do. Every day she waited was another day he spent locked up.

But it wouldn't kill him to be locked up. He'd egged on Owen with the white lightning, and besides that, he was an asshole who hit his girlfriend. It wouldn't hurt him to stay in jail an extra day or two. He might learn something. Maybe the cousin had helped Cane tie Owen up. Maybe the cousin had come back after she left, and she really wasn't guilty after all.

And anyway, if she'd be spending years in prison, maybe the rest of her *life* in prison, didn't she deserve some last good times? What would good times even look like?

Maybe a little bag of cocaine. She'd never tried cocaine. Maybe a night of dancing: fast music, songs she loved, and her body flowing and grooving, arms and legs and hips all feeling it, greased and in sync. And she wanted to fuck somebody, too, to be dropped out of her mind and into her body so completely that she forgot, even for just a little while, all the awful things she'd done. That was the best thing about fucking, how it took you off. She wanted to look somebody directly in the eyes while she fucked them, and she wanted them to look back. That had never happened, not in her whole entire life. Why hadn't anybody ever wanted to look into her eyes when they fucked her?

She wanted to ride a roller coaster and savor the drop and remember how it felt in her rib cage to plunge and survive it. She wished she could ride it with the kid named Randy—or maybe just have one more chance to let him pull her around on his float.

Then, too, she wanted to be at Teresa and Jen's again, hanging out, maybe fixing dinner together or playing some dumb board game—or even working, stacking boxes of premade sandwiches into the refrigeration unit on Jen's boat. But most especially she wanted more time with Teresa, even though Teresa could be a bitch. She was her *sister*, and she barely knew her. Now she never would.

Outside, in a nearby yard, some people got into a fight: a bellowing woman, a raging man, a thud and the clamor of a knocked-over garbage can. Dori peeked out the window but couldn't see anything. The woman was probably being beaten. If Dori ever got out of prison, if she ever got out of Hell, maybe one day she'd have a couch to offer another woman with no place to sleep. Or even a man. There were men who needed couches, too. All over the world people were in trouble. She could pluck them from convenience stores or church tree houses. What difference did it make if they spoke another language? No two people ever spoke the same language.

Before daylight, a baby woke up crying, and the older woman staggered down the hall to get a bottle. She must have forgotten that Dori was there because when she saw her curled up on her couch, she cried out, *"Ay Dios mio!"* waking the other children, and none of them got back to sleep after that. They all came into the living room and watched TV, the little kids crawling around her ankles and calves and singing songs in Spanish with the characters from *Sesame Street* while somebody fried bacon.

"Gracias," Dori said, taking a slab in a greasy paper towel. *"Muchas gracias."*

She wasn't in a hurry. She walked south along the highway, through high grasses in her flip-flops, trying not to think too much. She was probably thirty miles from Teresa and Jen's, maybe a little more. The Maryland state line was about the same distance behind her, but she'd never be a Marylander, and she knew that now. She'd made it maybe a mile past the trailer park, maybe two, when a truck pulling a big boat passed her and then slowed down and pulled off the road.

With a deep ditch on one side and asphalt on the other, there was no way around it, unless she stepped into the road itself, where other cars were whooshing past.

She almost stepped out anyway when she realized the boat had a "Waterkeeper" decal along the side. The driver was Eric. He left the truck running when he jumped out and trotted back to her.

"Dori?" he called. "What are you doing out here?"

She shrugged and said, "Walking."

"Where've you been?" he asked.

She dropped her head and started to cry.

"Are you hurt?" he asked. "Are you alright?" He pulled her to him, and she sobbed against his chest. He smelled like raw fish, but she didn't mind much. She didn't smell that great either.

"I did something horrible," she admitted.

He thought she was talking about Sugar and his tumor. "I heard," he told her. "But that cat's dying anyway! I can't believe it's not dead already. Get in the truck. I'll take you back."

"I can't go back there," she said.

Eric smiled. "You having a better time out here?"

She shrugged again.

"Come on," he said. "I've gotta make a quick stop at one of the barrier islands to post some 'No Trespassing' signs, but I'll give Teresa and Jen a call and let them know you're safe. They've been looking for you everywhere."

It gave her a jolt to think they'd been looking, a delicious, electric surge, so Dori agreed.

They drove to a boat ramp on the seaside. While Eric backed in the trailer, Dori stood along the dock and secured the ropes, tugging the skiff off the trailer and into the water and keeping it from floating away while Eric pulled out and parked.

"Hop in," he told her, and she did, and then they were trolling through creeks, with marsh grasses high and green on either side. It was like moving through a maze.

There were no other boats around, nobody fishing or swimming. It seemed they must be far from the world, far from everything, but Eric still had a cell signal. First he left a message for Teresa and Jen. Then he returned a call to someone from the harbor, giving his opinion of the new floating docks. "Hang on," he said to the person on the other end of the phone, and he told Dori to stretch out on the deck on her belly for a better view and a more fun ride.

So she did. She grasped the very front edge of the bow and bounced along as the water sprayed up and cooled her face. She lost herself in the thick ripples as the skiff crossed over water. It felt hypnotic and dreamy, and it made her sleepy. In the distance, she could glimpse the barrier islands that separated the bay from the ocean, and she wished that they could shipwreck there and live on an island forever, just her and Eric, protected by "No Trespassing" signs. In her mind, she gave them each a pair of magic flip-flops, so they could bounce from the island back to the mainland for groceries. Maybe once a week they could spring over to the movie theater in Chincoteague.

In a little while Eric pointed out a loggerhead to Dori. Its head was nearly as wide as the shell of the turtle she'd found dead on the rocks. He dropped the boat to idle so they could watch it swimming past before speeding up again.

Dori felt the vibrations of the boat in her hipbones and pelvis, a pleasant tingling, and she wondered if Eric ever had sex on his workboat or if maybe he felt like it on that day. She wondered who else he'd taken out to the barrier island where they were headed.

As they approached, Dori asked, "Is trespassing really a problem way out here? It doesn't look like the kind of place many people would be able to get to."

"You'd be surprised," Eric replied. "People pull their boats up right over there." He pointed to a sandy beach where they seemed to be headed.

"Why would anybody care?" Dori asked.

"Birds," said Eric. "It's their mating season, so we don't want anyone disturbing the nesting birds."

Dori snorted. They'd go to that trouble for *birds*? She imagined that she and Eric were birds, and wished they were birds. Maybe ospreys, with their white leggings beneath brown-speckled tail feathers.

Eric raised the motor to protect his propeller and drove the skiff directly into the sandbar. Dori climbed out into water mid-calf deep. "Shove me off and do some exploring," Eric instructed.

"I'll put out these signs and then come back to get you. Might take an hour."

"What about the nesting birds?" she asked.

"Don't bother 'em," Eric said and smiled.

The beach was covered with conch shells, some of them whole and unbroken. The ones higher up in the hot sand were empty, bleached and dry, but some of the ones near the waves still had animals living inside: thick, muscular, quivering mollusks. Dori examined them—they looked like tongues—then returned them to their wet habitats.

As long as she stayed near the shoreline, the birds didn't bother her. Whenever she walked inland, toward the driftwood that had washed into the shrubs and small trees, birds would screech and squawk and come after her, circling her head and warning her off. She could see Eric's boat down the way for a while. Then he disappeared, and it occurred to her that he might forget her. He could leave her there and never come back. She didn't know if that'd be a bad thing or not.

She stripped off all her clothes, but kept on her flip-flops, and went out into the waves and moved her legs like a frog. She lost a shoe, but luckily it floated, so she found it again. The rubber soles were sliced from all the broken shells along the sandy floor, but they were better than nothing. She put them on her hands and used them to buoy herself, lifting her legs and half-floating in that salty sea.

Then she put her shoes back on and allowed the currents to wash her in. She sat at the edge of the water, in a place where there weren't many shells, and sunbathed naked until Eric came back.

He walked right up on her, still holding his mallet and a single sign. "Whoa," he said, when he saw her unclothed. He turned away from Dori and toward the nesting birds to say, "Sorry." He laughed uncomfortably. "Didn't mean to catch you off guard."

"What makes you think you caught me off guard?" Dori teased.

Eric laughed and said, "I've only got this one sign left, and then we'll be ready to scoot."

"Fine," said Dori. "I'll help." She pushed herself up and walked directly over to him. Eric exhaled audibly and leaned against his "No Trespassing" sign like he needed it to support his weight. Dori pushed the sign from his hand, and it dropped to the ground. Then she kissed him full on the mouth, powerful and electric, and everything else in the world dissolved.

He let her kiss him for maybe three seconds. Maybe five. She felt him pull away and then come back toward her before he pulled away again. "No," he said. "No way," and he started walking away from her, leaving his sign in the sand.

"Why not?" she called.

"Because I'm in a relationship with somebody else for starters," he replied. "And because you're underage."

"Barely," she said.

But he kept counting off his reasons. "Ever heard of statutory rape?" he asked. "And on top of that, you're the little sister of one of my best friends."

"She wouldn't have to know," said Dori. "There's nobody here. The seagulls won't gossip."

He turned back around and looked at her. "Listen," he said, "you're a beautiful woman. You really are. You're going to make somebody a real special girlfriend and wife one day. But I need you to put your clothes on now and get in the boat."

It was his tone that made her mad—and then ashamed.

Or maybe she had it backward. Which came first? Shame or rage? Was one the mother of the other—or were they more like siblings, even twins?

Dori didn't talk to Eric at all on the ride back to the mainland. He kept trying, saying things like, "I won't mention it to a soul. I promise," or even, "Don't get me wrong. I'm *flattered*. It just can't happen. You understand that, right?" or pointing out land-marks, sharing tidbits about how the islands used to be, like Dori gave a good goddamn about any of that. Every time he said something, she wanted to pull out her revolver and shoot him in his sweaty crotch. But she didn't, because at the same time, she knew that she was the one who deserved to be shot.

He'd been nothing but gracious to her.

How did she get to be such a bad person? She should put a bullet between her own eyes and make the world a better place.

According to the scriptures, suicide was wrong, but so was everything else she'd done. It was hopeless, and there was no way out. Supposedly she'd burn in Hell for suicide, like sorry old Judas Iscariot, but at least the punishment would be underway. She was so sick of waiting to find out if she'd be punished, and how, and when, and for how long. And couldn't you say that Jesus himself committed suicide? He didn't *have* to be crucified. He could have recanted about the whole Son of God business and nobody would have blamed him, with his life on the line, but he didn't. He didn't resist death. He chose it.

She'd read that drug or alcohol addiction was a slow form of suicide, and plenty of people took that route. Surely they weren't all burning in Hell, too.

Maybe suicide wasn't so bad if you did it inadvertently, or if you did it like Jesus, knowing your choice would get you killed, but making that choice anyway out of love for other people and as a sacrifice. Maybe her suicide could be considered an act of love. Think of all the people she'd never have a chance to hurt or betray if she was dead.

Why did she always think about suicide, though, even when only little things went wrong? The smallest rejection and it popped right into her head. She had a low tolerance for frustration: that was her problem, or one of them anyway. But she *couldn't* die until she made things right, and she didn't know how to do that yet.

She wasn't ready to see Teresa and Jen yet, either. So when they stopped for gas at a station she recognized, the station where she'd given the clerk the Percocet and first learned the news of Owen's death, she told Eric she was going in for lemonade. He said he'd take one too and gave her a ten-dollar bill. She walked straight in the front door and right out the back. She dodged poison ivy and green briar as she rambled through some woods and came out the other side into the parking lot for the local pawn shop. It was cool in there, the air conditioner turned up so high that the windows fogged. That's where she found Randy's granny's mother's ring in a locked-up case.

"Wanna see it?" asked the woman behind the counter. "Size 7.5. Vintage sterling silver."

Dori tried it on.

"$69.99," said the clerk.

"I don't know."

"Won't be here long," she said. "Just came in a day or two ago. I'll tell you what," she said, "for you, it's $59.99. That's as low as I can go."

So Dori bought it.

That night, she rented a room at a roadside motel she'd stayed in before, different room, same roaches. But she couldn't sleep. She still had pills and almost took them, but ended up dumping them in the commode instead. She had to clear her head, rather than mucking it up again. Flushing the pills definitely helped.

She was so tired of running. All she'd done was trek up and down that sad highway, wearing a rut in it. To be or not to be. She paced the carpet in that dim room, asking the same tedious questions.

She needed a guidance counselor or somebody to help her think through her options. She needed somebody to give her a test, like the one she had taken just a few months before, to determine what career path fit her best. She'd gotten emergency services worker or nurse as top career choices, and the guidance counselor had recommended she sign up for EMT training. She could take the basic course and be ready for the exam by the time she graduated.

But now she'd blown that, too.

She wished her mom was there to say, "Dori, these are your options," but her mom had forbidden her to even call. She couldn't keep paying for motel rooms, even sleezy ones, and surviving on Hershey bars and vending machine popcorn. She needed some green beans or something. She didn't even like green beans, but she knew her body needed them. And she was so lonely. Even Eric didn't want her. There was no one to talk to except the roach that kept trying to steal kernels of the popcorn she'd dropped on the floor.

"What would you do if you were me?" she asked the roach. It was big and brown all over—eyes, antennae, shell, wings—looking like something from outer space, except it wasn't. She'd read that roaches could survive anything, even the apocalypse. They were built for survival.

Maybe she was built for survival, too.

She pulled out her revolver and pointed it at the roach. "Stick 'em up," she joked, but the roach just stood there, not even scurrying off.

"Oh, go ahead and eat," she told the roach. "I'm not really gonna shoot you."

She unlatched the gun's cylinder and dumped the bullets into her hand. They were cold and substantial, and they clinked more than jingled when she walked them to the bathroom and plunked them into the toilet, one by one: "You. Don't. Need. To. Die," she whispered as she watched each splash, and she understood for that short moment that the part of her that wanted to die was the part in so much pain, the cruel part.

But there was more to her than that.

The bullets wouldn't flush, though. They just sat there heavy on the bottom, the way ammunition does.

When she came out of the bathroom, the roach was still there, staring at her. She didn't even stomp it.

X.

In a shady corner of the backyard next to a blooming lilac, Jen dug Sugar's grave. Teresa sat on the edge of the nearby hammock, rocking Sugar, who was swaddled in a purple baby blanket in her arms. Feet on the ground, she straightened her knees and breathed in, then bent her knees and breathed out. The hammock swung gently with her, mechanically, back and forth, and that was how she endured the first hours after Sugar's death.

Jen shoveled dark earth one heap at a time, and Teresa watched, step by step: stomp down, tilt back, scrape up, heft the soil, and pour. The crater creates the mountain.

Every now and then Jen wiped her eyes on the shoulders of her T-shirt, dabbed at the sweat on her face, and Teresa knew she should go get her some ice water, but she couldn't put Sugar down that long. He was already about to disappear from her for good.

How did that work—that people and animals just disappeared as if they'd never even been there? And how did it work that the ones left behind survived it? One breath at a time.

Off to Jen's right, not five feet from the gravesite, a robin struggled with something in the grass, a worm, yanking it out of the soil bit by bit, but clearly trying not to break it. The robin kept tugging and giving, tugging and giving, like you'd give a big fish on the end of your hook a little more line to keep the line from popping. Finally the robin freed the worm from the earth.

Teresa watched it peck the thing to death with little stabs of its beak. Then it gathered up that worm like chitterlings and hopped all around the yard with it dangling from its mouth before flying off.

Was it feeding babies or feeding itself? Did it matter? The worm was dead regardless. Who would miss it?

When Jen finished the hole, she went inside and got her own glass of water. Then she returned and sat next to Teresa, pushed back the blanket from Sugar's face, and rubbed his little head. His lime-colored eyes were open, fixed and glazed. "You were a good boy," she said to Sugar. She cried easily and didn't wipe her face. She let her tears fall right onto Sugar's fur and blanket. "You did a good job on the planet," she said, and though Teresa wasn't sure what that meant in any practical way, she still agreed.

They didn't bury him right away. They climbed to different sides of the hammock, pulled up their feet and faced one another, and they took turns holding him as they rocked there.

"Remember how he used to sit in the suitcase whenever we were packing?" Teresa asked.

"I remember finding his toy mouse tucked between the stacks of clothes when we got to Paris that time."

"How long ago was that?" asked Teresa.

"Six or seven years," said Jen.

"We should bury his mouse with him," said Teresa.

"We should go back to Paris," said Jen. "A getaway would do us good."

It was hard to put him in the hole, harder still to cover him up. When they were done, Teresa went inside but couldn't stay there long. Just long enough to start a load of laundry. Then she went back to the hammock with a book and spent the afternoon reading near his grave, or pretending to. She never even moved the clothes to the dryer.

Jen brought dinner out to the yard, just cold cuts from the deli, but Teresa wasn't hungry. Nothing much mattered except being there near Sugar. It was a chore even to go inside to pee.

In a way, it was a relief to be pulled away from all the other parts of her life. Of course, she thought of Dori and whether they should call the crime line to say she'd been with them, or whether they should hire an investigator of their own to try to find her. But thoughts of Sugar kept taking over. Losing him bottomed out her heart. If there was anything good about grief, it was how completely it consumed. Grief demanded everything she had.

After dark, Jen collected pillows and sheets, and they lay in the hammock side-by-side, covered up to keep mosquitoes from biting their legs and toes. For a long time, they rested there in the quiet, fingers entwined, watching the stars.

"I hate to think of him underground," Teresa said finally. "It's his first night down there."

"His *body's* first night," Jen corrected. "His spirit's not buried."

"I can't stand it," Teresa said. She turned her face toward Jen, and Jen rubbed her cheek so lightly that she could feel her littlest hairs there rising up to meet her touch.

"We don't have a choice," said Jen.

"There's always a choice," Teresa replied, even though it didn't make sense to say such a thing. She realized that she'd changed the subject of the conversation in her mind. She wasn't talking about Sugar anymore. She was talking about having a baby, or trying to, or worrying whether they would or wouldn't or should or shouldn't. Somehow it became all the same thing. "What if we have a baby and something happens?" she asked. "If we have to bury it? I couldn't stand that."

Jen rubbed the edge of Teresa's ear, so gently, the way they'd stroked Sugar those last weeks. Her fingers played with Teresa's hair, tucking a strand behind her ear, grazing her neck. "Don't even go there," she said.

"I can't help it," Teresa replied. "What if our baby ends up being bullied or even killed—like that poor boy in North Carolina?"

"You're jumping the gun," said Jen.

173

Teresa pulled away and sat up. Her back was starting to ache. "Or what if our kid turns out to *be* the bully. You never know! Do you think Dori really had something to do with his death?"

"She must have," said Jen. "Why else would she run?"

"What if our baby turns out like Dori then?" Teresa asked.

"Shhh," said Jen. "You're going around in circles, T. You're just upset."

"I can't have a baby," Teresa said. "I'll be your worst nightmare if we have a baby, Jen. I'll worry all the time about what might happen."

Jen batted her softly with a pillow. "Well, if you're saying that, then you're probably pregnant for sure," she joked. "That's Murphy's Law, right?"

"If I am, what will we do?" Teresa asked.

"What do you mean?"

"I mean, if I *know* that I shouldn't have a baby, and if I'm pregnant, then what should I do?"

"The same thing millions of people before have done: deal with it."

"There are a lot of ways to deal with it," Teresa whispered.

"Really?" Jen said. "After all we've been through? You don't mean that. You're just wrecked right now."

"Get this straight," said Teresa. "I share genes with a homophobic mother and a sister who's potentially capable of kicking a gay kid *to death*. Do you really think *I* should be having children?"

"We shouldn't be having this conversation," Jen said. "You can't make these kinds of decisions when we've just buried Sugar. Let's talk about it later."

Though it was too dark by then to really see her, Teresa could hear that Jen had started crying. Her voice warbled, and she'd begun to sneeze. Crying always made her sneeze. Still, Teresa couldn't stop: "Don't try to shut me up," she said.

"I'm not trying to shut you up," Jen replied. "But it's been a long, exhausting, shitty day, and I just need for you to talk about something else."

"See!" said Teresa. "You're trying to shut me up!"

"God! Why are you doing this?"

"Doing what?" asked Teresa. "I'm just telling you what I'm thinking."

"Well, everything that crosses your mind doesn't need to come out of your mouth," said Jen. "Don't you know that yet?" She almost flipped the hammock when she got out and left Teresa there alone.

Teresa spent an agonizing night in the hammock. She kept hoping Jen would come back and apologize. At the same time, she knew she was the one who owed Jen the apology. But why couldn't Jen accept the obvious?

She felt crampy and couldn't tell if the pull in her uterus might be implantation or a symbol of the ache she felt at losing Sugar. He'd been her only baby for all those years.

She dreamed she was in a grave herself, clods of dirt embedded in her hair, up her nostrils, clotted inside her ears and mouth, and beetles tap-dancing across her face. She woke up slapping at her cheek. The bug was real. Later, she heard a cat cry out in the night, a cat in heat, but at first she thought it was Sugar, yowling from the grave. She imagined digging him up with her bare hands, like that would do a bit of good.

It wasn't until the next morning that Teresa went to make the coffee and saw Jen crashed out on the sofa, still in her clothes, and the three missed calls on her cell phone, all from the previous day. Two were from Eric: the first saying he'd found Dori and the next saying he'd lost her again up near the wharf. Then there was the third call, from Hilda, whispering for Teresa to meet her at lunchtime the next day, three hours down the interstate in North Carolina. Hilda gave her the address of what she'd determined to be the midway point between them. "Don't try to call me back, darling," she said. "My phone's tapped, and this here number I'm calling from is borrowed, so you can't reach me. I'll meet you tomorrow at the cigarette outlet. It's right off the exit ramp. You can't miss it."

There wasn't time to make up with Jen. Teresa passed along the basic information and hurried to the shower. She needed to be on the road in less than half an hour and didn't have a clue what traffic would be like.

But by the time she toweled off, Jen was already dressed. "I'm going with you," she said, toothbrush sticking out the side of her mouth.

"You can't," Teresa replied. "Don't you have orders for the Miss Suzie going out this afternoon?" The Miss Suzie was a charter fishing boat and one of Jen's most reliable customers.

Jen ran to the bathroom to spit, then called back, "I'll figure it out from the road."

"That's thirty sandwiches," Teresa continued. "That's thirty people without lunch."

"I said I'll figure it out," Jen repeated. "Do we need the backup GPS? The one in the Subaru sucks."

They stopped for gas and coffee, and then hurried down the highway and over the bridge connecting the eastern shore to Virginia Beach and inland. Jen called Eric, and he volunteered to take the floating deli to the mouth of the harbor to meet Miss Suzie at one.

"That's awfully generous," Teresa said.

"He feels guilty about losing Dori," Jen said. "I'll pay him back."

Traffic was surprisingly light for a Saturday morning in June, maybe because they were driving away from the beach, and it was a good thing since Teresa had the runs. She kept dashing into convenience stores and grungy truck-stop bathrooms.

"It's just nerves," Jen reassured her. She'd bought some Imodium while Teresa was on the toilet. "Try this."

"Thanks," said Teresa. "And thanks for coming with me. I feel awful. I can't tell if it's in my head or not."

So Jen took over the driving. Teresa reclined the passenger seat and closed her eyes, but even after they crossed the state line, they continued to debate whether they should call the authorities, now that they knew for certain Dori was still in Virginia, or whether they should wait until after they spoke with Hilda, since she might be able to shed light on parts of the story they didn't understand.

"To protect ourselves, I think we better call," Teresa said. "We weren't just harboring a runaway. We were harboring a fugitive."

"And you want to admit that?" Jen said. "Look, we don't know where she is, and back when she was with us, we didn't know what she'd done."

"Does that make us innocent?"

"Not completely, I guess," Jen replied. "But not guilty, either."

In a way, it was easier for Teresa to ruminate over the Dori problem than to face seeing Hilda. *That* was what made her feel so queasy. She tried to nap but couldn't. She reminded herself that there were people reconnecting with long-lost relatives all the time, adopted children finding birth parents, husbands or wives returning from long stints in prison, all kinds of reasons for protracted absences.

The last time she'd seen Hilda, they'd gone shopping for a computer, her very first one, a big Macintosh desktop that they'd purchased with award money she'd received for winning a state-wide essay contest for high school students. Her award check paid for only a third, but her mom put the rest on the credit card.

Her essay had been a research paper on the history of cloning. Dolly the sheep had just been cloned, and Teresa and Hilda had both followed the news religiously, Teresa riveted by the science and Hilda by the ethics.

As they were setting up the new computer and installing the software, Hilda kept talking about Dolly and whether her life was predestined, and whether animals had souls, and if so, whether a cloned animal had a cloned soul and what that meant. "You know, I don't believe in playing God," said Hilda, "but I'd sure love to have two chances at this one life."

"What do you mean?" Teresa asked her.

"Just to have two whole different sets of experiences," Hilda mused. "So if something went wrong in one life, you could make it right in the other."

"That's not how it works," Teresa said.

"Oh, I know," said Hilda. They loaded the little hard disks into the drive, one after the other, and Hilda said, "I'm so proud of you, sugar," and "you write us some more award-winning essays on this beauty," and she patted the big beige monitor like she was petting the head of a lamb. Then she squeezed Teresa's shoulder and left her there to explore the Internet.

The next morning Teresa woke up to find a fleecy sheep Beanie Baby balanced on top of that computer monitor, and her mom was gone.

When they were a mile from their exit, Jen patted Teresa's thigh. "Hey, T," she said, "You awake? We're almost there."

Teresa returned her seat to the upright position, but the sun was so bright that even after she blinked, she couldn't clear her vision. All she could see was a glowing. She glanced at Jen, and her face was a sonogram, a luminous moon of a face, partially concealed behind sunglasses, with only a dimpled line where her mouth should be. She looked almost transparent, there behind the wheel of the SUV, and in an instant Teresa knew what it would feel like to *be* her, warm in a womb, a room as smooth as the inside of her own lip.

But as they circled the exit ramp and moved out of the sun, she turned into regular old Jen again.

They pulled into the parking lot of the meeting place and Jen killed the engine. "What is it?" she asked. "What are you staring at?" She wiped her nose. "Do I have a booger?"

"No," said Teresa. "I just love you," she said. "Let's go."

To enter the cigarette outlet, they passed through a remarkable archway, a shrine to tobacco built from cartons of stacked-up cigarette boxes, all brands and colors, encircled in blinking Christmas lights. From there they passed along a corridor lined with shelves of cigar boxes, then pouches and hard bricks of chewing tobacco, and tins of loose pipe tobacco and snuff. It was like the gateway into Tobacco Heaven (which was also the name of the place).

Next to the shopping carts, they found tobacco leaf wreaths and vases and planters, even decorative duck decoys shellacked in leaves of cured tobacco.

Tobacco Heaven had a Western section, too, with rodeo boots and square-dance finery; a Christmas shop; a section with beach chairs and garden flags; a linen department; and an enormous toy display with dolls dressed as Indian chiefs and squaws. There was even a snack bar, with well-worn metal tables and chairs, and that's where they waited for Hilda, after they'd circled the store repeatedly, looking for any signs of her.

"I can't believe this," said Teresa. "I really can't. If we've driven all this way—"

"Be patient," said Jen. "Maybe there was a wreck or construction or something." She'd made a trip to the book aisle and returned with a how-to guide on home renovations. She flipped through the pages, showing Teresa ideas for how they might renovate Rooms 3 and 4. "We need to get started on 3 pretty soon," she said.

The plan was for their current guest room, Room 2, to become the nursery. They'd knock out a portion of the wall between their bedroom and Room 2, and once the crib and changing table were installed, they'd need Room 3 for any future guests.

"What do you think of a wall bed?" Jen asked. She showed Teresa pictures of a nautical room with one image of the bed opened up and another image of the bed folded into its cabinet. "I like the bookshelves on either side."

"It's nice," said Teresa. "It's fine."

She didn't really care. If Hilda was running late, why hadn't she called? She had her phone number, so she could have called. Unless she didn't have a cell phone herself. She saw someone over by the Bibles that might be Hilda, but then it wasn't. "Listen," she said. "I've gotta run to the bathroom again. Text me if you see her."

She sat there on the toilet too dizzy to stand. She'd started bleeding, and it made absolutely no sense. It wasn't time for her period. It'd been only a week since ovulation—if that second faint line really indicated ovulation—and the luteal phase should last twice that long. Had she hallucinated the second line? The luteal phase should last fourteen days. Even on the shortest cycle, it'd have to be ten days. What was wrong with her? She wiped again and, sure enough, the toilet tissue was stained deep pink.

Maybe it was implantation bleeding, but there seemed to be too much blood for that. She felt too crampy, but then again, she didn't know how crampy implantation could make her.

And she didn't know whether what she felt was relief or distress, disbelief or grief. Luckily, she found a pad in a side pocket of her bag. "Breathe, girl," she said to herself and slapped it into her underwear.

When she got back to the snack area, they'd brought out fresh pizza, and Jen had bought a slice. "Carbs," said Jen. "Just what I needed. Want some?" and she offered Teresa a bite.

Teresa shook her head and plopped down in the metal chair beside her. "I got my period," she said. The words buckled in her throat.

"Are you sure?" Jen asked. "Isn't spotting a part of it?"

"It's not just spotting. There's too much blood."

"How would you know, though?" Jen asked. "I mean, how would you know how much blood was too much?"

She had sauce on her cheek. Teresa dabbed it away with a napkin.

"A lot of people don't spot at all," she said. "I shouldn't be bleeding. It might be a miscarriage, I guess, unless it's too early to count as that. Who knows?"

"It's okay," Jen said. "Don't cry. We'll figure it out." She put down her pizza, scooted her chair closer, and Teresa leaned in and sobbed against her collarbone. Jen held her there in the middle of Tobacco Heaven, and Teresa was so grateful for her salty skin, and her lovely, messy hair, which she had to brush out of her own face, and for the solidness of her arms and their reassuring support. "We can try again if you want," Jen said. "Or not—"

"I'm sorry about last night," Teresa whispered.

"There are a lot of ways to live a happy life, T," Jen said. "We don't need kids to be happy."

"Yeah, yeah," said Teresa, and she kissed her on the neck.

That's when Hilda showed up—looking confused as she tried to decide whether or not she needed a cart.

"Is that her?" Jen asked.

Teresa sat up quickly and dabbed her eyes with the pizza-stained napkin. "Oh my god," she said. "I think it *is*." They watched as Hilda struggled to pull apart two carts and ended up leaving them together and rolling the unwieldy doubles over toward the big glass counter where a salesgirl took cigarette orders.

"She's not even looking for you, though," Jen said. "It can't be her."

"It is," Teresa replied.

Hilda wore jean capris belted tight around her narrow waist, high-heeled sandals, and a tank with a lacy short-sleeve jacket over it. Her hair was platinum blond and full and still had the shapes of hot rollers in it. But she looked put together and proper, and Teresa felt huge and ugly and sick.

"I can't do this," she said.

Jen pulled her to her feet, grabbed her by the elbow, and led the way.

∽ ∽ ∽

Their reunion wasn't as awkward as Teresa expected. Hilda acted like she reconnected with estranged daughters every day. She made it seem commonplace. "Well, look at you, baby," she said and squeezed both of Teresa's hands in hers. "All grown up. You're just as pretty as a picture. Just as pretty as ever."

"I thought you weren't coming," said Teresa.

"Well, it's no wonder you've got abandonment issues, I reckon," Hilda said. "I'm sorry I'm late. My tires are old as Methuselah. I had to go slow." She looked at her watch. "We said twelve-thirty, didn't we? I'm not too late."

Teresa didn't correct her about the time. "Mom, this is Jen," she said. "My life partner and lover." She wasn't sure why she said *lover*, except that her mouth didn't make the word *wife* when it needed to, and if she didn't add *lover*, Hilda would automatically turn her into a friend.

"Well, my goodness," Hilda replied.

Jen offered her hand, and like Dori's before, Hilda looked at it as though she wasn't sure what she should do. But she shook it and held onto Jen's hand long after she had every right to put it down. "It's good to meet you, sweetie," she said.

Teresa had no idea what to make of the scene unfolding before her—so she switched the subject quickly. "Dori's okay," she said. "She stayed with us a little while, but we made her mad, and she left a few days back. But she's alive."

"I *know* she's alive," said Hilda. "If she don't quit calling me, she's gonna be alive and locked up in the pokey. I've told her my phone's tapped, but she keeps on calling. She must *want* to get caught." She turned toward the cigarette counter and said, "Let me get a few cartons of Dorals while I'm here. You can't beat these prices. Then we'll sit and visit."

They visited for a while: Teresa, Jen, Hilda, and probably twenty cartons of cigarettes, enough cigarettes to take up their own space at the snack bar table where they settled. They had to push away one of the chairs to make room for the carts. Jen got them all slices of pizza and sodas, and Hilda said the blessing right there at the snack bar, thanking God for the food prepared for their bodies and asking Him to use it for His service. She told them what she knew of Dori's involvement: "She did *not* do that terrible thing," said Hilda. "There's *no way* Dori could hurt a soul. She was running with the wrong crowd, though, in the wrong place at the wrong time. I tried to get her away from that sorry-ass boy. He comes from strange people," she said. She pulled out a sealed envelope. "If you know where she's at, I want you to give this here to her. I sold every bit of my stock. It's all the money I've got."

It seemed so strange to Teresa that her mom would *own* stock.

"What kind of stock did you have?" Teresa asked, knowing it was the wrong question.

"I don't know, honey. The kind that doesn't make you rich. That's for sure!" and she shrugged. "The kind that doesn't sell alcohol to children. What do you call it? The socially defensible stuff."

Jen tried to get them back on track: "We don't know where Dori is," she admitted. "So you keep your money."

Hilda pushed the envelope to Jen. "Try to find her," she said. "I need to get it to her." Her bottom lip started quivering then, and her big green eyes filled. "You don't know. You have no idea what it's like, to not know where she's at, to not know if she's dead at the bottom of a river somewhere."

"She wasn't dead at the bottom of a river yesterday," said Teresa. "Our friend Eric saw her maybe half an hour up the road from where we live."

"She needs to turn herself in," Jen said. "It's her best chance."

"Darling, she can't," Hilda replied. "She's had charges before—nothing serious, not at all—but she's on probation, and it won't go good for her. They'll lock her up a long time. And it's my fault. It's all my fault. I was a terrible mother," she said. She turned to Teresa and added, "I had such a time getting off the pain pills. Who understands the Lord's will? I reckon the Lord let me slip so I could better minister to the afflicted, but I was a better mother with you than with Dori. I was too old with Dori. I don't know what happened."

Teresa almost choked on her Sprite. Better with her? She'd *abandoned* her. Twice.

Hilda lit up a cigarette. It had been a long time since Teresa had been in a place where people smoked indoors, but at the cigarette outlet almost everybody was smoking: workers behind the perfume counter were lighting up, security guards sitting on their stools by the exits were exhaling streams of smoke as they checked each receipt. It was like being on another planet.

And there in the snack bar her alien mother puffed away. "If you girls had children, you'd understand," she said. "When you don't know where your child is, or if she'll be alright—"

What made her assume they *didn't* have children? They *could've* had children. And moreover, Hilda hadn't known where *Teresa* was, not for years. There was no indication that she'd anguished over not knowing if *she* was alright.

Teresa felt light-headed. Everything inside her vibrated, like she had yellow jackets buzzing all around inside her. She felt stung. "Did you care if I was alright?" she asked. "After you left *me*, I mean?"

"I *knew* you were alright," Hilda said. "You had a good daddy who loved you and a new computer to do your college applications on."

Like that was all a person needed.

"But that doesn't excuse it," Teresa said. She looked down at her own lap and shook her head.

"No," Hilda said, "no ma'am, it does not." She lit up another cigarette even though she already had one burning in the ashtray. "I don't expect you to forgive me, honey, and I can't change the past. But the minute I found out you were looking for me, the minute I got that message, I called you. And here I am."

It was true, but it wasn't enough. "You left daddy with the credit card bill for the rest of my computer," Teresa exclaimed, her voice louder than she intended. "He didn't even know you'd *bought* it!"

"Well, he either paid it off or he didn't," Hilda said. "Nothing I can do about it now. What's done is done."

But Teresa couldn't stop. She didn't even care that a family of four, all decked-out in American flag T-shirts, picked up their cheeseburgers and switched tables. "And you didn't even *acknowledge* the invitation to our commitment ceremony." She grabbed Jen's hand and squeezed it. Jen's hand was unusually sweaty. "You could have sent a card or something, couldn't you?"

"It's taken me a while to get used to the idea of two women," Hilda admitted, "but I'm working on it."

"Good thing I didn't need your permission," Teresa said. "Still don't."

"You are a grown-ass woman," Hilda agreed. "You can live your life by your own rules."

Jen joined in with a spirited "Amen!" surprising them both, and Hilda cackled outright.

"I know this won't help you a smidgen," Hilda said, "but I'll tell you anyway that I never went a day without thinking about you, Teresa, and I checked on you, too. I looked you up on Facebook."

"I haven't used my Facebook in years," Teresa said.

"I know it," said Hilda. "You need to get with the program." And then she added, "But you probably ought to work on your privacy settings, too."

They were in the checkout line when Hilda offered the envelope of money again, Hilda with her cigarettes and Teresa with a jumbo box of tampons, a tin of mixed nuts, and some CBD oil to put beneath her tongue. Hopefully it would calm her down.

Hilda said, "If you don't see Dori for a while, spend the money on yourself. Have a spa day. Take your friend with you and both of you get your facials and pedicures, whatever you want."

"She's not my friend," said Teresa. "She's my wife."

Jen elbowed her gently, and when Teresa looked over, she mouthed the word, *Enough.*

Hilda cocked her head sideways. "Well, I still don't believe in any of that, but I love *you* just the same," said Hilda. "I've prayed for you *every day* of your life. I know you know that."

"In bed she makes me feel like an acrobat," Teresa continued, and Jen put her hand over her eyes and then left the checkout line and walked directly out the door and into the parking lot.

Hilda didn't say anything else until they'd paid for their purchases and left the store. "Walk with me to the car," she told Teresa. "I got something for you."

They crossed the hot pavement, maneuvering the cart full of Dorals between closely parked vehicles, and Teresa assumed they were headed to the battered subcompact with no hubcaps parked in the far row. But Hilda opened the trunk of an older model beige sedan. The trunk didn't look like Teresa imagined either. It wasn't stuffed with clothes, toys, or random yard sale junk. Instead, there was a gigantic package of toilet paper, unopened, a tire jack, and a single cardboard box.

Hilda loaded all the cigarette cartons back there before she reached into the box. "Here," she said. "I thought you'd appreciate this one." She handed Teresa a sculpture, a pink crocheted uterus, fallopian tubes and ovaries attached, with a cloth doll tucked inside it. The doll's face peeked out from the bottom. Through each of the doll's eyes, she'd jabbed a rusted knitting needle. The needles crossed one another in the middle, and Hilda had tethered them together at the X and glued a small, crucified Jesus at the juncture. The other ends of the needles were secured into a heavy wooden base, with the words painted in an unsteady hand: *For you created my inmost being; you knit me together in my mother's womb, Psalms 139:13.*

"Usually I prefer the King James version for my scriptures," said Hilda. "But I liked the use of *knitted* in this verse. The King James says *covered* and that's just not as poetical, do you think? Sometimes King James could be a real big dud." She laughed and coughed.

"Thank you," said Teresa.

"I hope you like it," Hilda said. "If you don't, you can pull out the doll and wear that womb to the next Women's March. It'll double as a 'pussy-hat.' Isn't that what they call it?"

"Ah, yeah," said Teresa. "I think so."

Jen pulled the car over beside them, and Hilda opened the back passenger door so Teresa could load up the sculpture.

"Do you need any toilet paper?" Hilda asked. She motioned toward the multipack there in her trunk.

"Sure," said Teresa, so Hilda gave her two rolls.

"How about cigarettes?"

"I don't smoke," said Teresa.

"Well, how about your acrobat wife?" she asked, and nosed toward Jen. "Does she need any cigarettes?"

"I don't smoke either," Jen called. "But thanks."

"Alrighty then," Hilda said. She opened her arms and Teresa moved into them, and Hilda gave her a hug, a real one, with both arms and her full chest. "I taped my business card to the bottom of that sculpture," she said. "So you got my phone number now. Feel free to use it."

Teresa nodded, even though she didn't know if she'd ever speak to Hilda again. As she got in the car, settled into the passenger seat, and fastened her seatbelt, Hilda stood there with her empty doubled-up shopping carts, watching them. Jen was just about to pull away when Teresa called out the window, "Hey, Mom, one more thing: we're starting a family, me and Jen."

"Really?" Hilda said. "Well, how about that?" She shook her head and added, "I always did want to be a granny."

Back on the Interstate and heading toward Virginia, they talked for most of the next hour, reliving the hour before, which is what people do: making every experience funny or tragic or not-to-be-believed, shaping their histories, choosing which parts to memorialize, which parts to seal off. They turned that short visit with Hilda like a kaleidoscope, marveling at every image, each a wondrous, different thing.

187

"She called you a grown-ass woman," Jen remembered. "That's classic."

"Yeah, but first she called us girls."

"Look how far you got in just one visit, though," Jen continued. "Not just to woman, but to *grown-ass* woman."

"The thing that really blew my mind was hearing her say she'd been a better mother to me than to Dori—and realizing that it was probably *true*."

"I know," said Jen. "Poor Dori."

"And the fact that she doesn't want Dori to get *caught*. That's just so messed up I don't know where to start. You'd think she'd be holding a televised press conference, telling Dori to do the right thing and turn herself in. Instead, she's financing her getaway, or trying to."

"How much money's in the envelope?"

Teresa opened it up and counted. "Two hundred and fifty-four dollars."

"What?" Jen howled. "She spent more than that on cigarettes!" And they both cracked up, but it pricked at Teresa's heart that Hilda had gone to so much trouble to get them so little money. Two hundred and fifty-four dollars wouldn't keep Dori afloat for a week, even if they had some way to get it to her.

She couldn't stop wondering where Dori might be, or where she would sleep. With some skeezy man, probably. She could end up trafficked. She could end up dead herself. Teresa couldn't let Dori keep drifting.

"I guess Hilda loves her, don't you think? But her love's as unstable as she is, so it's basically useless."

"Not true," Jen said. "You can't judge another person's love like that."

"Oh, yes I can," said Teresa. "Watch me. I'm judging it right now."

"It's just that Hilda's love isn't all that Dori needs, any more than a computer and a good daddy were all that you needed when she ran off with the preacher. But just because love isn't *enough* doesn't mean it isn't real."

"I never said it wasn't real." Teresa smarted.

She got quiet then. She'd hoped to have a better sense of what to do about Dori after talking with Hilda, but now her thoughts were even more muddled. She opened the mixed nuts, offered some to Jen, took a handful herself. "You know how when you're little you always worry about crazy things—like you think a monster might actually be hiding in your closet? I used to worry all the time about quicksand. I'd read about ranchers out in Arizona losing cows and horses in it, and I'd seen *Indiana Jones*."

"*The Princess Bride* had quicksand, too," Jen added. "Remember how fast she went down? Bloop!"

"Even though nobody I knew had ever gotten stuck in quicksand—or had even *seen* quicksand—I was always afraid I might accidentally step in it and get sucked down and die before anybody could save me." She sighed. "Of all the things to worry about! But it makes sense, in a way, 'cause living with Hilda could sometimes feel like that. You know, quicksand looks like regular sand, so you don't know you're about to sink until you're sinking."

"Damn," said Jen. "If Hilda's love has quicksand in it, we'd better toss Dori a rope."

They were still in North Carolina when Teresa called the chief of police who'd delivered Dori to their door a little over a week before. She still had his cell number in her contacts, from back when they served on the library board together, so she reached him directly, and she reported all that she'd learned: that her half sister was wanted for questioning in a hate crime, that neither she nor Jen had seen her since Tuesday, but that Eric had given her a ride the day before and lost her at the Shore Stop up the road. She provided a full description, but the chief remembered. "Green eyes, right? And was she still carrying that floweredy bag?" he asked.

"Probably," she said. Then she added, "Jen and I are out of town. Will you call me if you find her?"

"Yep," he replied. "Any chance she'll head back to your place, you reckon?"

"I doubt it," Teresa said. "She was furious when she left. Eric was trying to bring her back when she escaped him at the gas station. She definitely didn't want to see us."

"I'll get up with Eric then," the chief said. "I'll keep you posted."

She ended the call, pulled her heels onto the edge of the seat, and cried against her own knees. Jen said nothing but started to sneeze. Between them, they used half a roll of toilet tissue.

In a while, Teresa blew her nose and said, "Well, now I know how Benedict Arnold felt."

"Oh, come on," Jen replied. "Don't be a drama queen."

"I thought you liked drama queens."

"I must," Jen said and winked.

"Really, though, I just turned in my little sister to the police. That's heavy."

"You didn't have a choice," Jen comforted.

But there was always a choice—and always at least two ways to see every decision. Teresa hoped that one day Dori would understand.

But it seemed unlikely. Most people want things clear-cut and simple: a good guy and a bad guy, a right way and a wrong. With her high school students, Teresa used old Benedict Arnold himself to try to help them understand the complexity: to the Americans, he'd been a traitor; to the British, a hero and a patriot—at the exact same time. One year, her AP history students gave her a T-shirt to wear on the Fourth of July that said, "Happy Treason Day, Ungrateful Colonialists," with an angry picture of Queen Elizabeth wearing British flag sunshades. At least she'd helped that class understand.

It was all about perspective. The same thing was true for the Southern soldiers who fought for the Union, or even for that kid from Washington, DC, who joined up with the Taliban. Whether Teresa liked it or not, it was the same with Hilda, who had traded in one family for another. Everyone had their supporters and their haters. Hilda had her reasons.

It was easier for Teresa to find compassion for Benedict Arnold than for Hilda, though.

She suspected Dori would feel the same way about her.

But she wasn't a traitor to Owen Howe. At least there was that.

When they stopped at a rest area for a bathroom break, Teresa pulled down her visor and used the little mirror there to check her face. She looked dreadful, with her red-rimmed eyes, the lids all bloated, her nose like Rudolph's. Just as she was about to close the mirror, she caught a glimpse of Hilda's sculpture in the back seat behind her, reflected in the mirror and sitting exactly where a baby's car seat would go.

There was nothing artistic about that sculpture, if you could call it a sculpture at all. "I hate that thing," she told Jen. "I'm dumping it. I'm going to put it behind the car tire and back over it when we leave the rest stop."

"Great," said Jen. "Then we'll get a flat from those knitting needles, and you can blame Hilda for that, too."

"Hey now!" said Teresa.

But she didn't back over the sculpture. Instead, while Jen took a walk around the perimeter, stretching her legs, she sat at a picnic table and tore it apart, piece by piece, peeling the newborn doll out of the crocheted sack; prying superglue from around the dolly's eye sockets and wiggling free the rusted knitting needles that left the hollow head with two creepy, empty holes. She used her Swiss army knife to saw at the binding that held the knitting needles together and tethered the crucified savior to his cross. She stashed the tiny Jesus in her pocket, for Sugar Britches' grave, and threw the needles into the recycling bin.

Before tossing the sculpture's wooden base into the thicket of trees across the ditch from where they'd parked, she pulled off Hilda's business card. How bizarre that Hilda *had* a business card. It read, "Hilda Baxter, Folk Artist and Peacemaker," written in curlicue calligraphy and providing both a phone number and an email address. She tucked the card into her pocket and was just about to unravel the knitted uterus, using her teeth if she had to, when Jen appeared and took it from her hands.

"I hope you don't regret this later," she said. She tugged the pussy hat onto her head, fallopian tubes and ovaries sprouting like ponytails.

"I won't," Teresa assured her. She debated whether to throw out the mutilated plastic doll. There was no repairing those gouged-out eyes, but she couldn't stop thinking that the doll might have been Dori's once upon a time. In the end, she swaddled it in a reusable grocery bag and tucked it beneath the passenger seat with an umbrella and a can of Fix-a-Flat.

When they crossed the Virginia state line, past the big, happy welcome sign with its cardinal and flowers making the whole state seem cartoonishly hospitable, Jen said, "We did the right thing, you know? Owen's family deserves to know what happened. Maybe Dori can tell them."

Teresa pictured the scene of Dori's apprehension: sirens, officers drawing their guns, handcuffs. Would Dori go quietly or put up a fight? "I still don't want to be around when they arrest her," she said.

"Me neither," Jen agreed.

So they made a left, rather than a right, and headed away from the coast and toward the lush green hills that would lead them eventually to mountains.

"What if she gets the death penalty?" Teresa asked.

"That's really unlikely."

"She *could*," said Teresa.

"I doubt it," said Jen. "But if you want, we'll hire her a lawyer."

"What will we pay for a lawyer with? Hilda's stock returns won't even cover the initial consultation."

"We've got the baby's college fund. It's a place to start."

Teresa cut her a look.

"I'm serious," said Jen. "If we end up having a baby, we'll save up again." Teresa reached across the console and took her hand, and they drove high over hills, and plunged back down. Past woods and fields, through tiny town after tiny town, at higher and higher altitudes, they drove on unfamiliar roads.

Since neither of them had worn walking shoes, they took a detour at an outdoor outfitter and spent the money from Hilda's cashed-out stocks on their feet. From there, they headed to the Blue Ridge hiking trails to decompress and shape new plans.

It made a good story, really: two lesbians paying for an attorney for a girl who committed a hate crime against a gay boy. Maybe a good enough story that one day they could sell the movie rights to Lifetime and replenish their baby's college fund.

XI.

The driver of the transit van recognized Dori and delivered her all the way to the gazebo at the beachfront. For a while, she sat on a bench in the shade, working up her nerve to go see Teresa and Jen. She hoped they'd help her map her next move, but that also meant she had to confess. Would it be better to turn herself in there in Virginia, or should she go back to North Carolina? And if so, could they drive her?

She was scared they might hate her.

She walked along the pier and then headed down their street, feeling braver when she didn't see Teresa's car out front. When she knocked and no one answered, she was disappointed, but also relieved. She checked the deli to see if Jen was working, but the manager said they'd had a family emergency and left town.

"Did somebody die?" Dori asked.

"I don't think so," said the manager. "They're supposed to be back tonight."

Dori ordered a sandwich and took it outside to eat.

She sat at a small table at the far corner of the patio. Both the trellis next to her and the pergola above were covered with delicious-smelling honeysuckle vines. For dessert, she picked a few flowers and sipped at the nectar, then watched butterflies and even a hummingbird come and go. She noticed that the honeysuckle vines had grown beyond the trellis, crossing into the branches of three young neighboring crepe myrtle trees. The vines twined around and crisscrossed their limbs, and honeysuckle flowers draped softly from each tree's canopy.

She needed to warn Jen to prune those vines. Otherwise they might choke out the little trees they decorated so spectacularly.

It seemed strange and sad that something as tender as honeysuckle could also be deadly. But then everything seemed strange and sad.

Dori waited there until closing time. The manager who came to take her plate and water glass asked, "You okay?"

"Yeah," Dori said.

"You need me to call them for you?"

"Oh, no," said Dori. "I'm just enjoying the butterflies."

"I've gotta lock up," the manager said apologetically, but Dori still had the key to Room 2. She pulled it out to show her and said, "I'm fine. I'll just walk around front in a little bit."

When it was late, nearly dark, and Teresa and Jen hadn't yet returned, Dori let herself into Room 2. It felt sort of like breaking and entering, but also not, since she still had the key. Immediately, she felt better and safer. She'd missed that room, with the crazy mash-up of colors on the walls, bedspread, and pillows, and she pretended it was still her bedroom.

Though she kept the curtains drawn, she loved it that her bedroom had such a big window. There wouldn't be windows in her prison cell, probably. She loved it that she had a bathroom of her own and knew it might be a long time before she had privacy again.

She settled on the bed without pulling down the covers, so she wouldn't dirty it much. Her feet and shins both throbbed. She was wearing the mother's ring she'd stolen from Randy's granny, a simple band with four small stones—an aquamarine, a garnet, a topaz, and a peridot—and she played with it on her finger, spinning it around. She knew all the stones because she'd ordered her high school ring the month before. She'd ordered topaz because that was her birthstone, but she'd liked the peridot better. She wondered what Owen Howe had ordered. Now he'd never get to wear his high school ring.

Neither would she, probably, and her mom would still be left paying the balance.

Randy's granny's mother's ring had almost the same colors as Room 2, a coincidence that also seemed like a sign. She wondered if Randy's granny had four children, or if the stones were for her grandchildren. Maybe one of them was Randy's birthstone.

She wondered if there would ever be a ring with a stone in it for her, and if so who might possibly wear it.

The next day when Teresa and Jen still weren't home by lunchtime, Dori dropped the letter she'd written through their mail slot, along with the key to Room 2, and headed for the police station a few blocks away. But it was closed on Sundays, locked up tight, with a sign on the door providing a non-emergency number, plus instructions for anyone who saw a crime being committed to dial 911.

She walked back to Teresa and Jen's but had no way into the room anymore. She picked a couple of cucumbers and a tomato from their garden and munched them as she headed to the beach, figuring sooner or later she'd see a police car to flag down.

When she arrived at the abandoned ferry dock, Randy was already there, out in the water with his dad, pulling in crabs. Dori settled in the sand and watched for a while before he spotted her.

"Hey, Dori!" he called, and he splashed toward her to show her that he'd lost a tooth.

"Cool," she said. It was one of his top teeth. His gum was still bloody and uneven; it looked shocked about being so exposed.

Randy pushed his tongue in and out of the hole. "It *just* come out," he said. "I'll tell you what happened. I was swimming out there, and I had my mouth open, and this crab reached right in, with the big claw, not the little one, and yanked that thing!"

"How'd the crab know which tooth was loose?" she asked.

Randy shrugged. "I'm just teasing," he said. "I made that up."

"It's a good story," Dori replied and smiled.

He pointed at her mouth. "What happened to your broke tooth?"

"I bumped it on a bottle," she lied.

"Like a baby bottle?" he asked.

"No," she said. "A glass bottle. I was drinking a Mountain Dew."

"I didn't know that came in glass bottles," Randy replied. "All my Mountain Dew comes in plastic bottles or else cans."

Her tooth had actually been broken in the tussle with Owen. She'd been trying to untie him, but he'd thought she was attacking, and he got her with his elbow. Served her right. Now she had something to always remember him by.

"I got my tooth in my pocket somewhere," Randy said. He reached into his cutoffs and pulled out some change, a shell, a couple of rocks, and finally the tiniest, whitest tooth Dori had ever seen, all ringed with darkness around its irregular top. "I'm saving it for the tooth fairy," said Randy. "She'll probably swing by tonight."

Dori rolled his tooth around in her fingers, pushed her skin against the sharp, darker portion. She wanted to keep the tooth, but she gave it back.

"Let's go show my momma," said Randy. "She's rolling my granny's hair."

Dori grabbed her bag and followed Randy around the rocks, up the bank, through the field, and into his granny's yard, where chickens clucked around their ankles as they headed to the door.

"Watch out for chicken shit," Randy warned.

They walked right into the house, letting the screen door slam behind them. "Hey!" Randy called. "Look!" He ran through the living room and into the kitchen, and Dori followed. She knew the floor plan well. She watched him stand before the two women, pushing his tongue in and out of the new slot in his mouth.

Randy's momma and granny looked surprised to see her, but they both smiled, and his momma said, "Well, who's this?"

"Dori!" Randy said. "My girlfriend from the beach. I told you about her over and over!"

"Hi," said Dori.

"Well, my mercy," said the granny. "We thought he'd *made you up*!"

And Dori was amazed—amazed to think that all the time she'd been breaking and entering, popping pills, running from the law, all the time she was working so hard to impress Teresa and Jen, to face what she'd done to Owen Howe, as far as Randy's momma and granny were concerned she was an invention, no more real than a tooth-stealing crab or a magic flip-flop.

It was a great relief, actually, realizing that she wasn't at the center of every story.

"Y'all don't never believe nothing I say," Randy complained, and Dori laughed.

Randy's momma put down her comb and cut them each a slice of lemon pie.

"Get 'em some tea," said the granny, and so Dori and Randy sat at the kitchen table and dined while the momma sectioned the granny's hair into little squares and rolled it up in hard pink plastic curlers.

Randy told them the story of the crab that pulled his tooth, but this time he pretended that the crab had gotten away— swimming out into the channel and taking the tooth with him—and at that very minute his brave daddy was chasing down that crab to retrieve it.

In a little while, with a magician's *voilà*, he produced the tooth. "I'm just teasing!" he said. "Here it goes," and he passed the tiny tooth to his granny, who held it in her palsied fingers and *ooh*ed and *aah*ed about it.

Dori knew it would be a long time before she'd have lemon pie at anybody's table again. She savored every bite, marveling at how not so long ago she'd wanted to be dead. But now that Owen had died and charges against her were sure to land her in prison, she wanted to live.

"Can I use your bathroom before I go?" Dori asked the granny.

"Why, sure," she said. "It's right around that corner."

Dori left the mother's ring, the wedding band, and the little diamond in the dish by the sink, perched right on top of the white bar of soap. Randy's granny was sure to see them the next time she washed her hands.

She left the handgun, too, but not in plain view. She hid it high inside the medicine cabinet, in case Randy came into the bathroom behind her. She folded up all the remaining money and tucked it beneath a tube of denture cream.

After that, the two of them raced back to the beach, and they played there the rest of the afternoon. They retrieved the blue float, and Dori held it while Randy tried to surf, and then Randy pulled her around and among the pilings. When they were tired of being in the water, they went back to the sand to build castles.

As they played, Dori remembered other times at the beach. She remembered what it felt like to be seven, to have a missing tooth. She ran her tongue against her broken tooth, and a rush of excitement bucked through her.

She sieved gritty sand between her fingers, licked salt from her lips, let her hair fall into her eyes, let her toes crimp into the ground and spring her back up to search for shells to make windows and doorways for her castle.

She patted the sand down hard, flattening the top of her castle, and the castle became a wedding cake. She dribbled wet sand over it, and her wedding cake melted before her eyes.

It was Randy's idea for them to transform their shoes into magic flip-flops that could bounce them as far as they could imagine, all the way up to Heaven, he said. They both had flip-flops already, but just the cheap rubber kind you could buy at the drugstore. Randy rolled green sea lettuce into cigars around the thongs of his flip-flops. Dori gathered feathers—three big feathers and one smaller—and tried to weave them around her thongs, but it was hard to keep the quills between her toes, even when she knotted them together with strings of dried sea-grass. Still, they gave off the impression of magic flip-flops sometimes. The two of them searched for tiny shells, the very smallest ones, and embedded them into their magic flip-flops. But the shells kept slipping off. No matter how delicately they walked around the beach, they couldn't prevent their magic shoes from falling completely apart.

Then Randy's dad waded out of the water with his five-gallon bucket clicking with crabs.

"Bye," said Randy. "See you next week!"

"Okeydokey," said Dori.

"Okeydokey, Artichokie," said Randy. He called back several times, "Okeydokey!"

Dori grabbed the float and headed back to the water, and she drifted there among the posts, resting on her belly and letting the currents decide which way to take her.

As the sun dropped low, it seemed she grew younger and younger, so little in the end that she probably had no business floating around the bay by herself.

In her mind she pictured her mom calling her to dinner: "It's getting late, darling," she heard her say. "Time to come inside." But then her mom morphed into Teresa, beckoning from the edges of the surf. "Let's go," Teresa urged, and Dori wished Teresa'd been her mom.

Sounds echoed and amplified around her. She heard a call from the distant horizon: "Let's go." The sun was going down, a pink and fiery smear. She could just make out someone who resembled Owen Howe splashing at the place where melted sun met water. It looked warm out there where he was. Strangely, she felt cold.

Then a voice shouted from the rock jetty, "Come on in!" She turned and saw the chief of police. "Don't make me come after you!" he hollered. There were others in uniform standing along the beach, waving, but she was so dreamy by then that she thought for a minute they were calling her to dinner.

She'd been out there drifting a long time. Her fingers had shriveled. She studied her fingers and they seemed so strange, not like fingers at all, but maybe what came before fingers, the predecessors to fingers. She couldn't remember exactly what she was doing out there floating on the bay.

Let's go, the different voices sang until the sounds themselves grew otherworldly: songs of sunsets, angels, ghosts. She closed her eyes, and the voices spiraled, throbbing in and out. She couldn't tell if they were coming closer or moving away.

The raft slipped from beneath her, and Dori was surprised to find that she wasn't out as deep as she had thought.

She knelt against the soft, silty bottom of the bay, the surface of the water circling her shoulders, and she felt her own blood rush, her own heart pulse, her own voice humming deep inside her: *rise up.*

"Okay," she answered, and she stood. "Okay. I'm coming," she called. She raised her hands up toward the sky and waded deliberately to shore.

Acknowledgments

This book took many years to come together, and a lot of great friends, readers, and editors helped and supported me along the way. I especially wish to thank Marcy Posner, Christin Lore Weber, Joy Bloom, and Amy Tudor for their close and detailed readings and for asking me hard questions—architectural, spiritual, and ethical—that helped me shape this story. Longtime readers Andrew Follmer and Jenean Hall also weighed in with helpful responses, along with the spectacular women in my family who tell me just what works for them and what doesn't, starting with my sweet momma, Patsy Reynolds, my aunt Sammie Jordan, my sister Genie Blanton, my niece Caroline Gleason, and my cousins Mary Beth Byrd and Lexie Jordan.

I am grateful to have landed at Bywater Books and appreciate so much the help I've received from Fay Jacobs, who first approached me about submitting the book to Bywater; Salem West, who has moved me steadily through the editorial process and cracked me up with every email; Ann McMan, who designed so many amazing covers and then redid it again at the eleventh hour; and Elizabeth Sims, whose editorial suggestions showed me not just weak spots in the book, but weak spots in my own character—which I'm working on!

Most especially, I thank my beloved wife and partner-in-crime for more than twenty years, Barbara Marie Brown, who has listened to me read, question, and rewrite so many scenes in this book that she could probably recite it. In Spanish.

About the Author

Sheri Reynolds is the author of the novels *Bitterroot Landing*, *The Rapture of Canaan* (an Oprah Book Club selection and *New York Times* bestseller), *A Gracious Plenty*, *Firefly Cloak*, *The Sweet In-Between*, *The Homespun Wisdom of Myrtle T. Cribb*, and the full-length play, *Orabelle's Wheelbarrow*. She teaches creative writing and literature at Old Dominion University, where she is the Ruth and Perry Morgan Chair of Southern Literature and serves as Department Chair of English. She lives in the town of Cape Charles on Virginia's eastern shore. Learn more about her at *www.sherireynolds.com*.

At Bywater Books we love good books about lesbians
just like you do, and we're committed to bringing
the best of contemporary lesbian writing
to our avid readers. Our editorial team is dedicated
to finding and developing outstanding writers
who create books you won't want to put down.

For more information about Bywater Books,
our authors, and our titles, please visit our website.

www.bywaterbooks.com